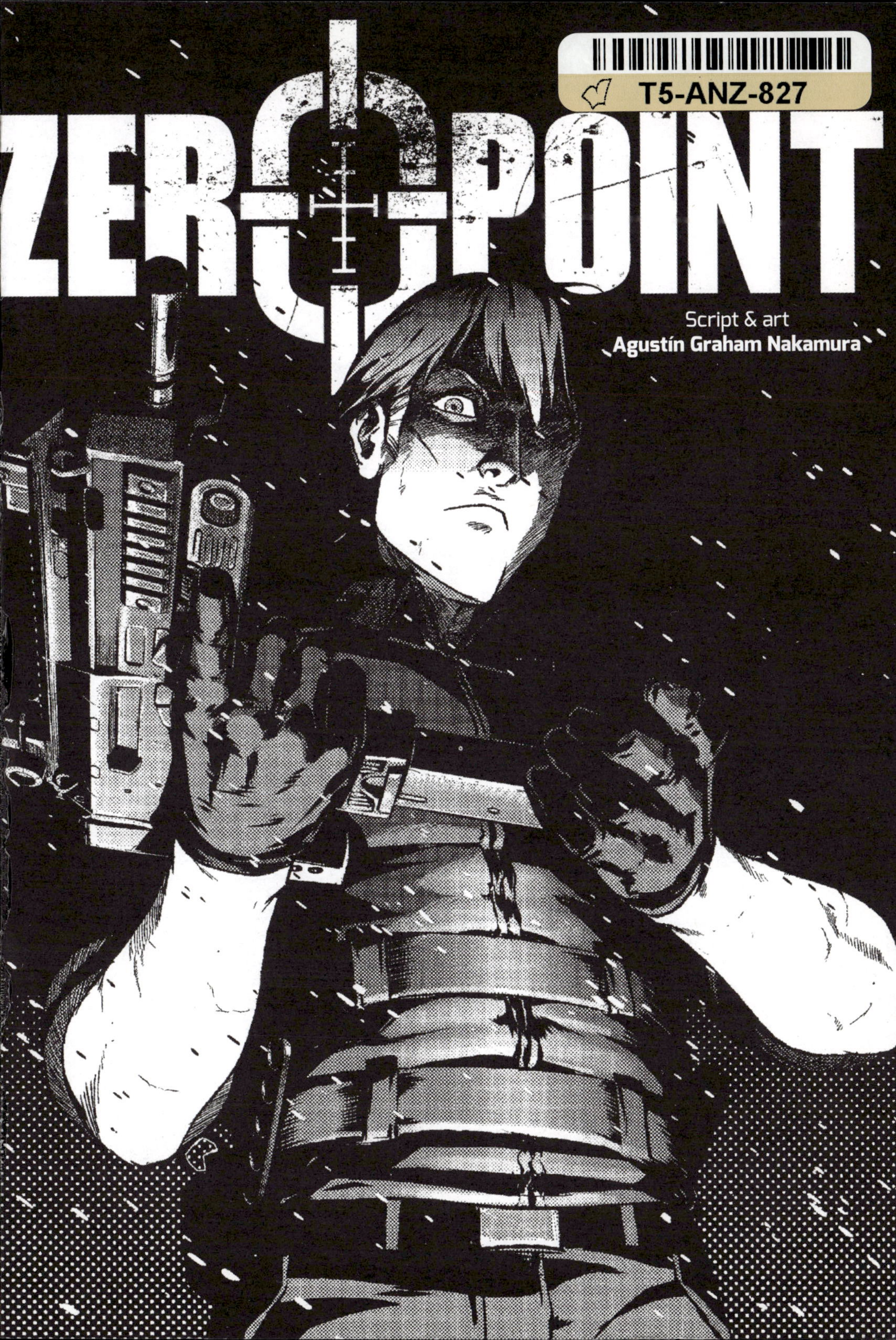
ZERO POINT
Script & art
Agustín Graham Nakamura

ALIEN BOOKS

DIRECTOR
Matías Timarchi

SENIOR EDITOR
Lysa Hawkins

EDITOR
Martín Casanova

ASSISTANT EDITOR
Inés Moguillanes

SALES & OPERATIONS
Danielle Ward

TRANSLATION
Lea Paolini Somers

REVISION
Ignacio Gonzalez

LETTERING
Camila Jorge

FINANCE DIRECTOR
Fabricio Castellano

PR & SOCIAL MEDIA
Rodrigo Molina

Special thanks to
Diego Agrimbau
Ramón I. Bunge

February 2024. First printing.
ZERO POINT and all related characters are © Agustin Graham Nakamura - Punkbot Comic Books LLC. All rights reserved.
Printed in China.

Except for review purposes, no portion of this publication may be reproduced or transmitted, in any form or by any means, without the express written permission of Alien Books. Published by Alien Books.
www.alienbooks.com
info@alienbooks.com
f aliencomicbooks
 aliencomicbooks

PROLOGUE

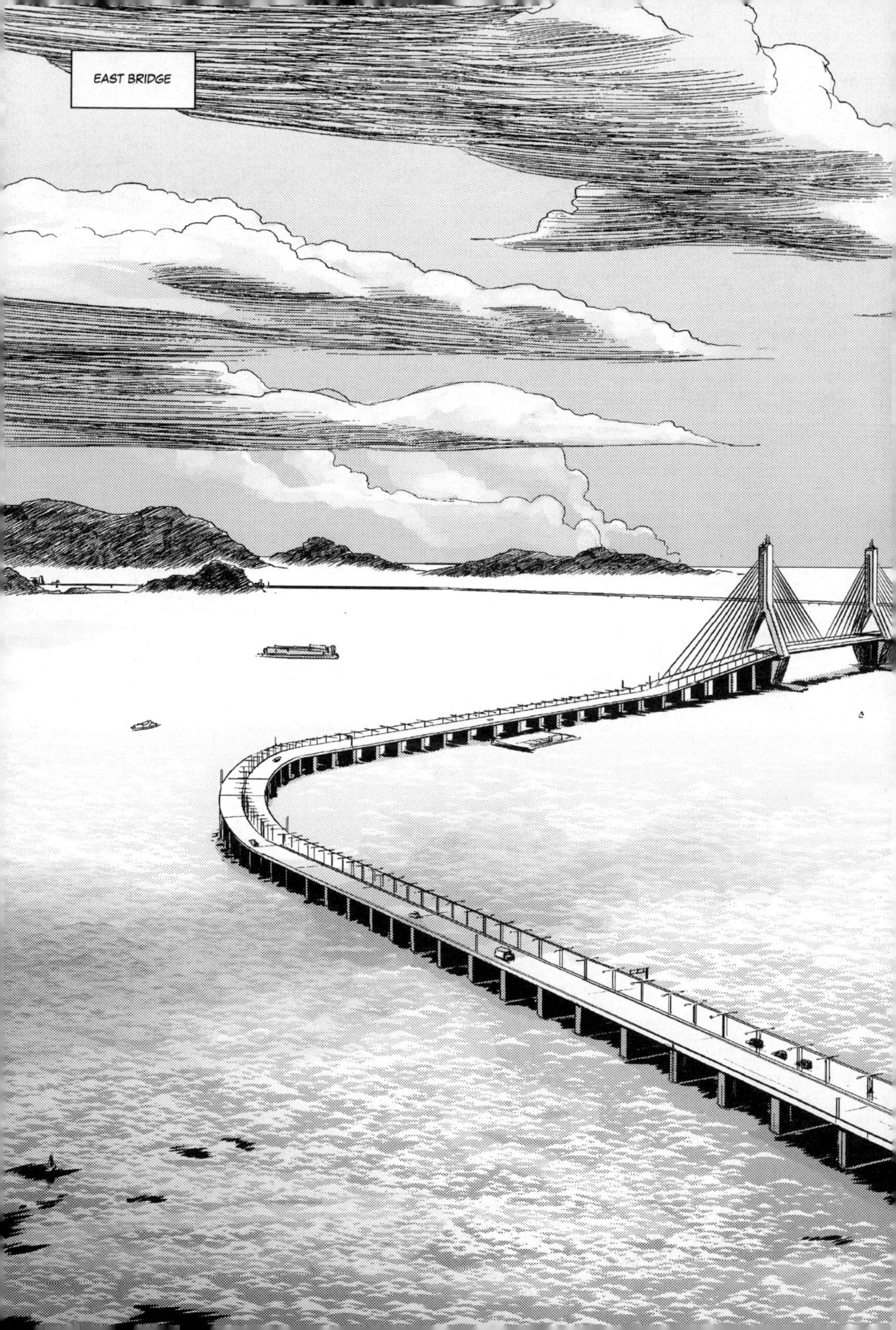
EAST BRIDGE

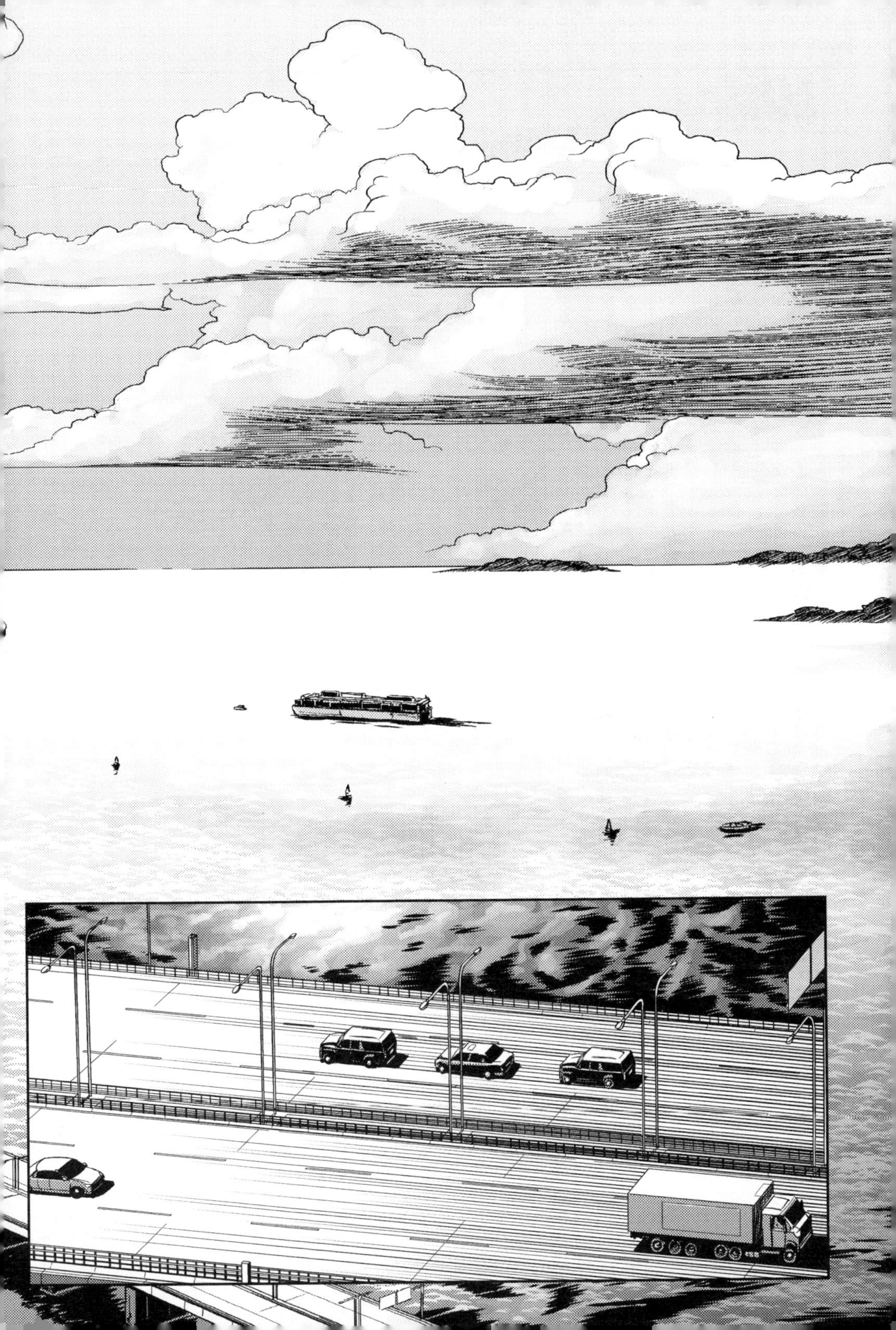

WROOOOOOOOOOOOOOOOO
WE'LL BE THERE IN 40 MINUTES.
OF COURSE I'VE GOT THE MONEY WITH ME.
BY THE WAY, THANKS FOR THE BACKUP.
IT'S ALWAYS A PLEASURE DOING BUSINESS WITH YOUR GOVERNMENT!

01 HERE. EVERYTHING'S COOL...
WHAT?
WAIT, SOMEONE STOPPED IN THE MIDDLE OF THE ROAD...
SPANG
SPANG
SKREEEEEEEEEEEECHHHH

CRASH

CRASH

THE FUCK IS GOING ON?!?

GET DOWN, SIR!

02 HERE. WE'VE LOST 01!

COPY. DON'T STOP!
GO STRAIGHT TO THE RENDEZVOUS POINT...
SPANG
SHIT!
GET US OUT OF HERE!
SPANG
SPANG

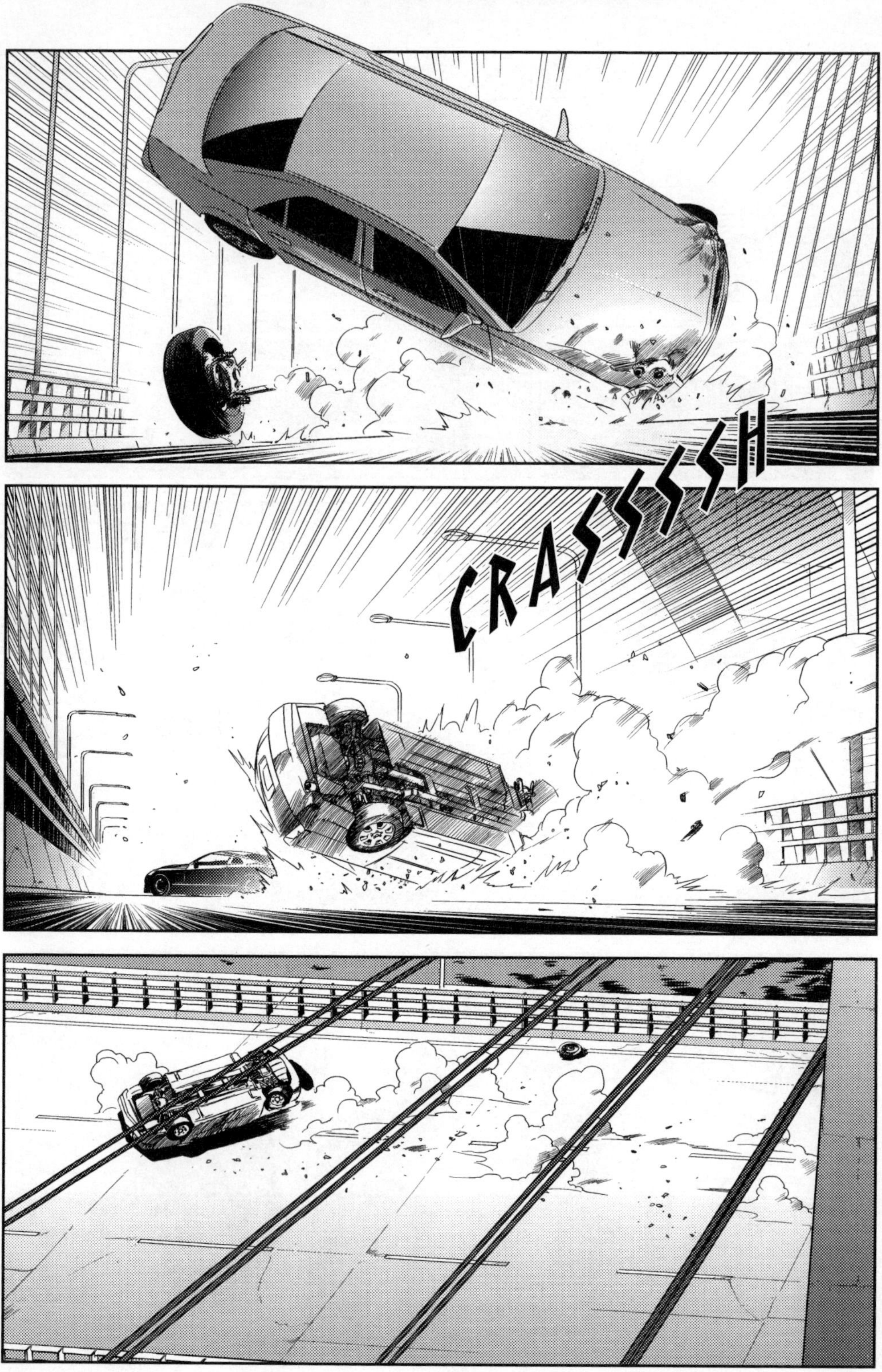
CRASSSSSH

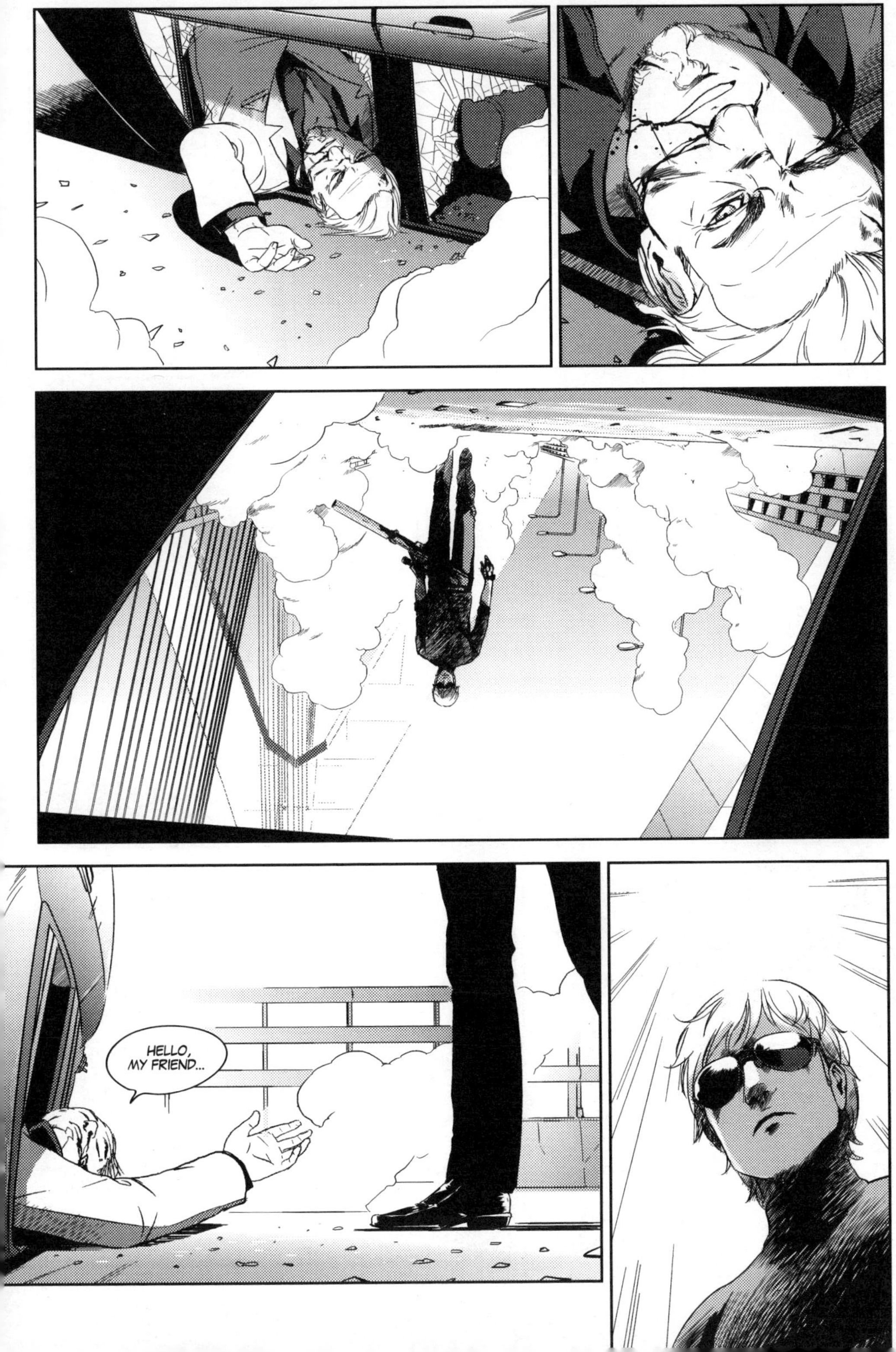
HELLO, MY FRIEND...

YOU DID A FINE JOB BACK THERE... NO UNNECESSARY CASUALTIES...
RIGHT?
YOU LOOK LIKE A SMART GUY. HOW ABOUT WE MAKE A DEAL...
LISTEN. I HAVE A SMALL FORTUNE ON ME RIGHT NOW... SURELY MORE THAN WHAT YOU'RE GETTING PAID FOR ME.
KEEP THE MONEY. LET ME GO. HOW'S THAT SOUND?
WHY GET MORE BLOOD ON YOUR HANDS WHEN YOU CAN FILL THEM WITH CASH INSTEAD? C'MON! EVEN SOMEONE LIKE YOU WOULD KNOW THAT'S A GOOD DEAL!
HMM...
NICE TRY.
BUT DESTROYING YOUR CARGO IS ALSO PART OF THE JOB.

BECAUSE I LIKE YOU, I'LL GIVE YOU A SMALL CHANCE.
OK?
CLICK
THIS IS AN INCENDIARY GRENADE. IT TAKES A WHILE TO DETONATE.
IT'S SIMPLE. IF YOU CAN PUT THE PIN BACK IN, YOU WIN.
PLIK
YOU HAVE TEN SECONDS.
GOOD LUCK.
YOU CALL THIS A CHANCE?
COME BACK!
SON OF A BITCH!
YOU ARE A DEAD MAN. YOU HEAR ME?!?
YOU THINK I CAN'T DO IT?
YOU'LL SEE...
THERE!
K-CLICK

KA-BOOOOSH!!!
CONGRATULATIONS. YOU DID IT, "MY FRIEND."
SKREEEEEEEEECH

01

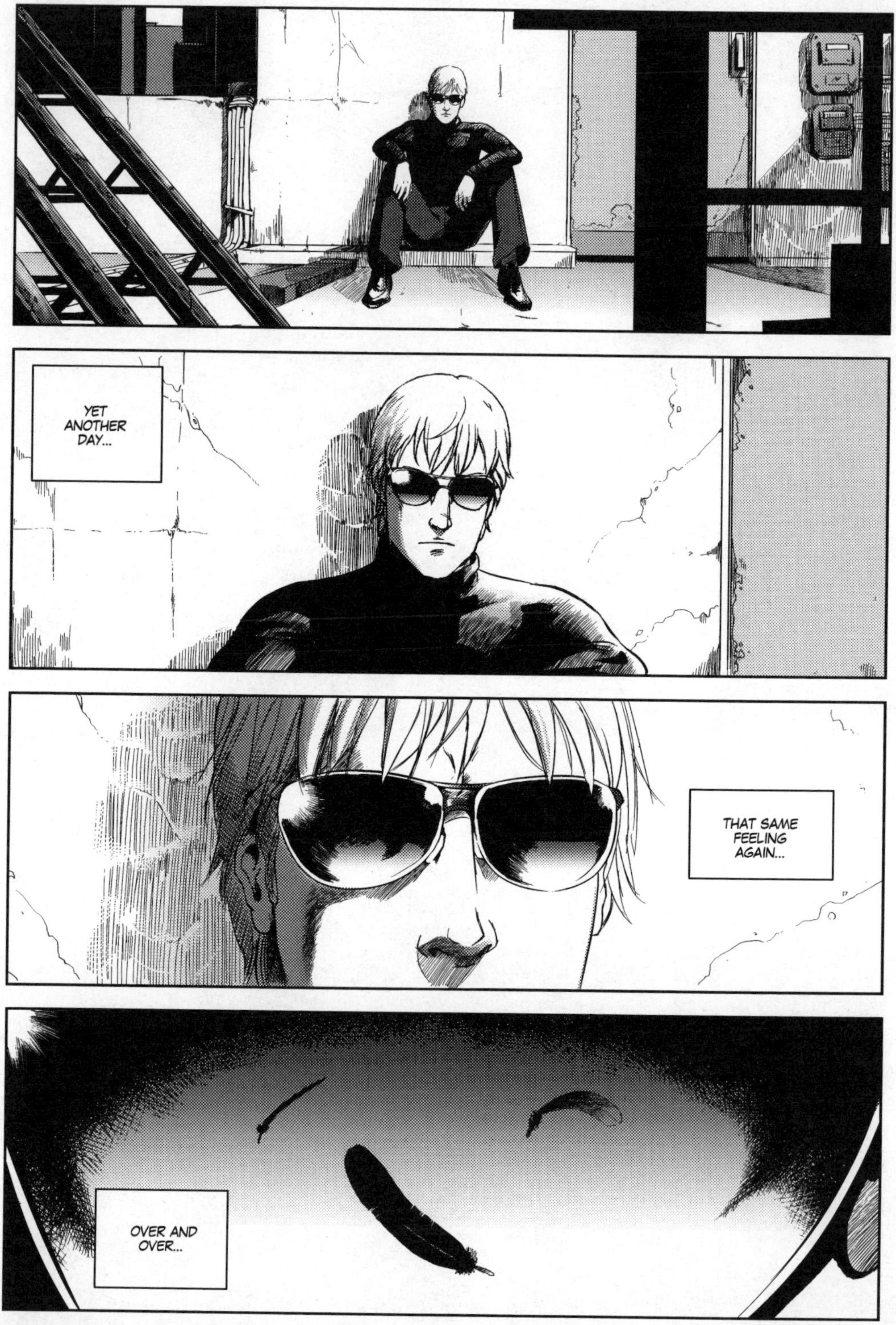
YET ANOTHER DAY...
THAT SAME FEELING AGAIN...
OVER AND OVER...

WE SHOULD ALL KNOW THE EXACT MOMENT THAT WE'RE GOING TO DIE...

...SO THAT WE CAN KNOW WHAT FACE TO PUT ON AS WE WELCOME OUR DEATH.

CLIK

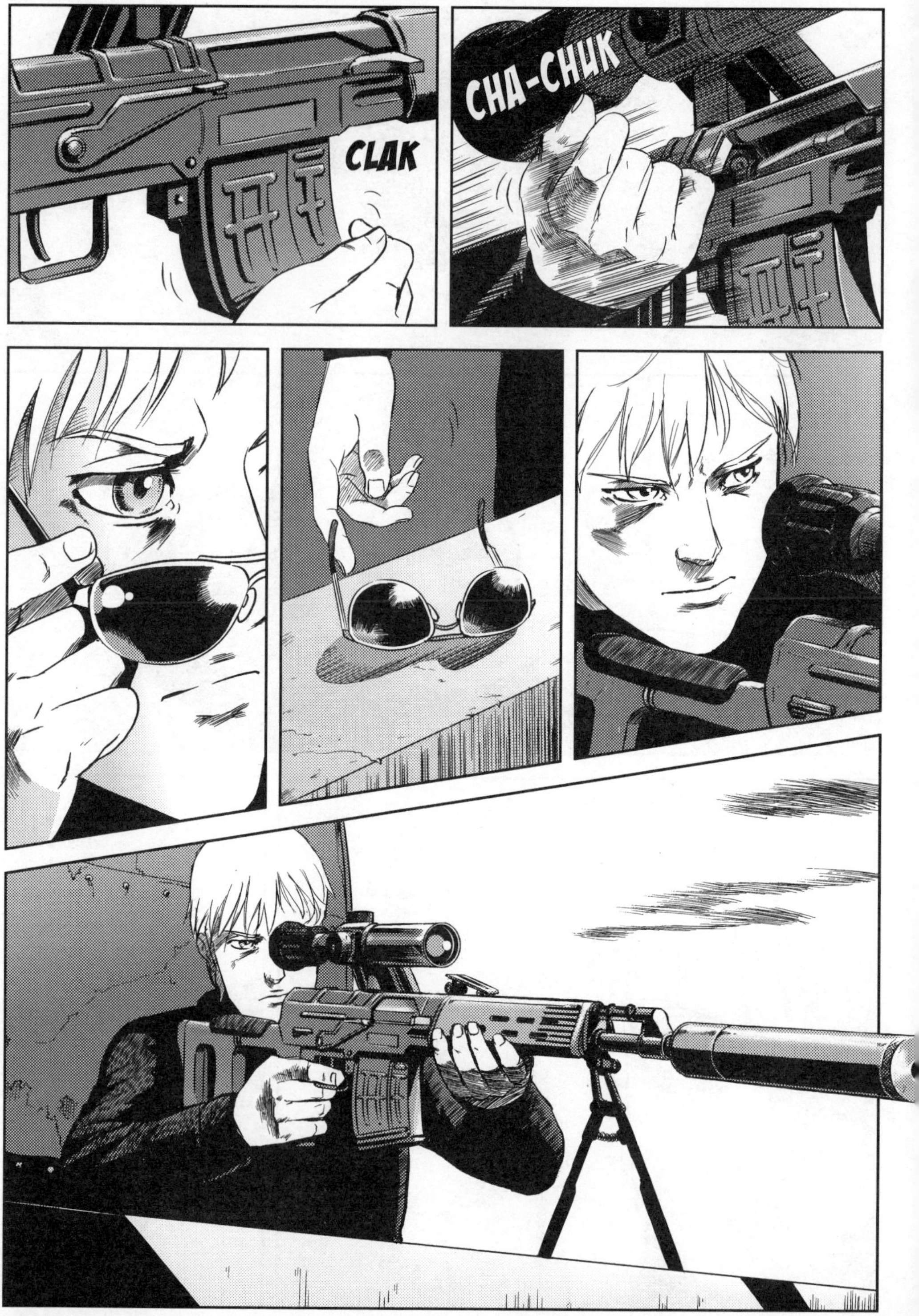
CHA-CHUK
CLAK

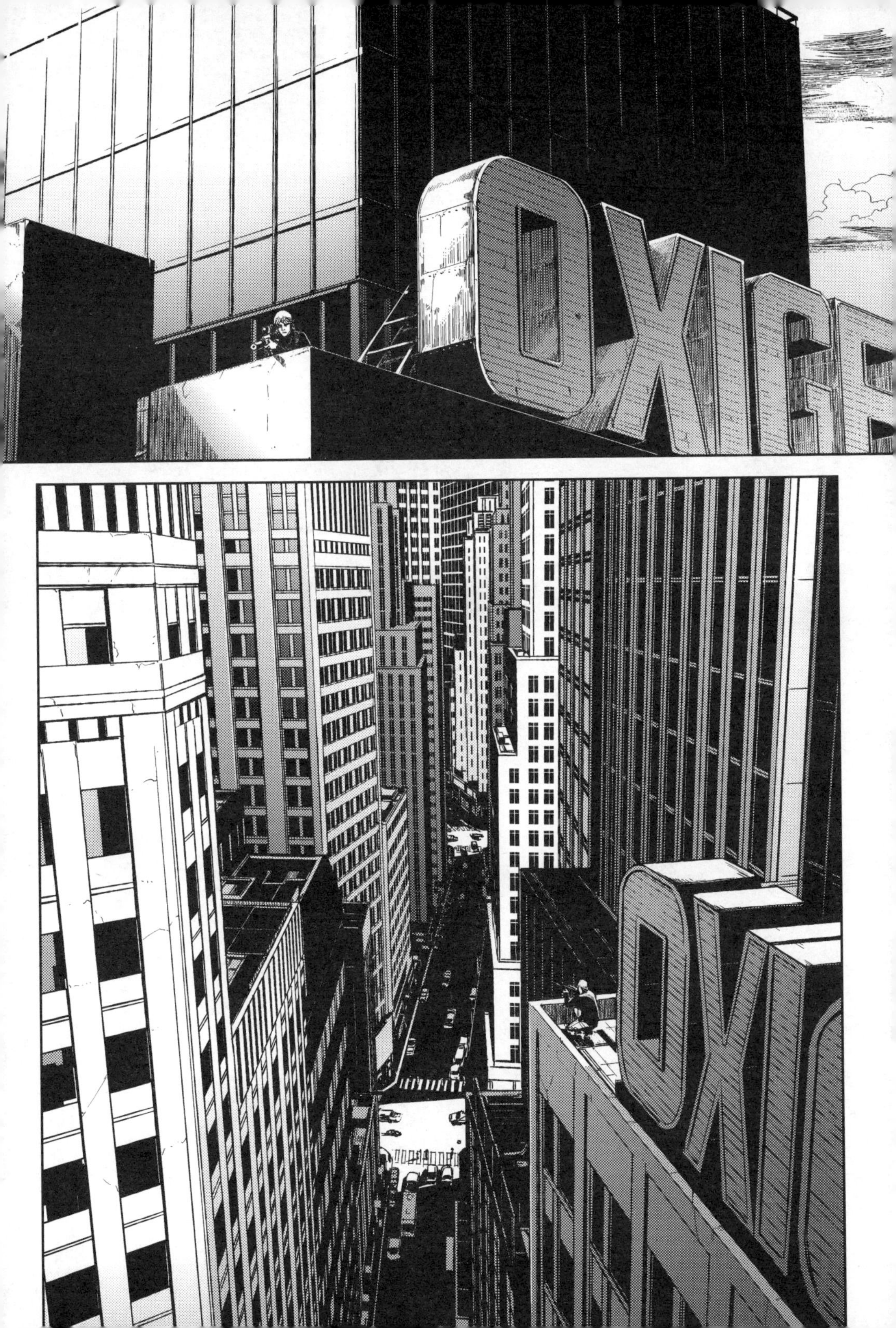

HE'LL HAVE FOUR ARMED GUARDS.
TONY'S OPEN 24 HRS
BREAKFAST
CAFE
DINNER
LUNCH
OPEN 24 HOURS
HE'LL GO TO A MEETING IN THE IMPERIAL HOTEL THE DAY AFTER TOMORROW.
50% UP FRONT, AND 50% WHEN IT'S ALL DONE.
JUST LIKE YOU REQUESTED.
TAP
OK, BIRD?

I THOUGHT THE PREVIOUS JOB WAS GOING TO BE OUR LAST ONE...
WELL...
NO DEAL. TAKE THE MONEY.
WAIT!
DO YOU THINK YOU HAVE A CHOICE?
WE CLEARED YOUR NAME IN EXCHANGE FOR YOUR SERVICES!
YOU WERE THE ONE THAT CAME TO US!
IF YOU WANT TO BACK OUT OF EVERYTHING NOW, FINE BY ME.
I'LL TAKE YOUR MONEY ONE MORE TIME...
GRAB
...BUT OUR ARRANGEMENT IS ALMOST OVER.
TONY! COMMISSIONER WHELAN IS TAKING OVER MY TAB THIS MONTH!
SURE THING, BUDDY.
HEHEHE...

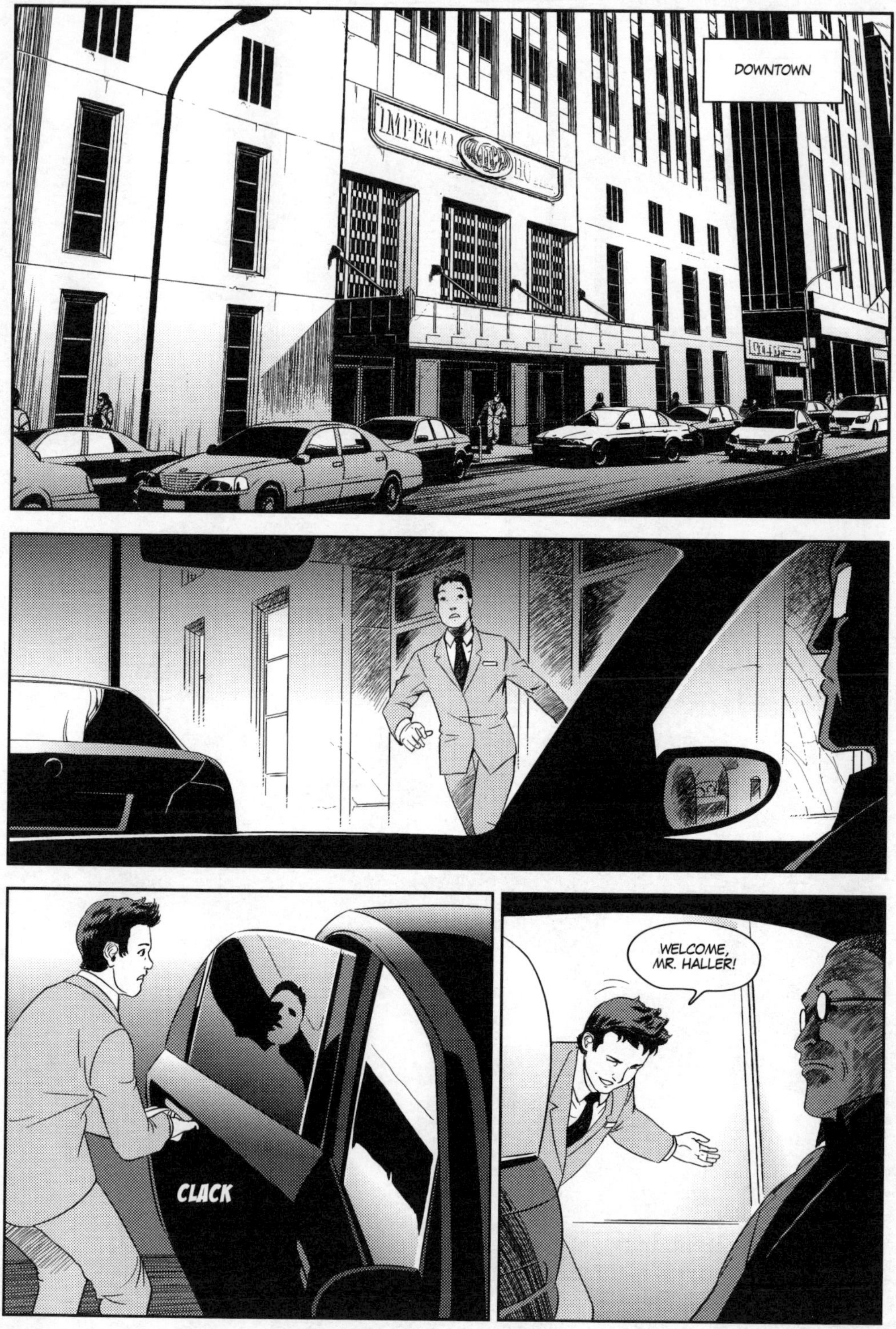
DOWNTOWN
CLACK
WELCOME, MR. HALLER!

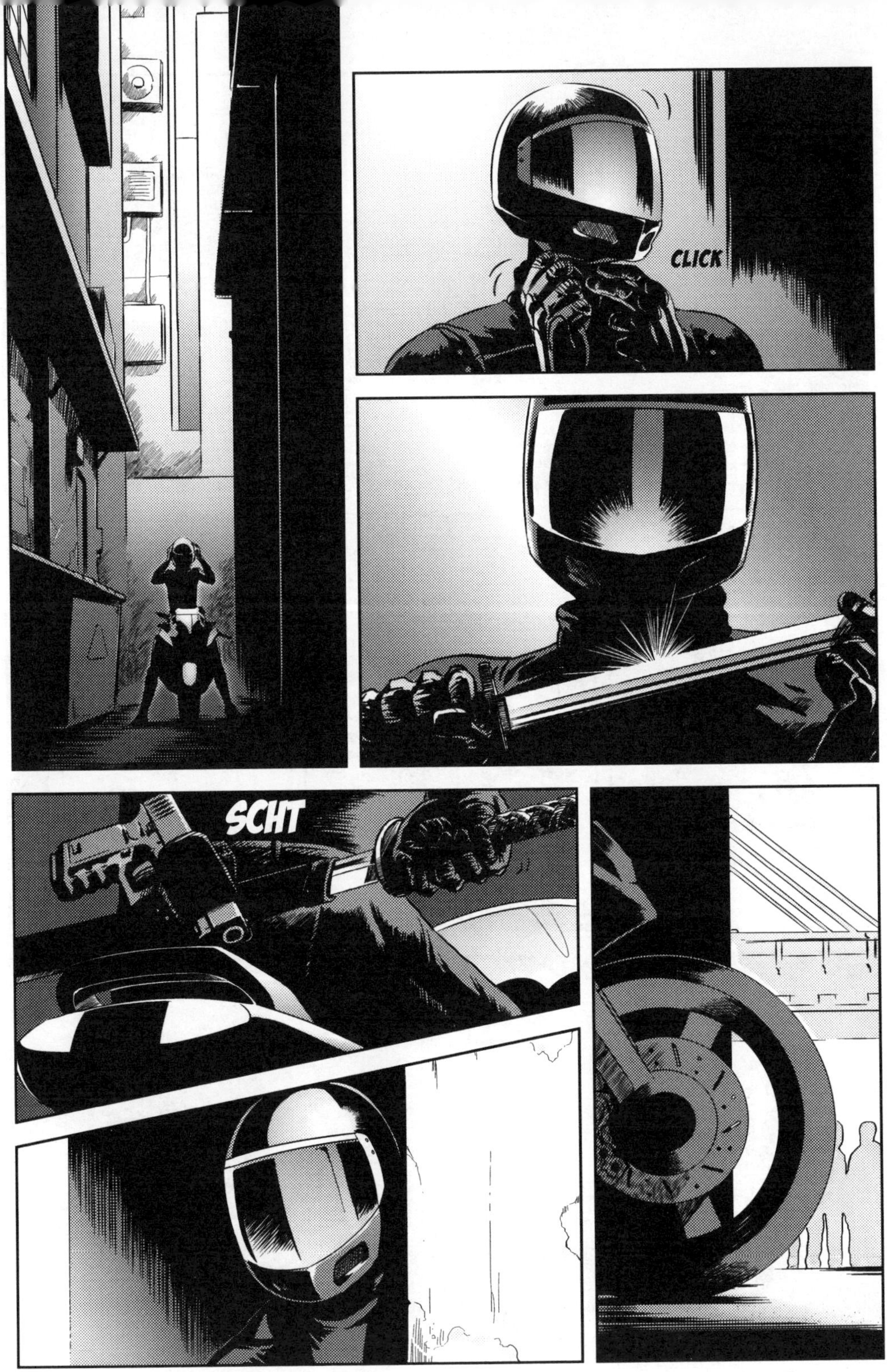
CLICK
SCHT

HELLO, BUDDY.

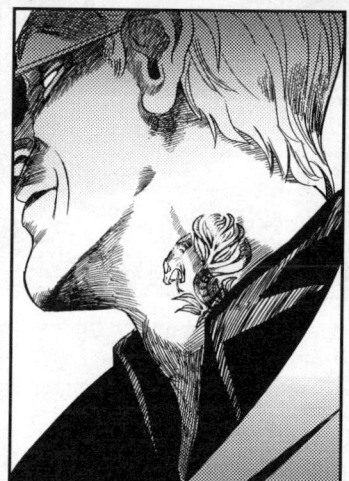

CLICK

TIME TO DIE...

LET'S SEE WHAT FACE YOU MAKE!
SKREEEEEEEE
HUH?
RRRRRRRRRRRRRRRR

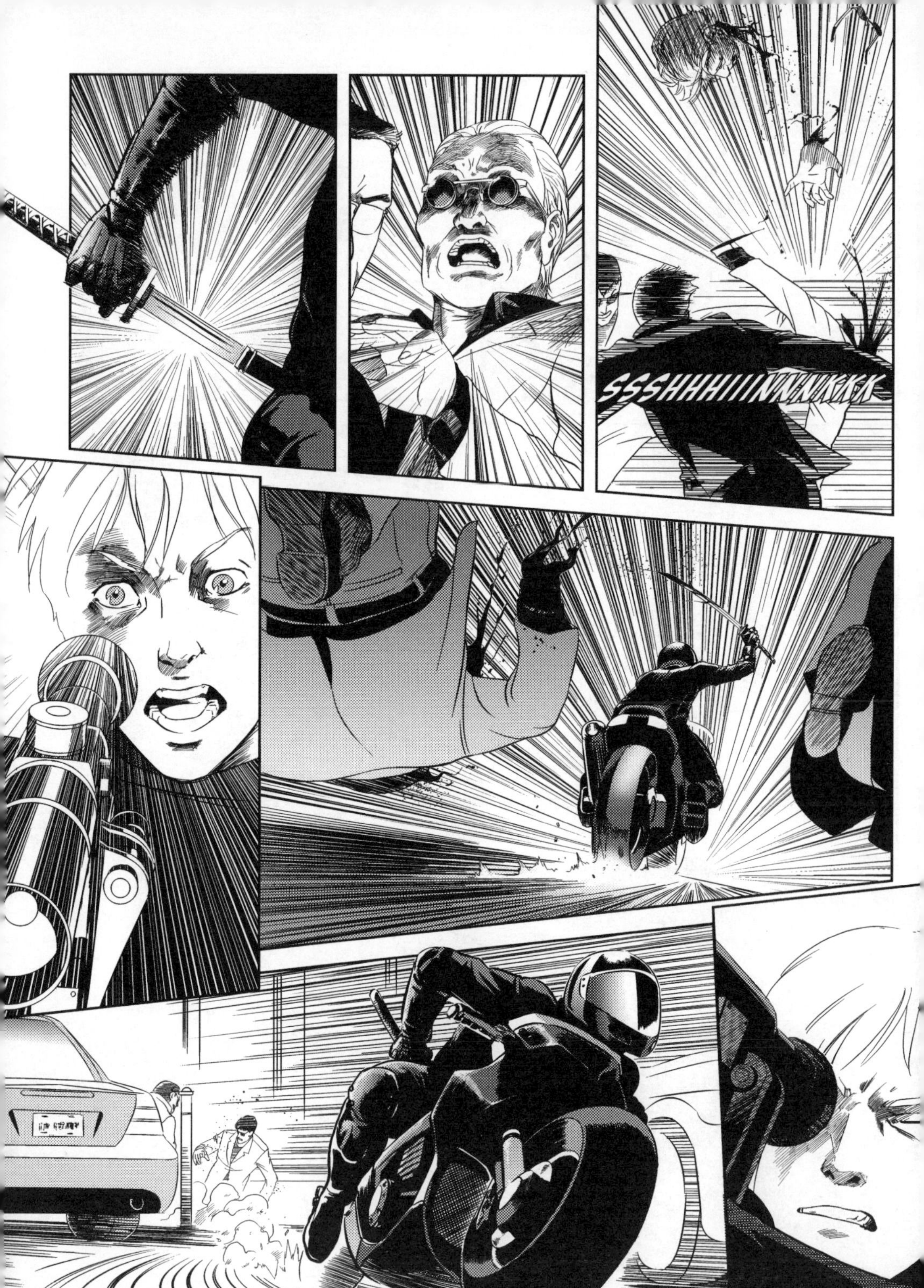
SSSHHHIIINNNKKK

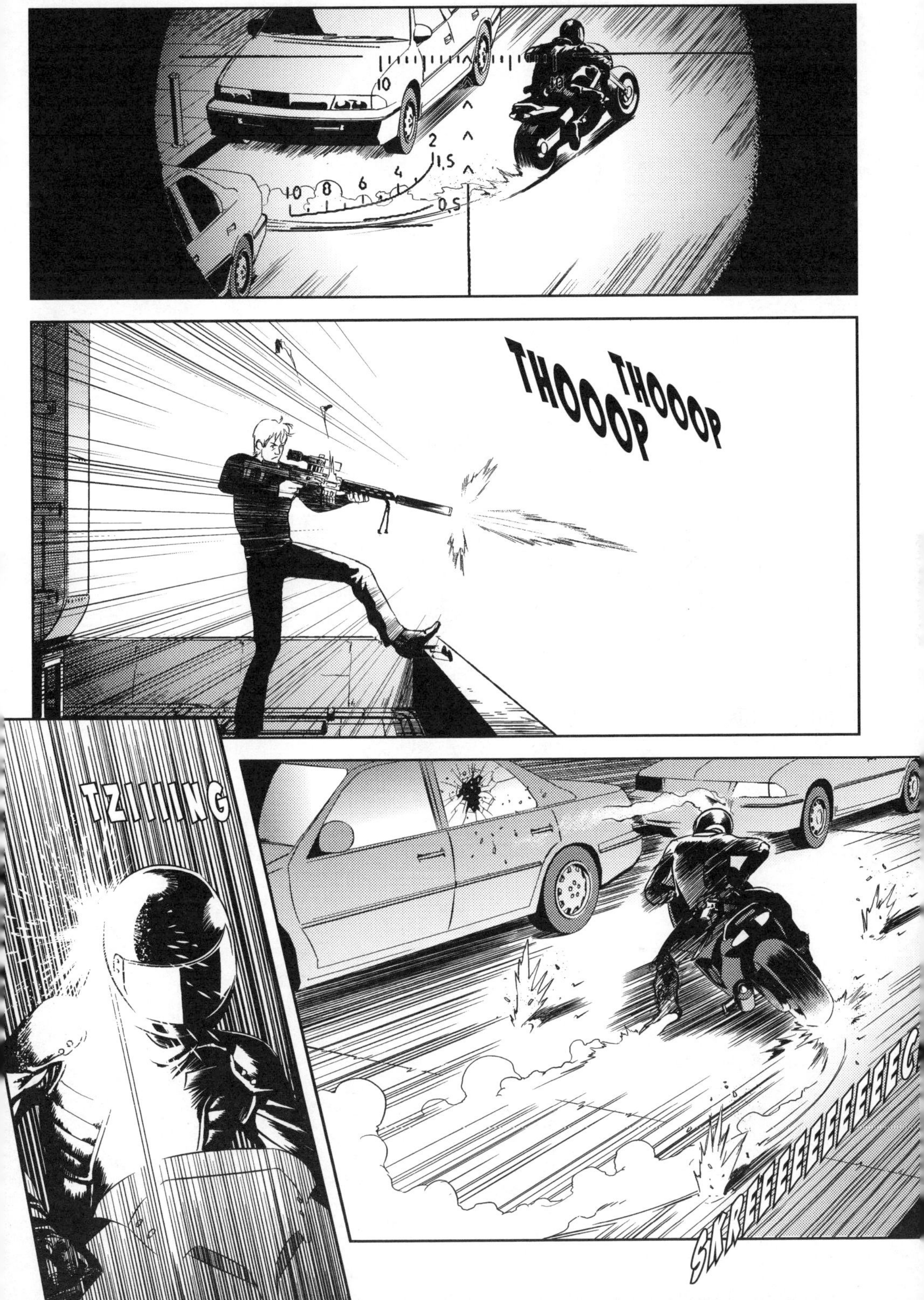
THOOOP THOOOP
TZIIIING

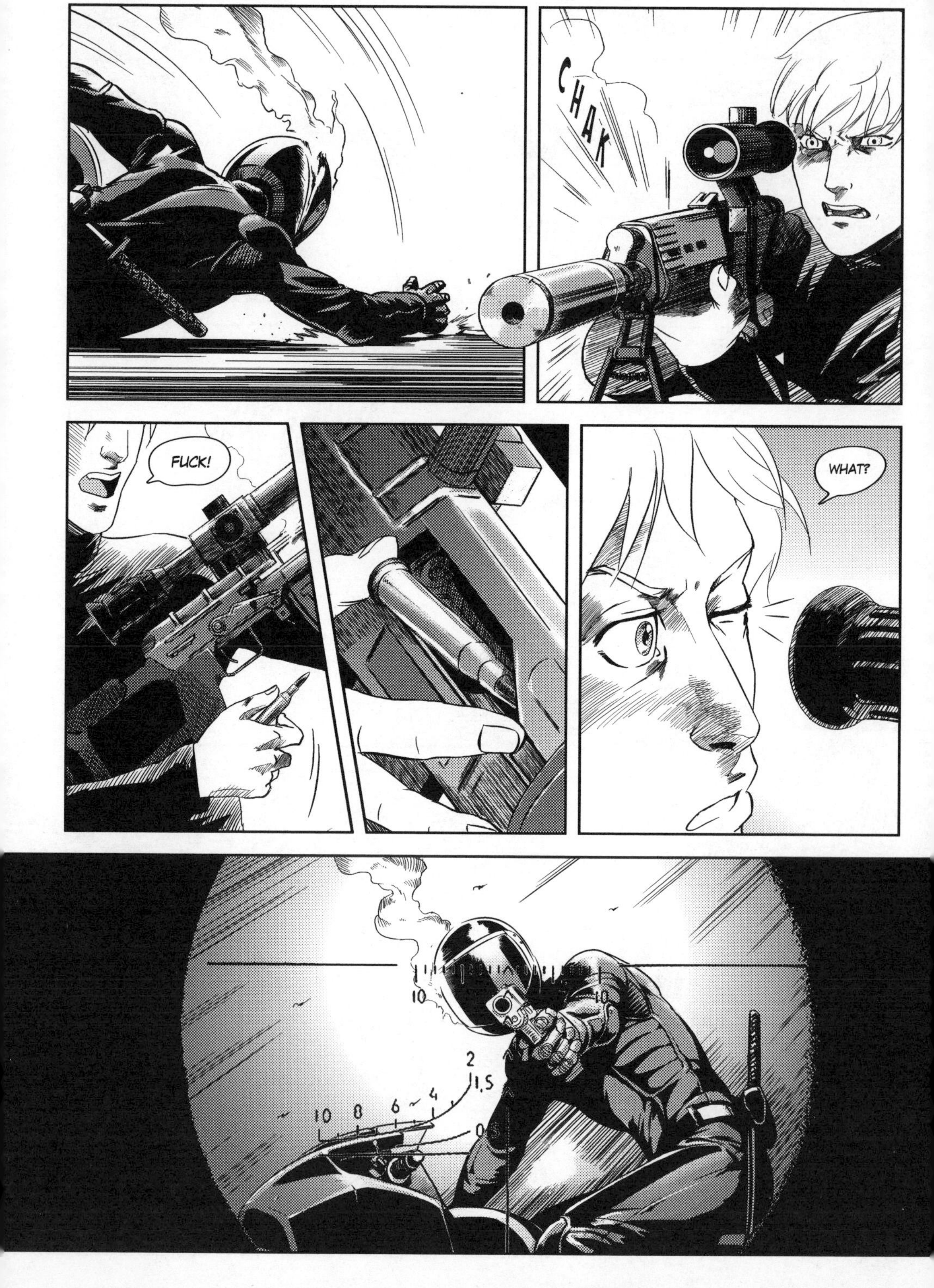
CHAK
FUCK!
WHAT?

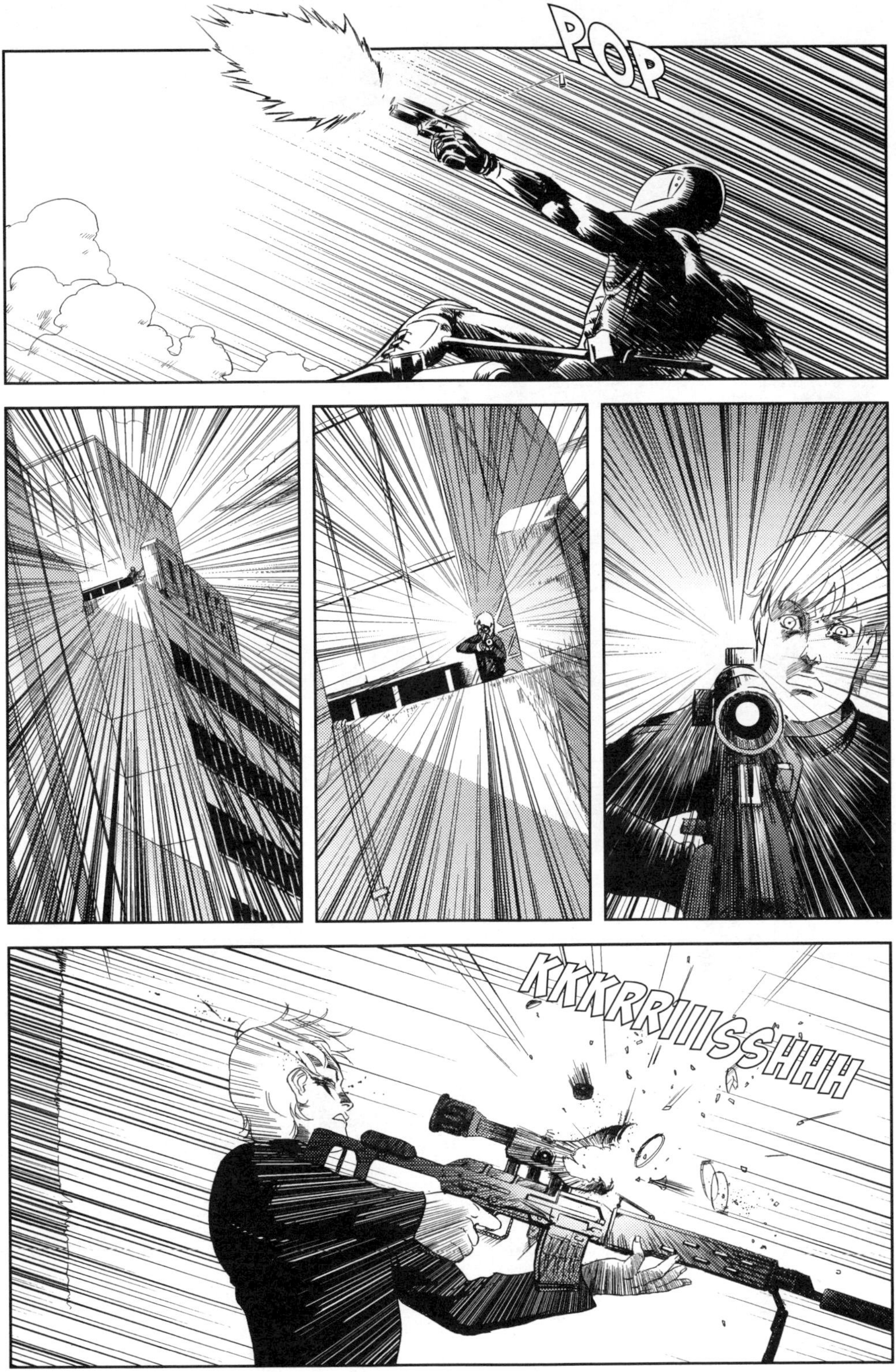
POP
KKKRRIIISSHHH

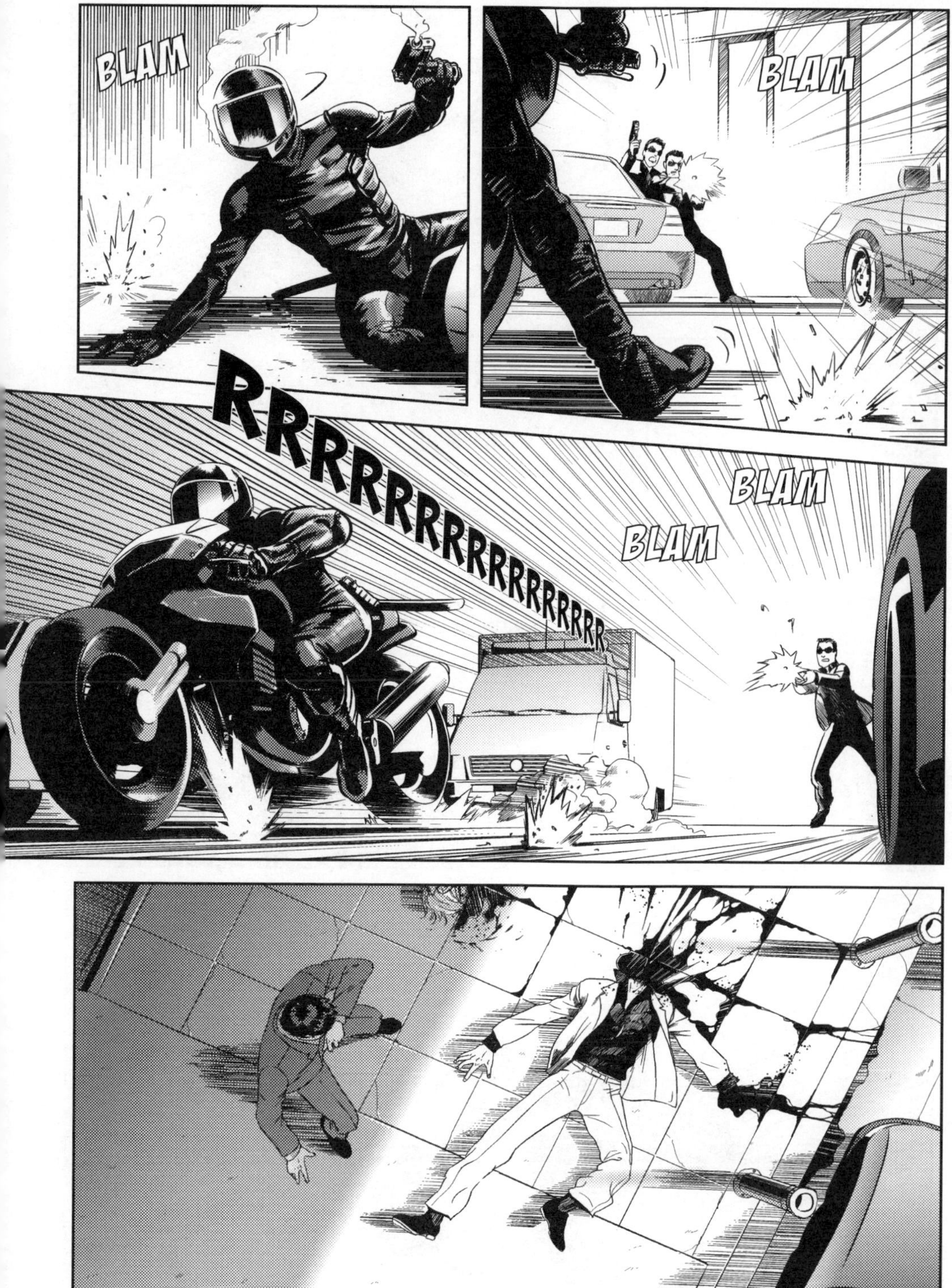
BLAM
BLAM
RRRRRRRRRRRRRRRRRR
BLAM
BLAM

SHIT.

MORE THAN 200 YARDS AWAY, WITH A HANDGUN...

HE'S A PRO.

THINGS WILL GET UGLIER FROM HERE ON OUT...

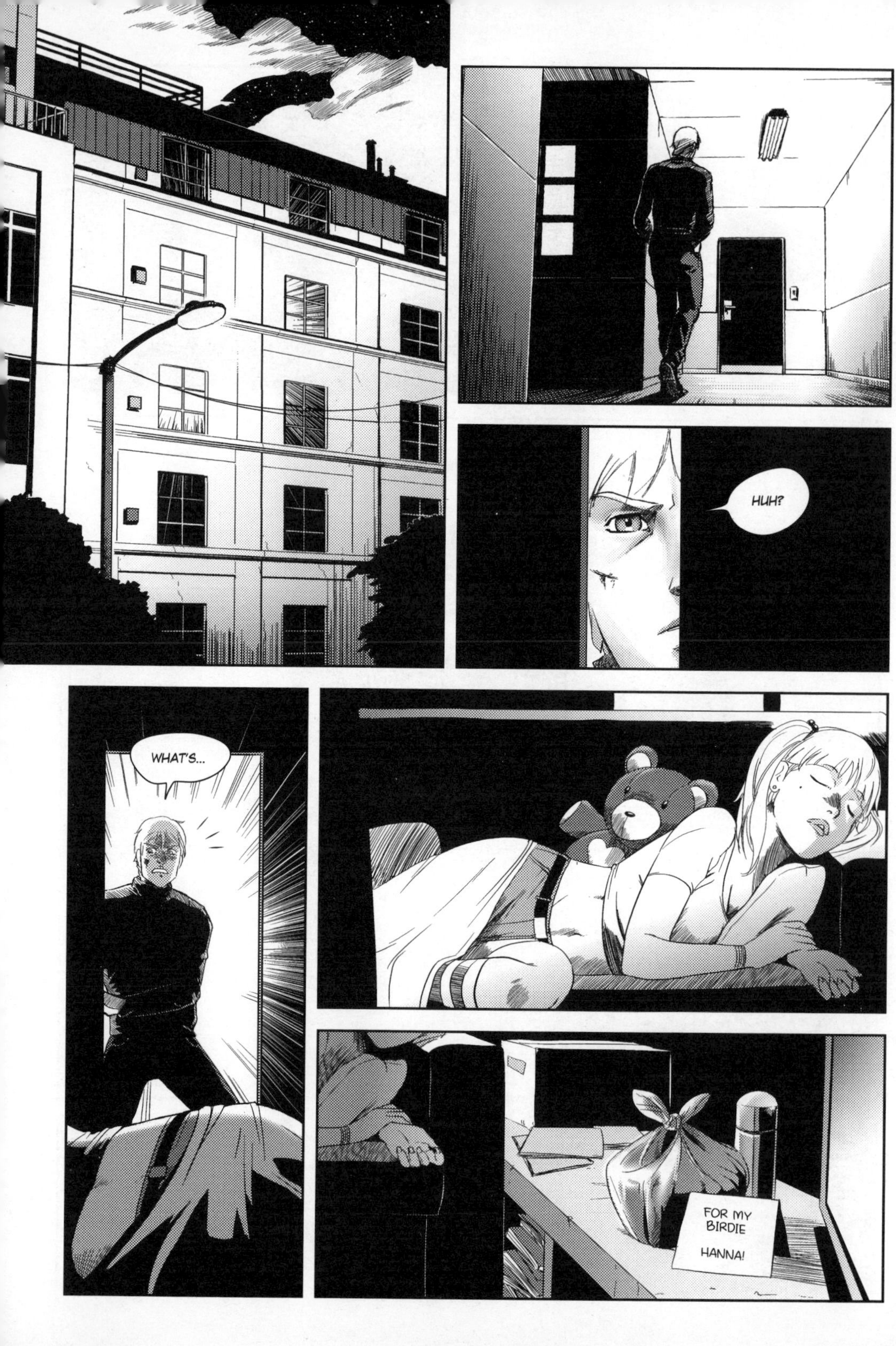
HUH?
WHAT'S...
FOR MY BIRDIE
HANNA!

FOR MY
BIRDIE
HANNA!
NOT AGAIN!
ALWAYS WITH HER IDIOTIC...
SHAAA
WAKE UP!
OUT!
SLAM
UNGRATEFUL DICK!
CAN'T YOU SEE ALL THAT I DO FOR YOU?!?
BLEHHHHH!

TSK...
I'M GONNA HAVE TO RETURN THE MONEY...
AND HAVE A GOOD EXPLA- NATION FOR ALL THIS...
SHIT!

"GET OUTTA HERE!"

"THIS IS MY CRIME SCENE. GET OUTTA HERE."

"THIS IS A SWAT JOB. IT'S NOT FOR DESK RATS!"

"SPEAKING OF RATS..."

"OR SHOULD I START INVESTIGATING YOUR BULLSHIT INSTEAD?"

"YES, MA'AM!"

"DETECTIVE MIKERS. I WAS TRANSFERRED OVER FROM ARCHIVES..."

"A PAPER PUSHER AFTER ALL..."

"LT. McMILLAN. THIS IS INVESTIGATION WORK. DON'T EXPECT ANYONE TO BE NICE TO YOU. WHAT'S THE SITUATION?"

WE HAVE A VICTIM. MALE, CAUCASIAN. AROUND 60 YEARS OLD.
NOBODY'S TALKING. I GUESS THEY WANT TO PROTECT THEIR BUSINESS CLIENTS.
WE HAVE TWO SHOOTERS. ONE HERE, AND ONE ON A ROOF 200 YARDS AWAY.
THE VICTIM WAS DECAPITATED. WITH A SWORD, I GUESS.
DECAPITATED?
LET ME SEE THE BODY...
I KNEW IT!
MIKERS, C'MERE!
YOU'RE NEW AND YOU PROBABLY DON'T RECOGNIZE HIM.
THIS AIN'T NO BUSINESS CLIENT. THIS WAS A STRAIGHT-UP VENDETTA.
THIS IS H. HALLER, THE BOSS OF ONE OF THE CITY'S BIGGEST MAFIA FAMILIES.

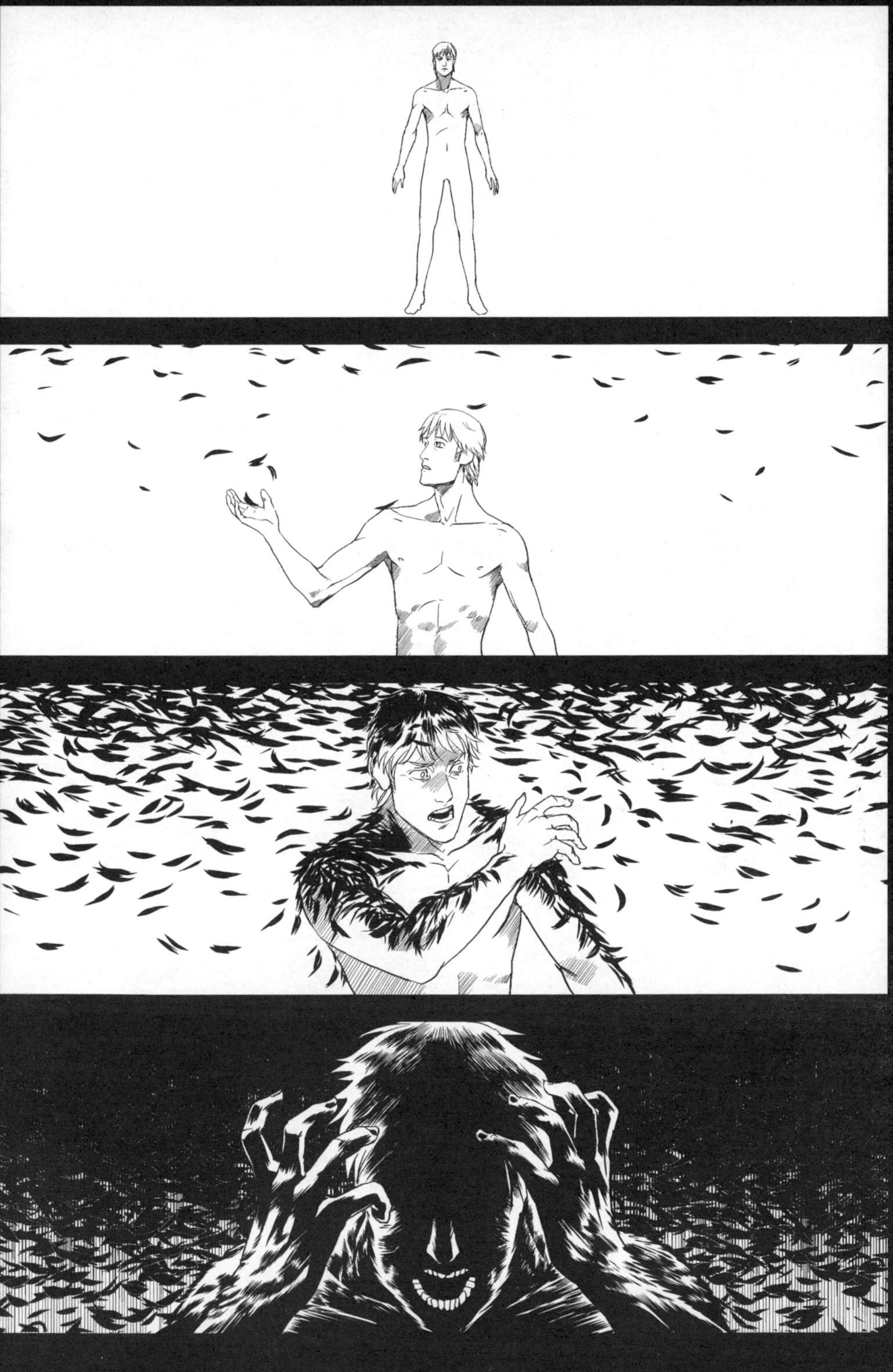

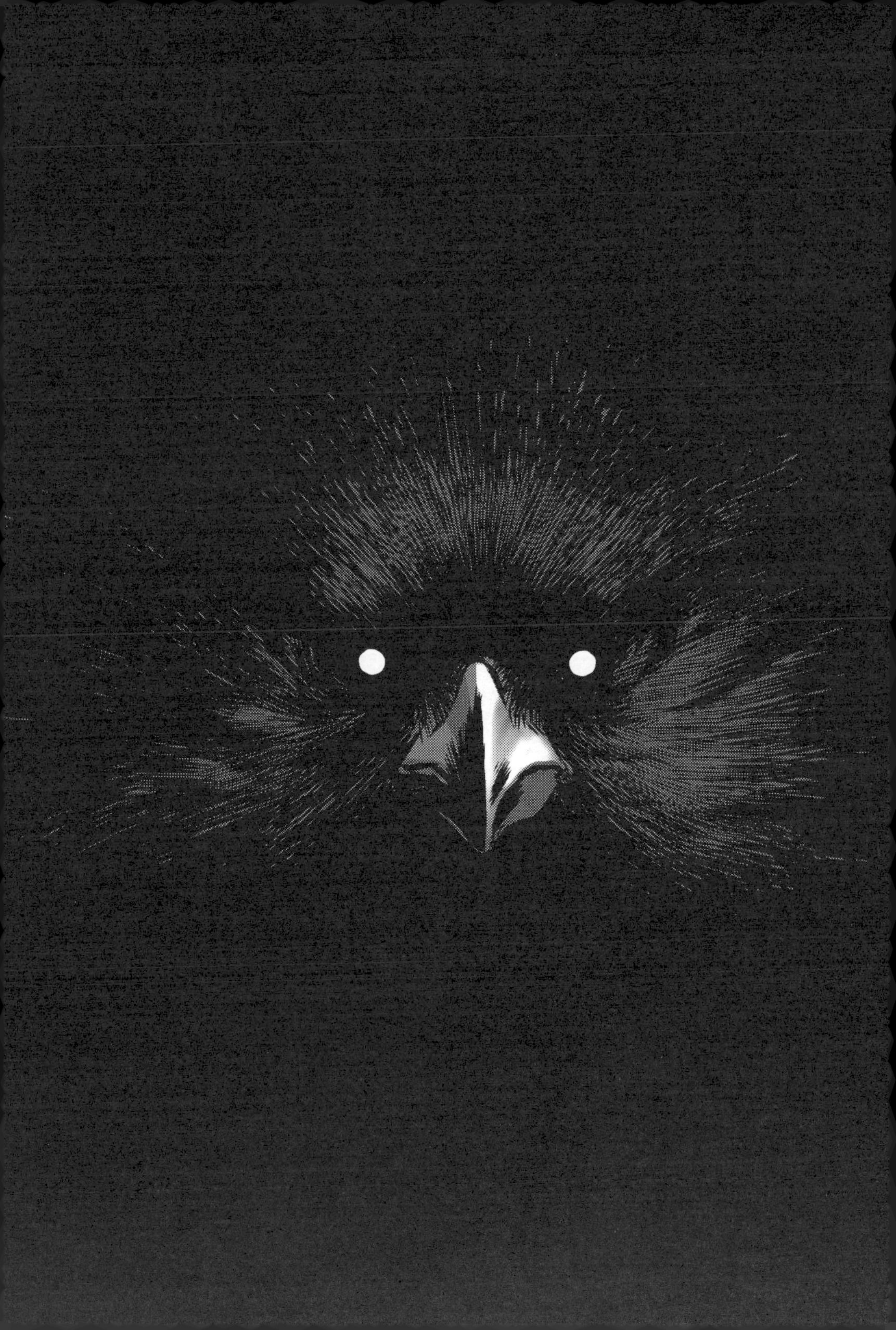

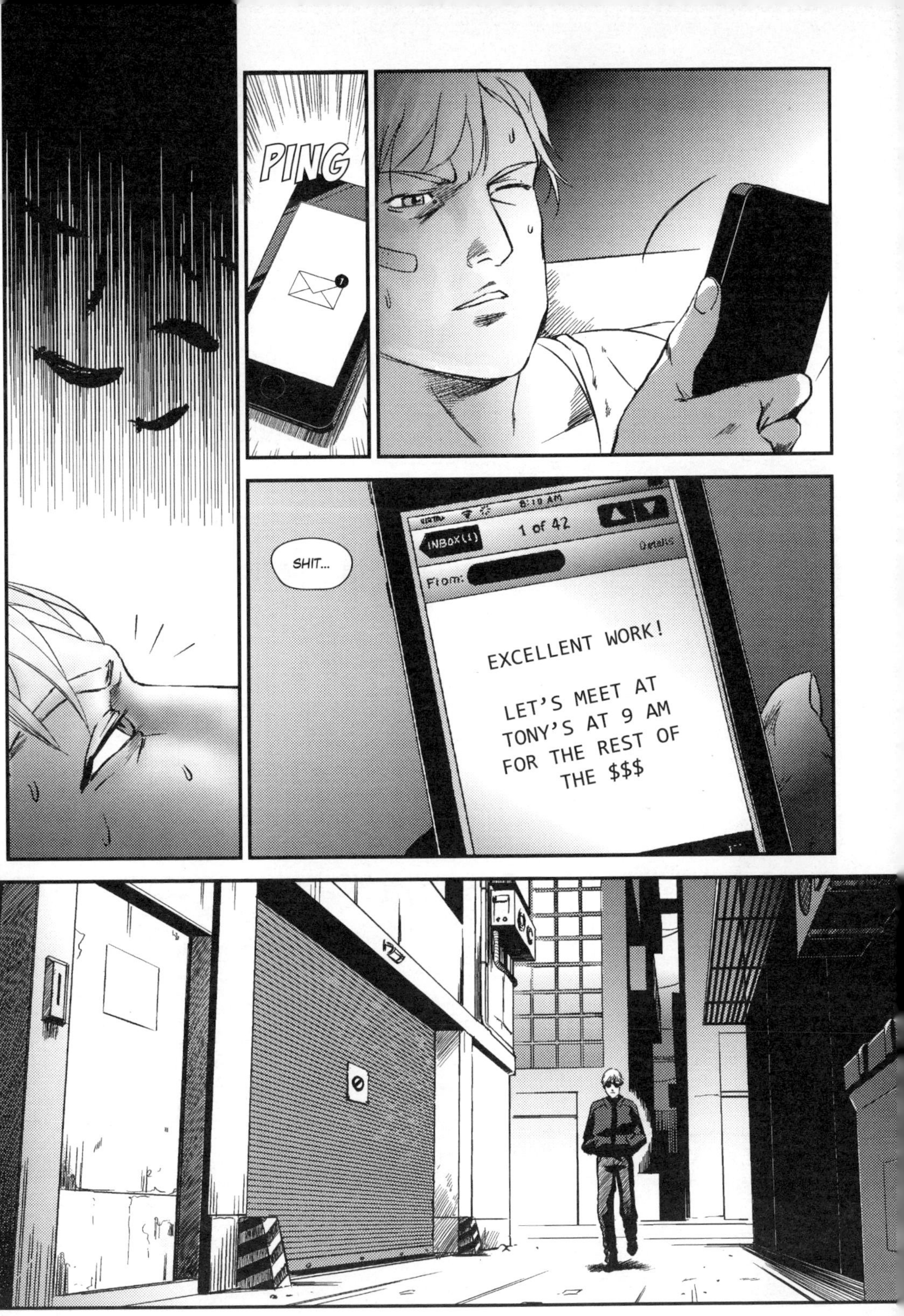

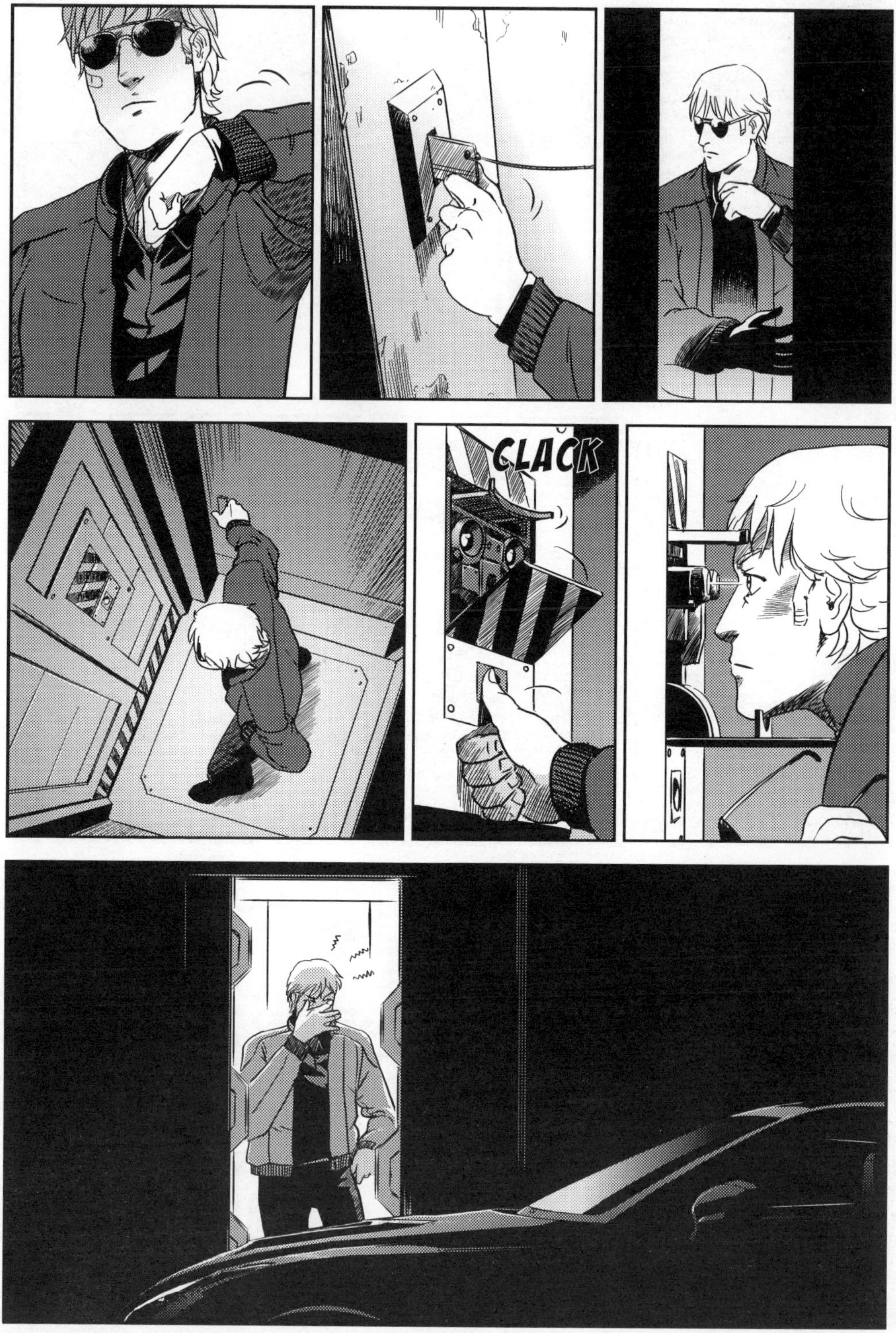
CLACK

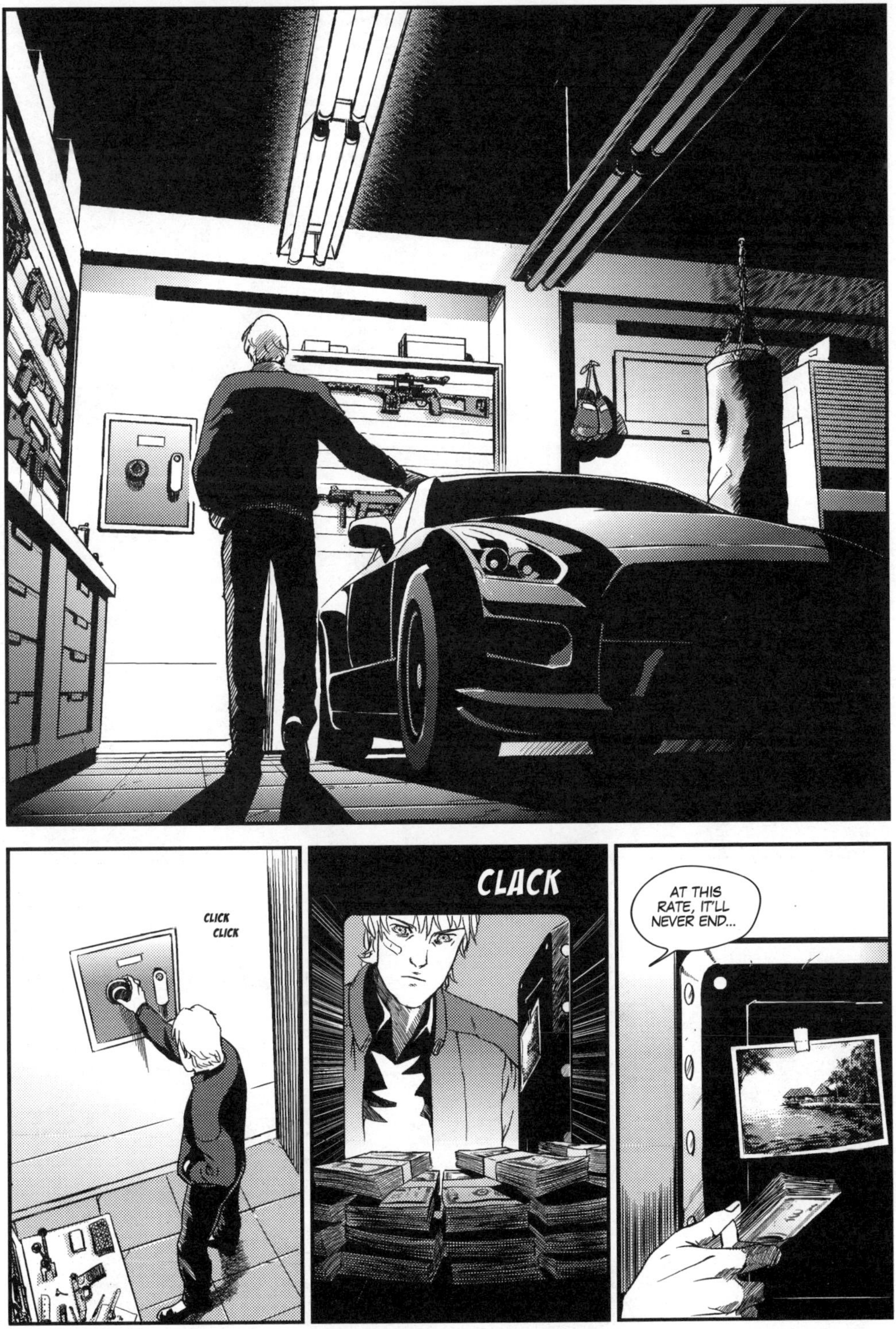
CLICK
CLICK
CLACK
AT THIS RATE, IT'LL NEVER END...

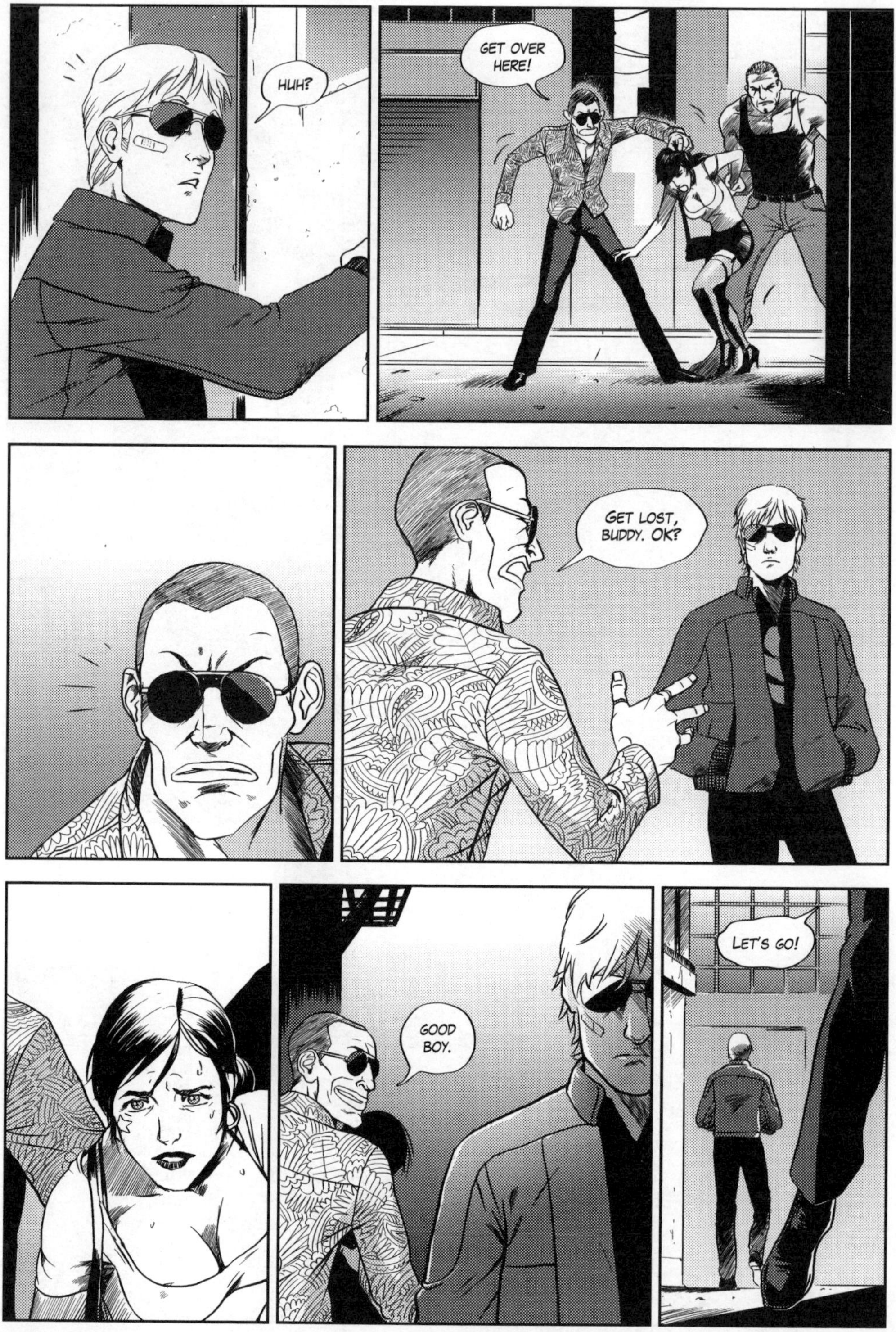
HUH?
GET OVER HERE!
GET LOST, BUDDY. OK?
GOOD BOY.
LET'S GO!

DON'T LIE TO ME!
YOU EXPECT ME TO BELIEVE THAT THIS IS ALL THE MONEY YOU GOT FROM A FULL DAY'S WORK?
WELL THEN, WE'LL HAVE TO FIND ANOTHER WAY FOR YOU TO PAY US, DARLING!
NO!
HE, HE, HE!
WHAT ARE YOU GUYS DOING?
FUCKER...
CLICK

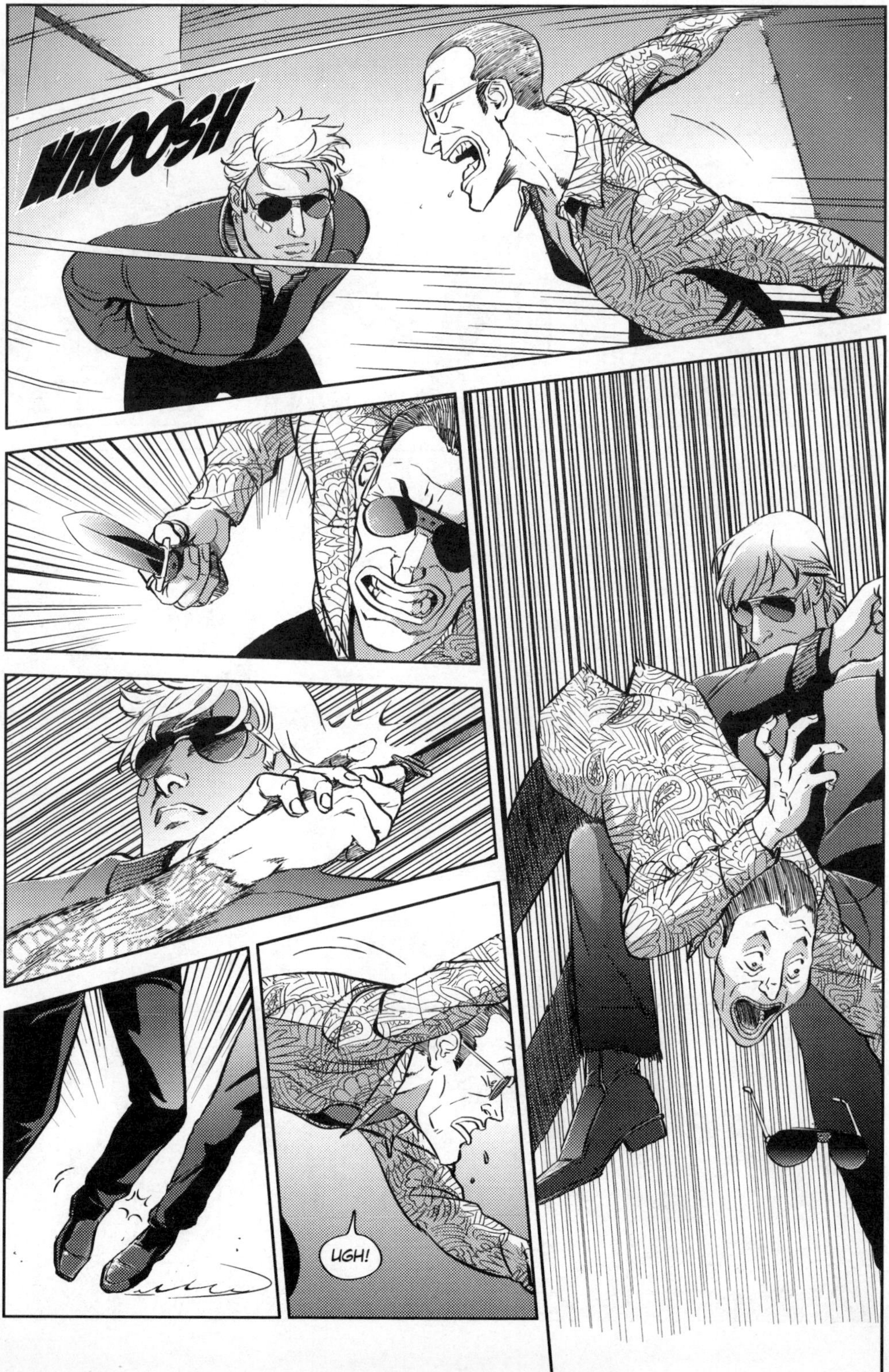
WHOOSH
UGH!

BLAM
THAT'S ENOUGH, BUDDY!
NOW BE A GOOD BOY AND OPEN THAT GARAGE DOOR, OK?
TOO LATE FOR THAT.
WHAT? ARE YOU CRAZY?

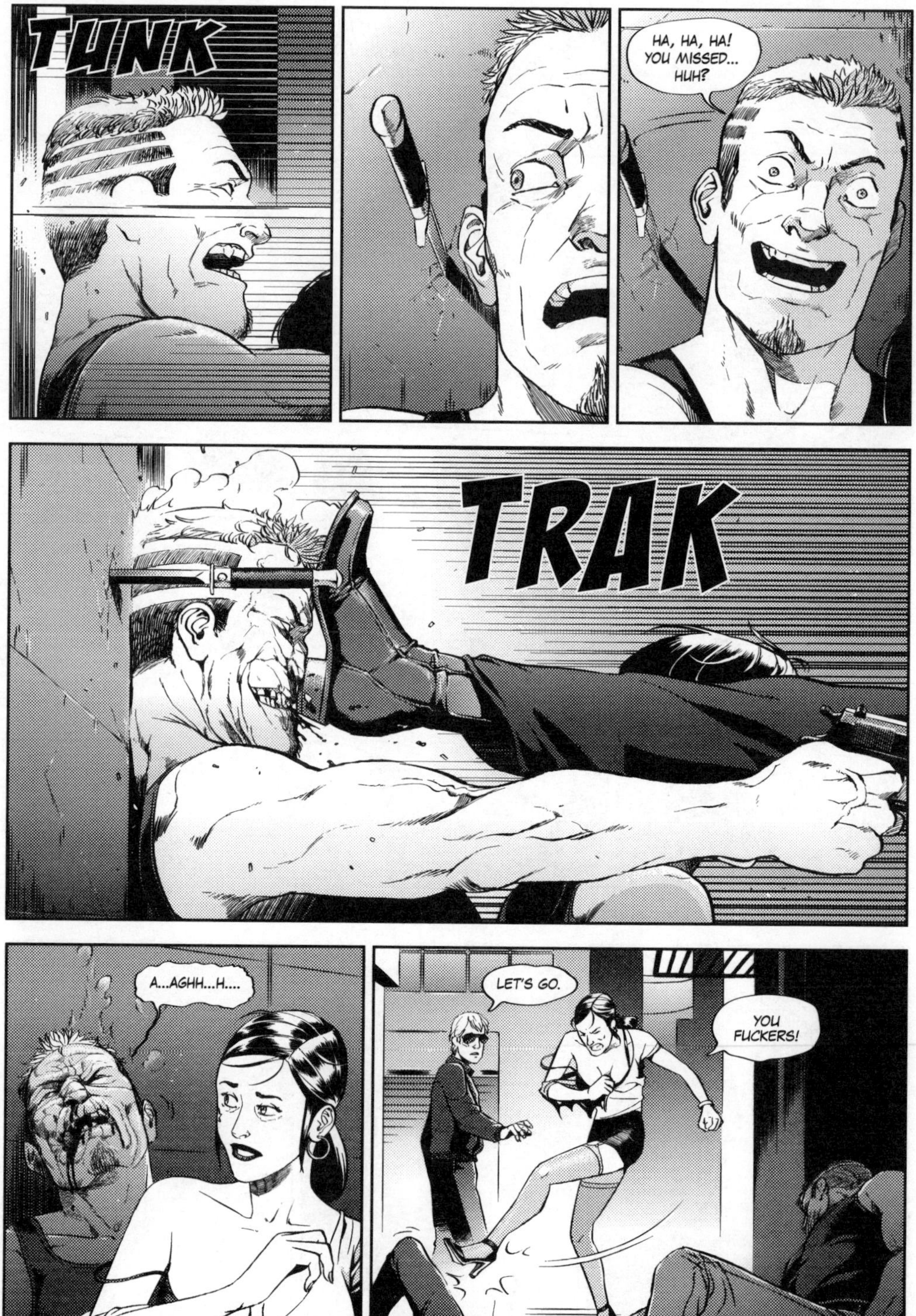
TUNK
HA, HA, HA! YOU MISSED... HUH?
TRAK
A...AGHH...H....
LET'S GO.
YOU FUCKERS!

MY HERO! THANK YOU!
I SWEAR I'VE NEVER SEEN THOSE GUYS BEFORE!
WHAT CAN I DO TO REWARD MY SAVIOR?
YEAH, YEAH... THERE'S JUST ONE THING THOUGH...
I KNOW THEY PAID YOU WELL FOR THAT LITTLE SCENE.
IF I EVER SEE YOU AROUND HERE AGAIN, YOU'RE GETTING THE SAME TREATMENT AS THEM. GOT IT?
CAFE
DINNER
LUNCH
open 24

GOOD MORNING!
GOOD MORNING! GOT UP EARLY FOR A CHANGE?
TOO EARLY FOR MY LIKING...
WHAT'S IT GONNA BE?
A LATTE AND A CROISSANT.
WORKING LATE?
TONY, I TOLD YOU NOT TO ASK ABOUT MY JOB, MAN.
YAWN
YOU DON'T WANT TO KNOW WHAT I DO... BELIEVE ME!
OK, OK. A LATTE COMING UP FOR MR. MYSTERY!
TONY, WE'VE KNOWN EACH OTHER FOR A WHILE NOW.
SOMETIMES I THINK YOU'RE THE ONLY ONE THAT ACTUALLY CARES ABOUT ME.

PHISSHHHH
MAKES ME THINK I SHOULD GET A NORMAL JOB SOMEDAY...
WITH A CLEARER FUTURE...
DRIP
DRIP
SOMETHING QUIETER, MORE PREDICTABLE...
MAYBE SOMEDAY...
TUNK

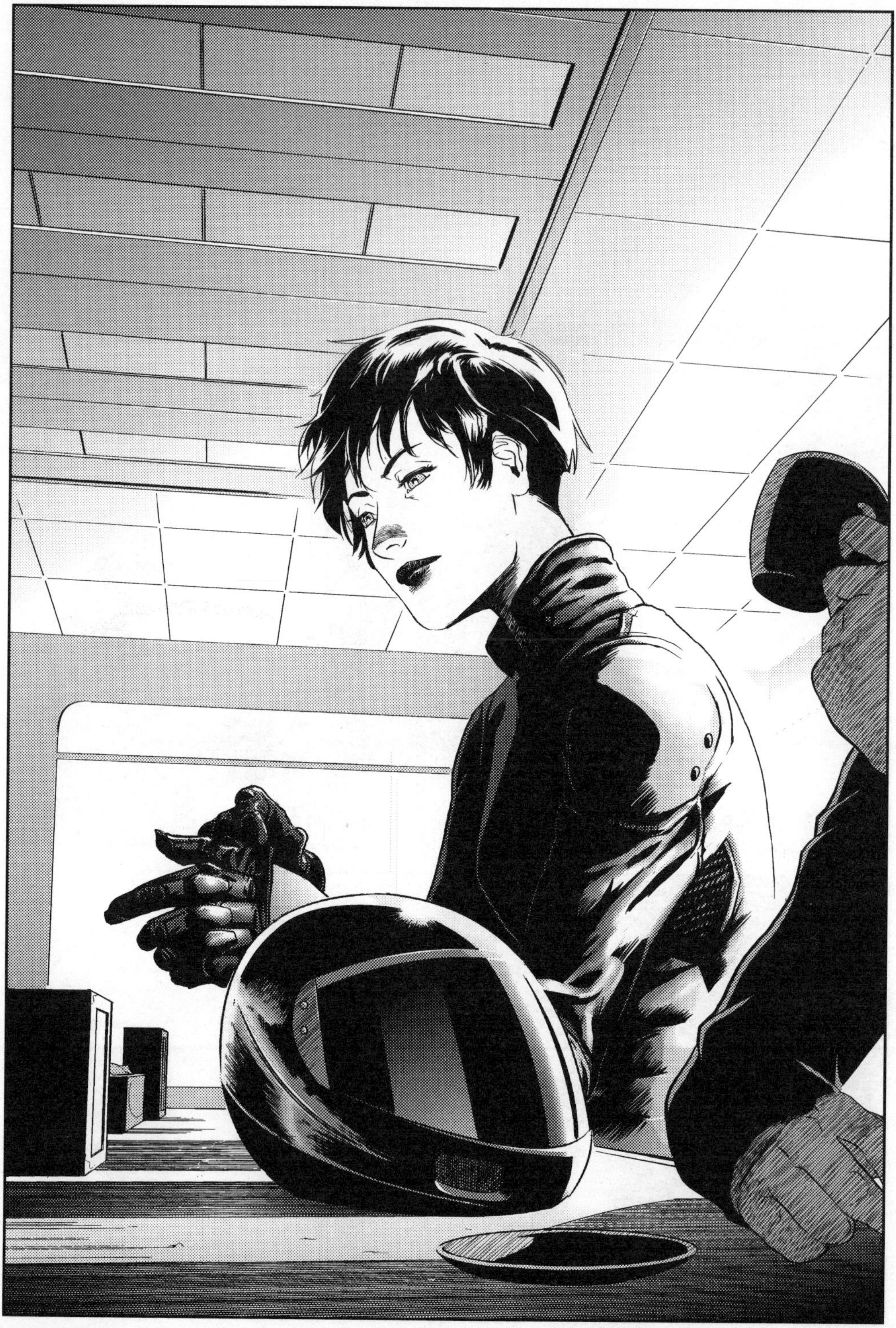

02

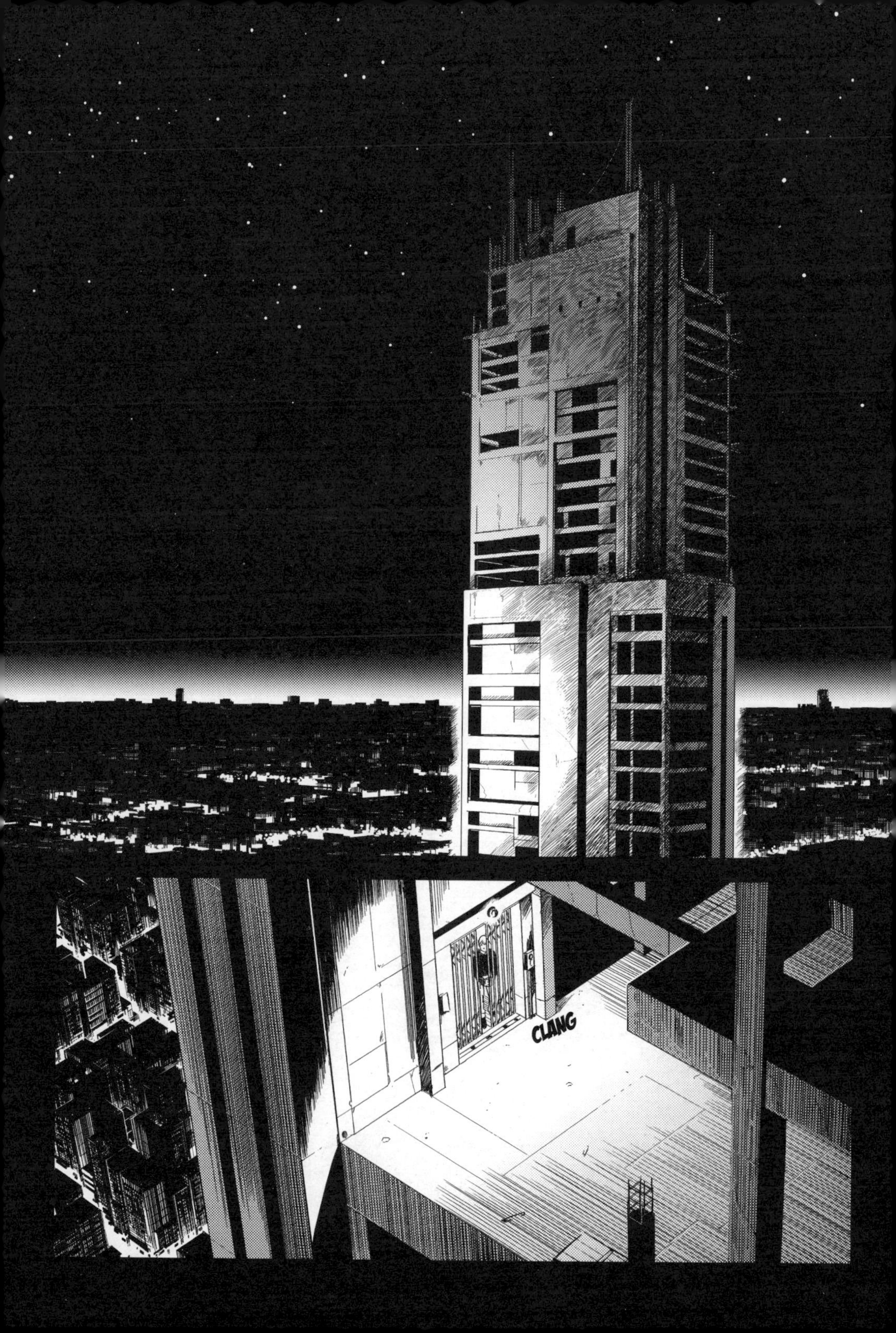
CLANG

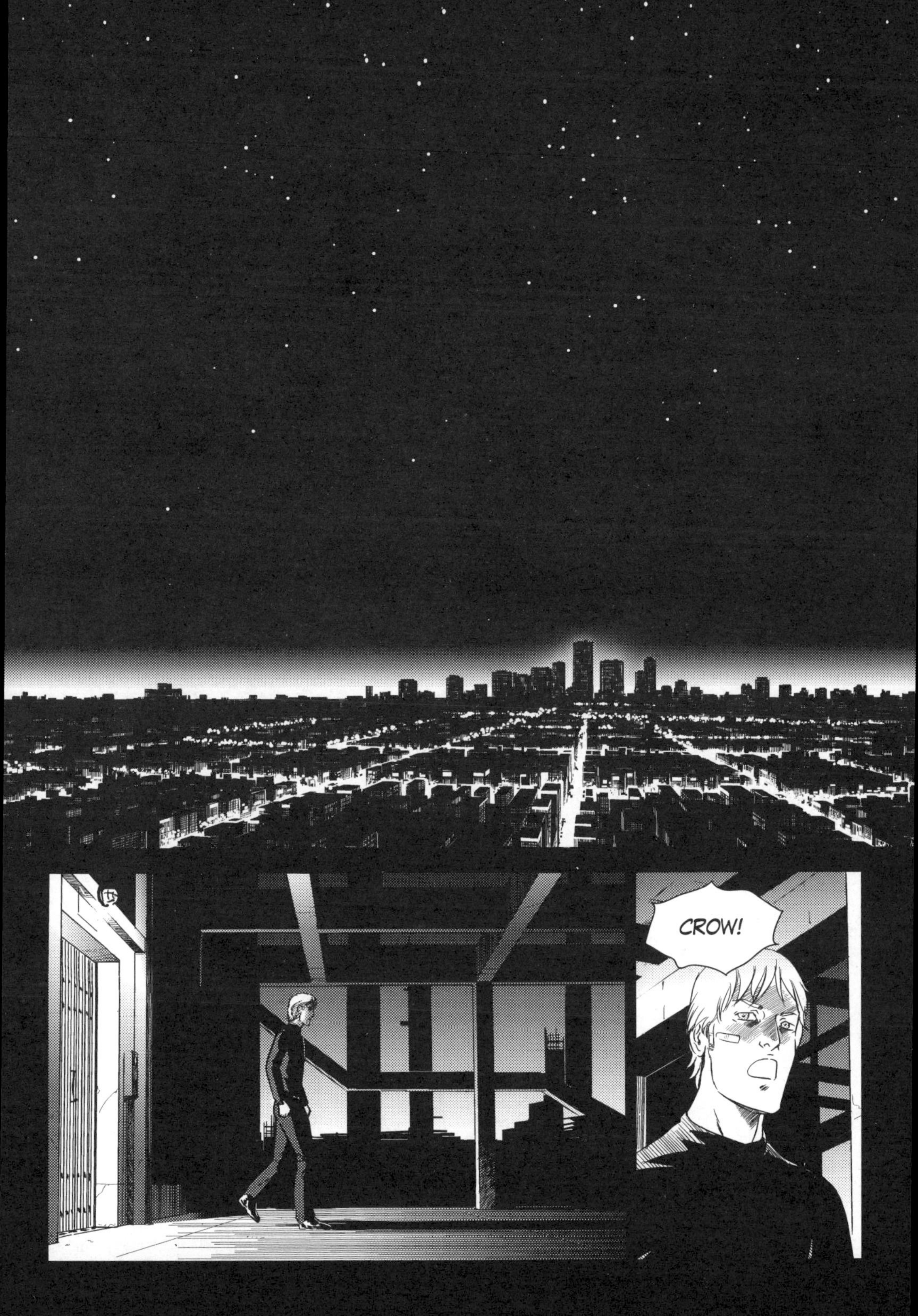
CROW!

LOOK WHO DECIDED TO SHOW UP!
OVER HERE...
IT'S BEEN A WHILE, BIRD.
I'VE BEEN BUSY LATELY. YOU KNOW...
HOW ARE YOU?
WHAT DO YOU WANT
I'D IMAGINE YOU'RE NOT HERE TO CATCH UP...
?
I NEED INFORMATION A NEW ASSASSIN'S IN TOWN

HE'S YOUNG. TWENTY-SOMETHING.
RIDES A BLACK MOTORCYCLE.
GOOD WITH BLADES. EXCELLENT WITH HANDGUNS
HA, HA, HA!
IS IT JUST ME, OR IS LITTLE BIRD HAVING FANTASIES ABOUT AN UNBEATA-BLE ADVERSARY?
OR ARE YOU ASKING BECAUSE OF SOMETHING ELSE?
OH... I GET IT!
IS IT BECAUSE THEY CAUSED YOU TO FAIL A MISSION FOR THE FIRST TIME EVER?
HA, HA, HA!
HOW MANY TIMES DO I HAVE TO TELL YOU THAT THERE'S NO ROOM FOR EGO IN THIS JOB?

WE GET PAID TO KILL. THAT'S IT.
DOING THE POLICE'S DIRTY WORK DOESN'T CHANGE THINGS EITHER.
CROW, I DIDN'T COME HERE TO GET LECTURED. I'M HERE BECAUSE I NEED YOUR HELP.
OK, OK. COME ON UP. I WANT YOU TO SEE SOMETHING.
THIS IS MY NEW TOY!
WINDRUNNER M200. .50 CALIBER. EFFECTIVE RANGE OF 2,000 YARDS.
NEXT TO THIS BEAST, EVEN A BARRETT LOOKS LIKE A TOY.

GRAB THE SPOTTER. I WANNA SHOW YOU SOME-THING.
LET'S GO VISIT SOME FRIENDS.
FOLLOW ME.
THIRD BUILDING, EAST.
TOP FLOOR. RIGHT WINDOW.

TYPICAL NEWLYWED. SMOKING BEHIND HIS WIFE'S BACK AGAIN.
TWO FLOORS DOWN...
LOOK, THE LITTLE ONE'S FINALLY TAKING HIS FIRST STEPS!
SAME FLOOR, TO THE LEFT...
THE USUAL GEEK LIVING IN FRONT OF A COMPUTER SCREEN. PATHETIC!
ONE FLOOR DOWN, SECOND WINDOW TO THE LEFT.
HERE WE HAVE MY LITTLE LOLA...
OR AT LEAST THAT'S WHAT I LIKE TO CALL HER...
A STUDENT. 20 YEARS OLD.
YOUR AVERAGE ANGSTY GIRL.
SHE'S EVEN CONVINCED THAT SHE'S UGLY. CAN YOU BELIEVE THAT?
YOU DO AGREE THAT THEY'RE ALL MEDIOCRE PEOPLE, RIGHT, BIRD?

I GUESS... WHAT'S YOUR POINT?		I WONDER IF I'VE ZEROED THE SCOPE CORRECTLY, OR IF I'LL NEED TO TAKE MORE THAN ONE SHOT.

DO YOU WANT TO KNOW WHAT I REALLY THINK WHEN I LOOK AT THEM?

I ASK MYSELF HOW THE BODY WILL FALL AFTER IMPACT.

KA-CLAK

HUH?

WILL THE WALLS GET STAINED BY THE GREY MATTER?

I GUESS THERE'S ONLY ONE WAY TO FIND OUT...

NO!!!

CHAK
YOU SEE?
I VIEW THEM AS OBJECTIVES. TARGETS.
YOU VIEW THEM AS PEOPLE.
THAT'S ALWAYS BEEN THE BIG DIFFERENCE BETWEEN YOU AND ME...
DAMN, I'M TURNING INTO A CRANKY OLD MAN!
LISTEN. I'M GLAD YOU REACHED OUT AND ASKED FOR MY HELP AGAIN.

LET ME SEE WHAT I CAN FIND OUT ABOUT YOUR FRIEND.
I'LL LET YOU KNOW IF I FIND SOMETHING.
WORKING TOGETHER, JUST LIKE OLD TIMES.
RIGHT, BIRD?
GOODBYE, CROW.

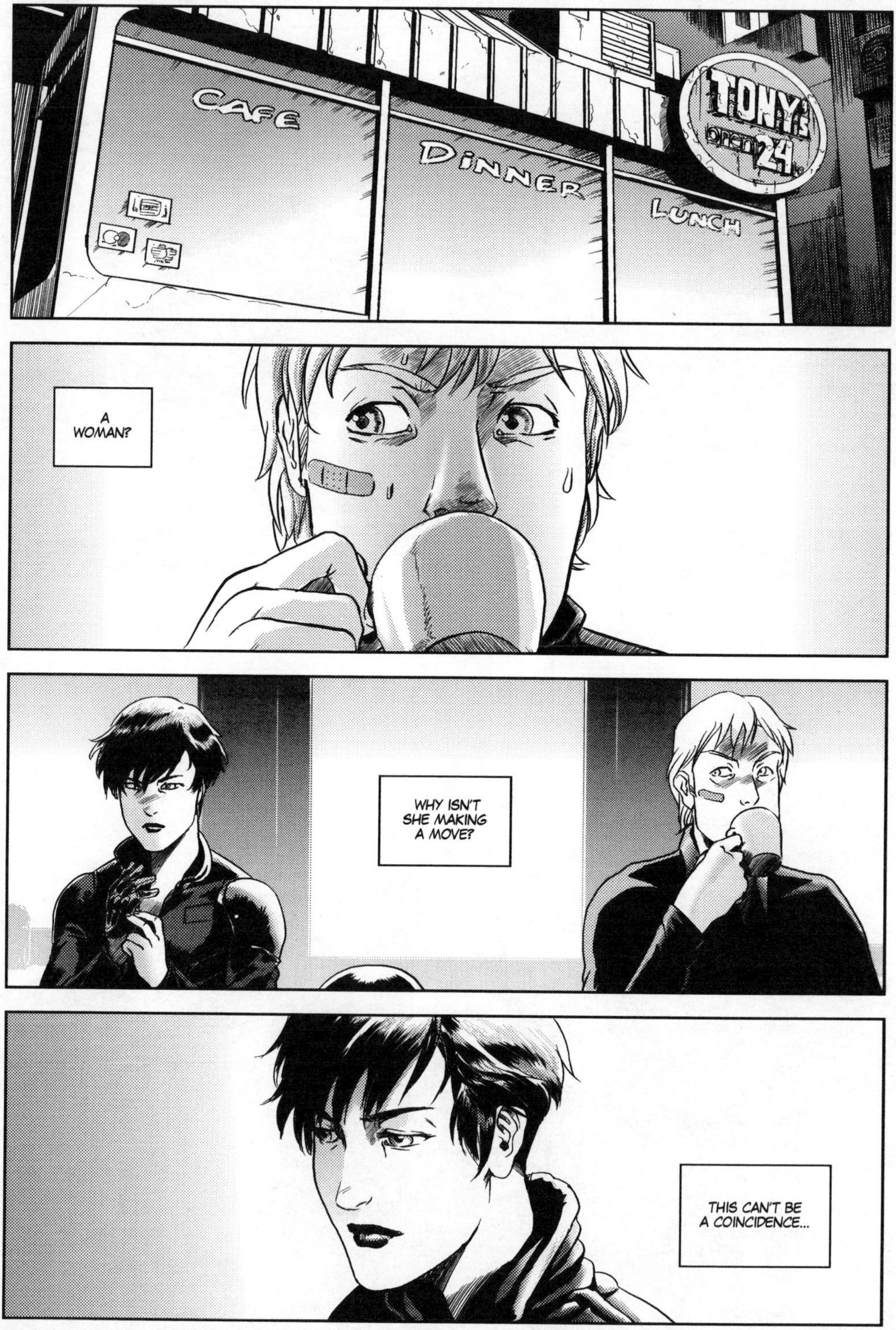
CAFE
DINNER
LUNCH
TONY'S
OPEN 24
A WOMAN?
WHY ISN'T SHE MAKING A MOVE?
THIS CAN'T BE A COINCIDENCE...

WAIT... MAYBE SHE DOESN'T KNOW WHO I AM.
I GOTTA BE QUICK...
I'M HEADING OUT, TONY! THANS FOR THE COFFEE...
CHANK
YOU LEAVING ALREADY? YOUR CROISSANT'S ALMOST DONE!
NO, NO. THANKS, BUT I'M NOT THAT HUNGRY ANYMORE. HOW MUCH IS IT?
C'MON, I'LL PUT IT ON YOUR TAB LIKE I USUALLY DO.
TONY...
TODAY I FEEL LIKE ACTUALLY PAYING YOU!
DON'T...

I DON'T KNOW WHY YOU'RE ABOUT TO DO THAT...
HUH?
I'M NOT HERE FOR YOU.
BESIDES...
ONLY A FOOL WOULD TRY TO ATTACK ME.
KANG

I TOLD YOU I'M NOT HERE FOR YOU!
SO WHAT ARE YOU DOING HERE THEN?
THAT'S NONE OF YOUR BUSINESS!
WHAP

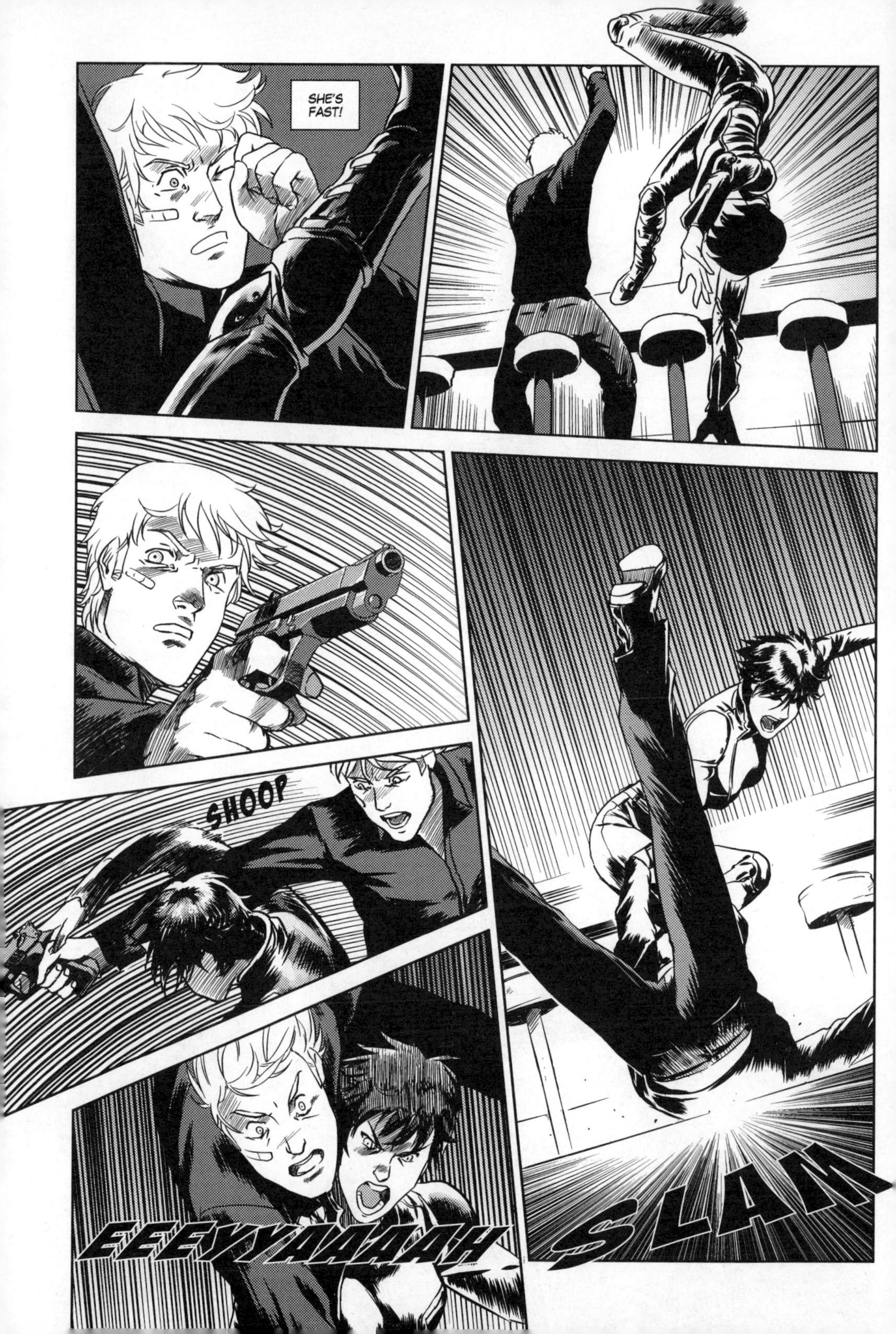
SHE'S FAST!
SHOOP
EEEYYAAAAAH
SLAM

AH!
GET UP!
YOU'RE GOOD, ALTHOUGH YOU'RE A BIT CLUMSY IN MY EYES.
LET'S START WITH YOU TELLING ME WHY YOU'RE HERE.
LADIES FIRST!
KA-CHAK

LET ME HANDLE THIS, TONY!
JUST LIKE YOU'VE BEEN HANDLING IT SO FAR?
AND YOU BETTER HAVE A GOOD EXPLANATION TOO, OR I'M CALLING THE COPS!
OK, BIRD?
BIRD?
CRASH

BUROOOOM

DONE!

LET'S GO!

ARE YOU SURE THEY'RE DEAD?

OF COURSE! NOBODY COULD SURVIVE...

HUH?

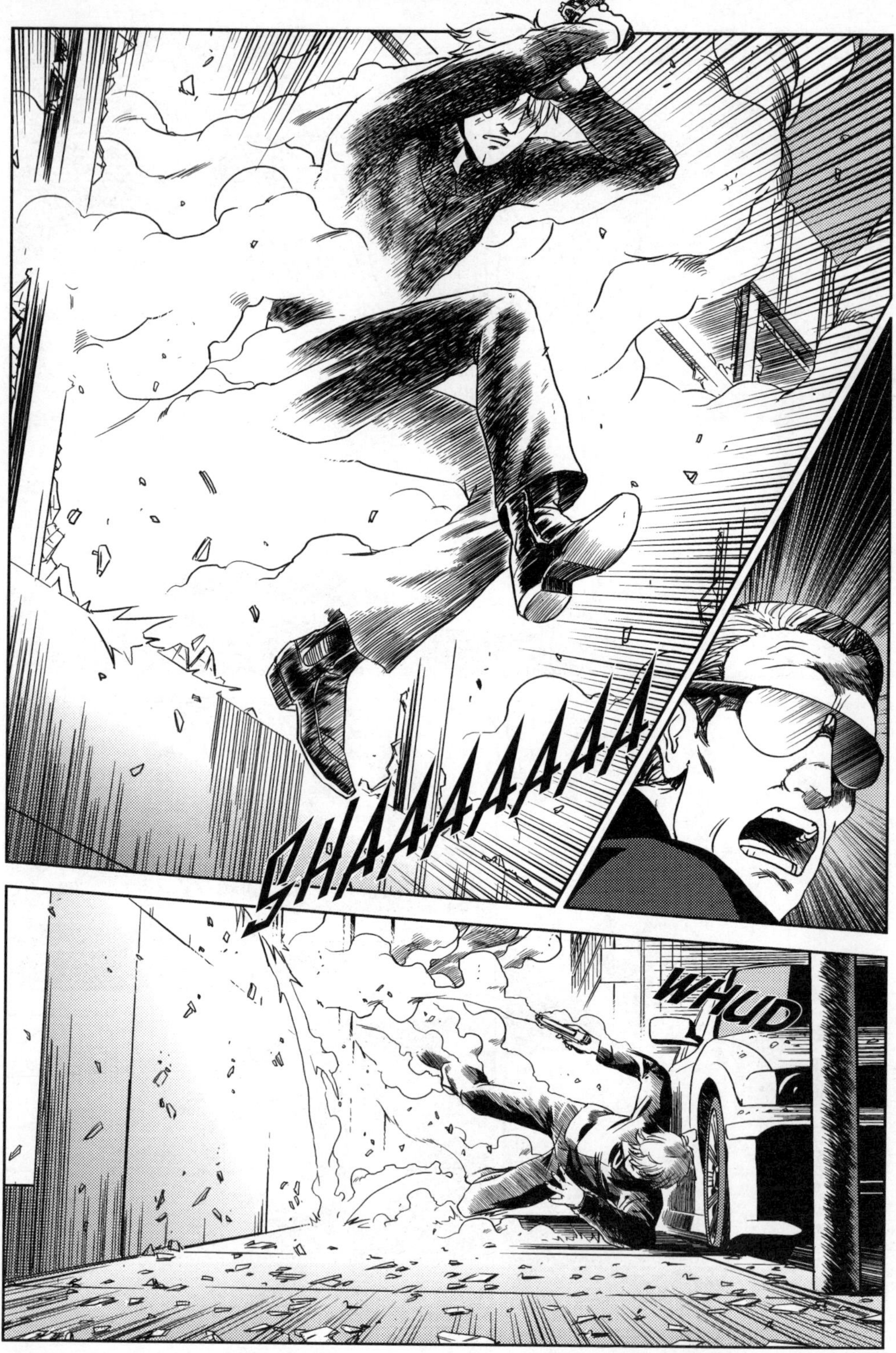
SHAAAAAAAA
WHUD

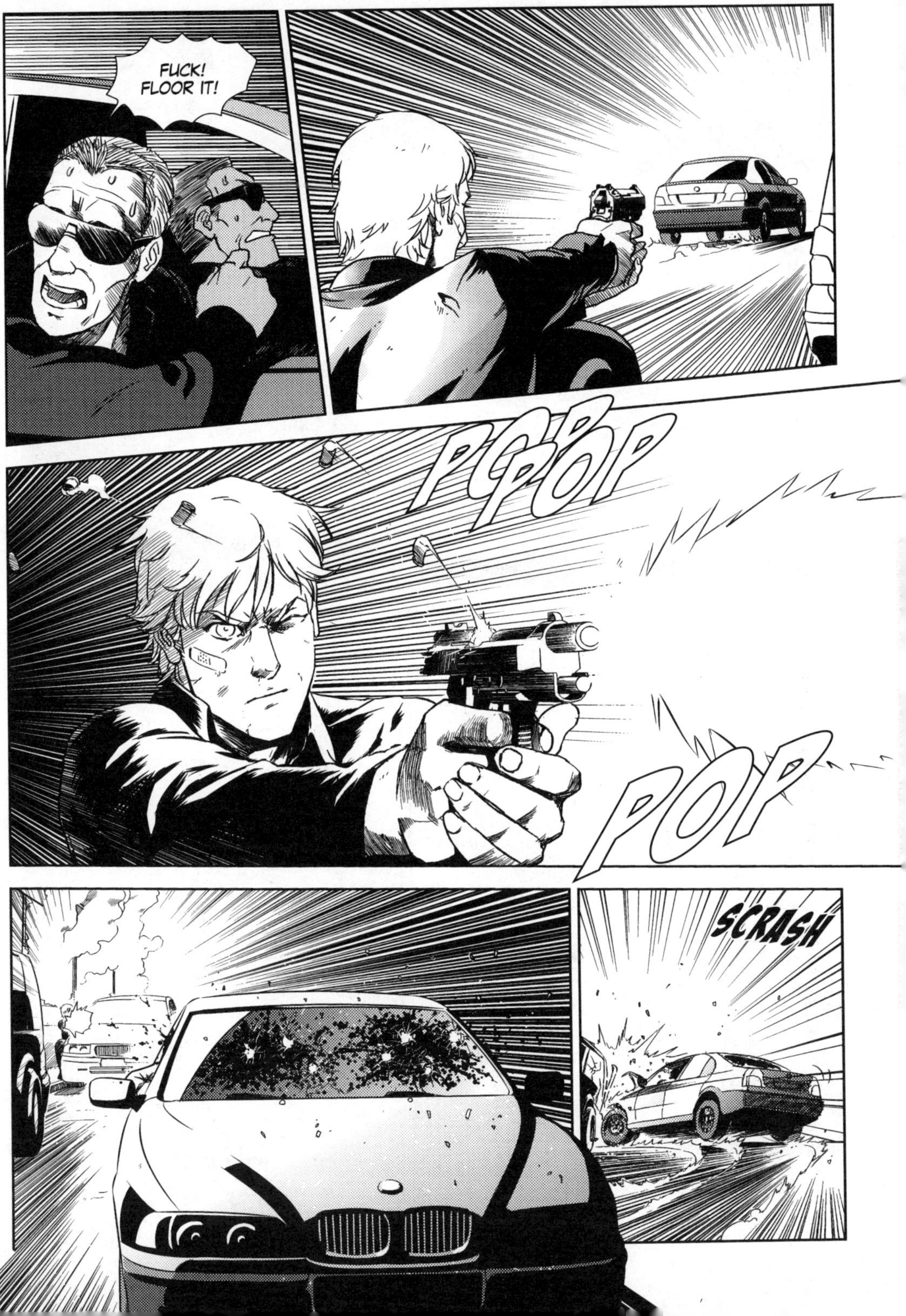
FUCK! FLOOR IT!
POP POP
POP
SCRASH

BOOOOM

IT'S OVER...

THAT WAS TOO CLOSE FOR ME...

IF IT WEREN'T FOR THE BAR COUNTER, WE'D BE HISTORY...

THE GIRL CAUGHT THE WORST OF THE BLAST.

YOU KNOW, BIRD...
I USED TO THINK YOU WERE A NICE KID...
BUT I WAS WRONG...
TONY, I...
FORGET IT.
DON'T EVER COME BACK HERE.
UNDERSTAND?
AND TAKE YOUR FRIEND WITH YOU.
IN THE STATE SHE'S IN SHE WON'T LAST MUCH LONGER...

AH!
WHERE...
HUH?
WHAT THE FUCK?!?
I'M GOING TO ASK YOU SOME QUESTIONS, AND I EXPECT ANSWERS...

03

SHIT
ARE YOU SURE HE'S COMING?
HUH?
BLIP
BLIP
HELLO?
I'M FREEZING MY ASS OFF HERE!
I DON'T HAVE ALL DAY, BUDDY!
IF YOU'RE NOT HERE IN 10 SECONDS, I'M LEAVING!
I TOLD YOU TO COME ALONE...
PLACE THE PACKAGE IN THE TRASH CAN...
WHO THE HELL DO YOU THINK YOU'RE TALKING TO?
WE DON'T WORK THAT WAY, PAL!
THE DEAL IS OFF!

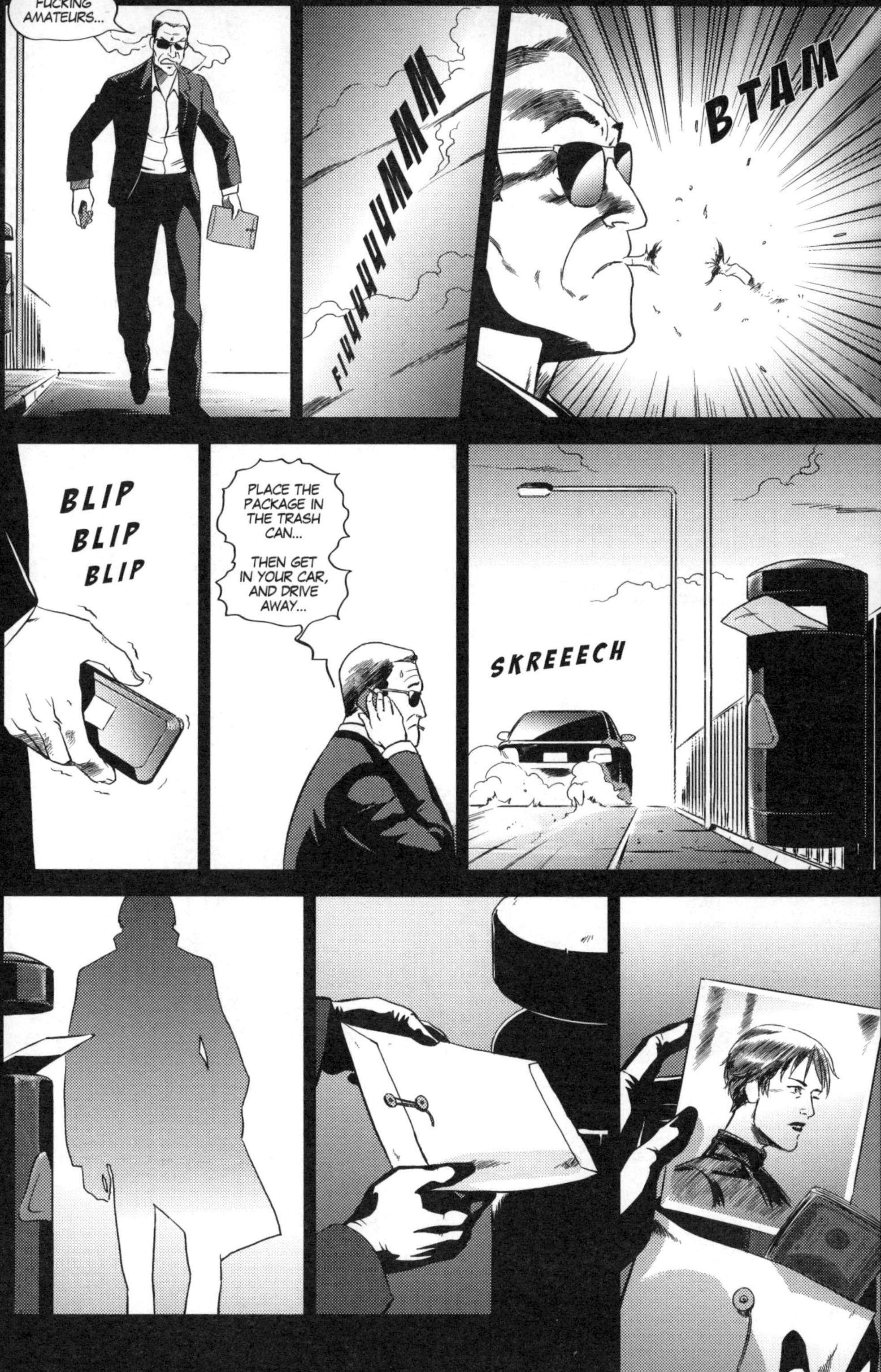
FUCKING AMATEURS...
FIUUUUUUMMM
BTAM
BLIP
BLIP
BLIP
PLACE THE PACKAGE IN THE TRASH CAN...
THEN GET IN YOUR CAR, AND DRIVE AWAY...
SKREEECH

"I DON'T KNOW WHAT YOU'RE TALKING ABOUT--"

"I ALREADY TOLD YOUR SWAT FRIENDS THAT THE EXPLOSION WAS BECAUSE OF A GAS LEAK!"

"TONY, THE TWO GUYS THAT WERE GUNNED DOWN WERE IN THE MAFIA."

"CALL ME IF YOU FEEL LIKE TALKING, OK?"

"I WILL. SEE YOU LATER, HONEY."

"YOU DON'T WANT TO GET INVOLVED WITH THE MOB, TONY. BELIEVE ME."

LAST WEEK THEY KILLED A MAFIA BOSS, AND TODAY WE HAVE TWO MORE MOBSTERS GUNNED DOWN.
THIS CAN'T BE A COINCIDENCE.
ANY NEWS ABOUT THE VICTIM'S IDENTITIES?
SPEAKING OF COINCIDENCES...
GOOD MORNING, COMMISSIONER.
YOUR SWAT FRIENDS ARE INTERFERING WITH MY WORK!
ISN'T THAT WHY WE HAVE INTERNAL AFFAIRS?
I WANT TO BE THE FIRST TO READ THE REPORT, OK?
WHAT THE HELL?

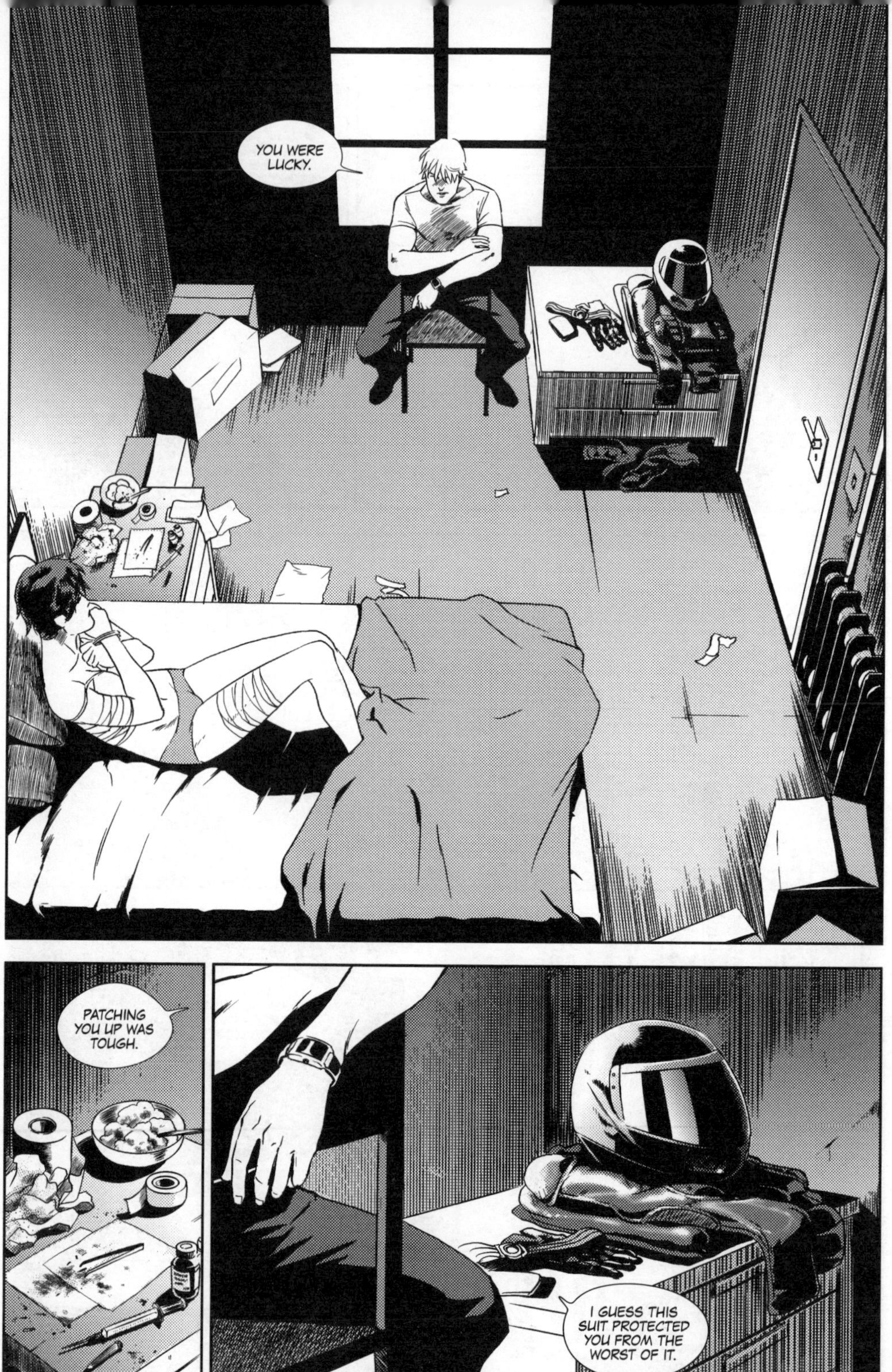
YOU WERE LUCKY.
PATCHING YOU UP WAS TOUGH.
I GUESS THIS SUIT PROTECTED YOU FROM THE WORST OF IT.

DO YOU THINK THIS IS GOING TO WORK?
THIS IS NO WAY TO TREAT A GIRL, "BIRD."
CUTE NAME!
I'M KAT. NICE TO MEET YOU.
I STILL CAN'T FIGURE IT OUT...
WHAT WOULD'VE HAPPENED IF I HAD TAKEN YOU DOWN DURING THAT MISSION?
OH!
YOU WERE THE OTHER SHOOTER... IS THAT WHAT THIS IS ABOUT? ARE YOU HAVING A HARD TIME GETTING PAID?
HA, HA!
I'M SORRY ABOUT YOUR FACE...

THERE AREN'T ANY REASONS WHY ANYBODY WOULD'VE WANTED TO GET RID OF ME BACK IN THE DINER...
SO THE TARGET MUST HAVE BEEN YOU.
YOU'RE GOOD, BUT I CAN RECOG-NIZE A FELLOW PROFESSIONAL WHEN I SEE THEM...
AND YOU'RE DEFINITELY NOT ONE OF THOSE.
SO... LET'S JUST CUT THE CRAP. WHO ARE YOU, AND WHAT WERE YOU DOING THERE?

WHY DID YOU KILL... HUH?
CLAK
MORNING, BIRDIE!
HOW DARE YOU BRING A SLUT HERE!
YOU SICK PERVERT!
SLAM
PIG!
OUT!

AM I NOT ENOUGH FOR YOU?
GET OUTTA HERE AND DON'T COME BACK!
WHERE WERE WE?
UMM...

WHAP
WHUMP
STOP!
YOU DON'T STAND A CHANCE LIKE THAT!
WHAT WERE YOU DOING THERE ON THAT DAY?

I WAS AVENGING MY DEAD FATHER!
HAPPY?
WHAT WERE YOU DOING?
I...
SIGH...
I'M SORRY...
I DON'T NEED YOUR PITY...
LET'S JUST DROP IT, OK?
YOU CAN GO.

THE SUBWAY STATION'S ONLY A FEW BLOCKS AWAY. JUST KEEP GOING STRAIGHT.
FOR YOUR SAKE, I HOPE WE DON'T SEE EACH OTHER AGAIN.
WHATEVER... IT SEEMS THAT YOU'RE NOT VERY GOOD AT AVENGING, ARE YOU?
...

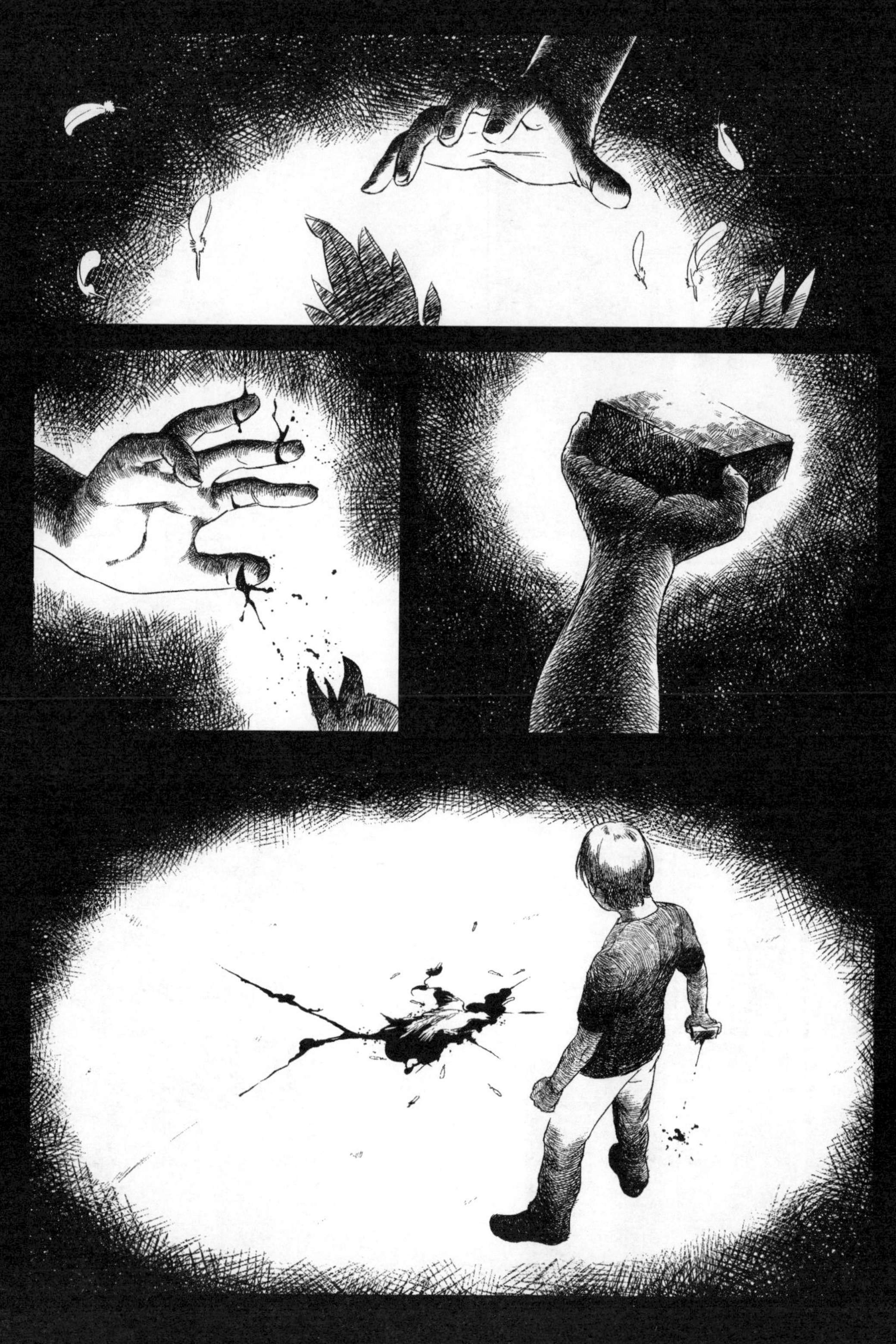

WHUD
UGH...
HUH?
MEOW?
CLANG
LA LA LA!
HEY! LOOK WHO WOKE UP!
GOOD MORNING!

HANNA... HOW MANY TIMES DO I HAVE TO TELL YOU?
CAN YOU JUST SHUT UP FOR A SECOND AND LISTEN TO WHAT I'M ABOUT TO SAY?!?
WHAM
AHEM...
ALTHOUGH I AM JEALOUS, I'M NOT GOING TO INTERFERE IN YOUR NEW RELATIONSHIP.
BESIDES, I THINK AN OLDER WOMAN IS MORE SUITABLE FOR YOU.
BYE BIRDIE!
WHO COULD UNDERSTAND WOMEN?

WHAT DO YOU MEAN THE TERMS HAVE CHANGED?
IF YOU WANT TO BE PART OF THIS FAMILY, WE NEED YOUR UNCONDITIONAL SUPPORT.
BUT, SIR, THAT WAS NOT THE DEAL!
I DID MY PART! I CAN'T PUT MY MEN UP TO THIS!
IT WOULD BE TOO OBVIOUS!
USE YOUR FORCES AND HURRY UP WITH IT OR I'LL HAVE TO EXCLUDE YOU FROM THE DEAL.
GOODBYE.
WHAT?!?
TAK

THAT SON OF A BITCH!
NOW HE WANTS TO KIDNAP A CIVILIAN?
MY MEN AND I CAN HANDLE IT.
FOR YOUR SAKE, I HOPE YOU CAN MAKE GOOD ON YOUR PROMISE TO GET US INTO THE MERGER.
SWAT
THERE'S NO NEED FOR YOU TO THREATEN ME TOO.
I'LL FIGURE OUT HOW TO GET IT DONE.
POLICE DEPARTMENT
THIS IS GETTING DANGEROUS!
...
CLICK
DRIVE.

IF YOU TELL THE TRUTH, YOU HAVE A BETTER CHANCE OF COMING OUT OF THIS ALIVE.
WHAT THE HELL IS THIS?
LET'S START FROM THE BEGINNING.
WHY ARE THEY TRYING TO ELIM-INATE ME?
NOBODY WANTS TO GET YOU!
WHO ARE YOU WORKING FOR?
I WORK FOR THE ZASTAVA FAMILY. THEY PAY BETTER THAN A COP'S SALARY, OK?
AND THIS WHOLE TIME YOU'VE BEEN USING ME TO DO THEIR DIRTY WORK...
I'M SORRY, PAL! BUT BUSI-NESS IS BUSINESS, RIGHT?
GO INTO THE NEXT CONSTRUCTION SITE.
C'MON, BIRD. YOU DON'T HAVE TO DO THIS!

WHAT ABOUT THE GIRL?

WHAT GIRL?

THE ONE THAT BEAT ME TO IT.

I DON'T KNOW WHAT YOU'RE TALKING ABOUT...

I DIDN'T TAKE DOWN THE LAST TARGET YOU ASSIGNED TO ME. ANOTHER ASSASSIN GOT TO HIM FIRST. A GIRL THAT SAYS SHE'S AVENGING HER FATHER.

I THOUGHT YOU HAD DONE THE JOB!

THEY TOLD ME THEY WANTED TO MEET YOU AT TONY'S PLACE... BUT I NEVER IMAGINED THEY WANTED YOU DEAD!

I THINK THEY'VE BEEN PLAYING US THIS WHOLE TIME! PLEASE, LET ME GO! I... I HAVE FAMILY TO TAKE CARE OF!

I PROMISE YOU'LL NEVER SEE ME AGAIN!

WHAT DO YOU SAY?

HUH?

UFF! I'M GONNA HAVE A HEART ATTACK...

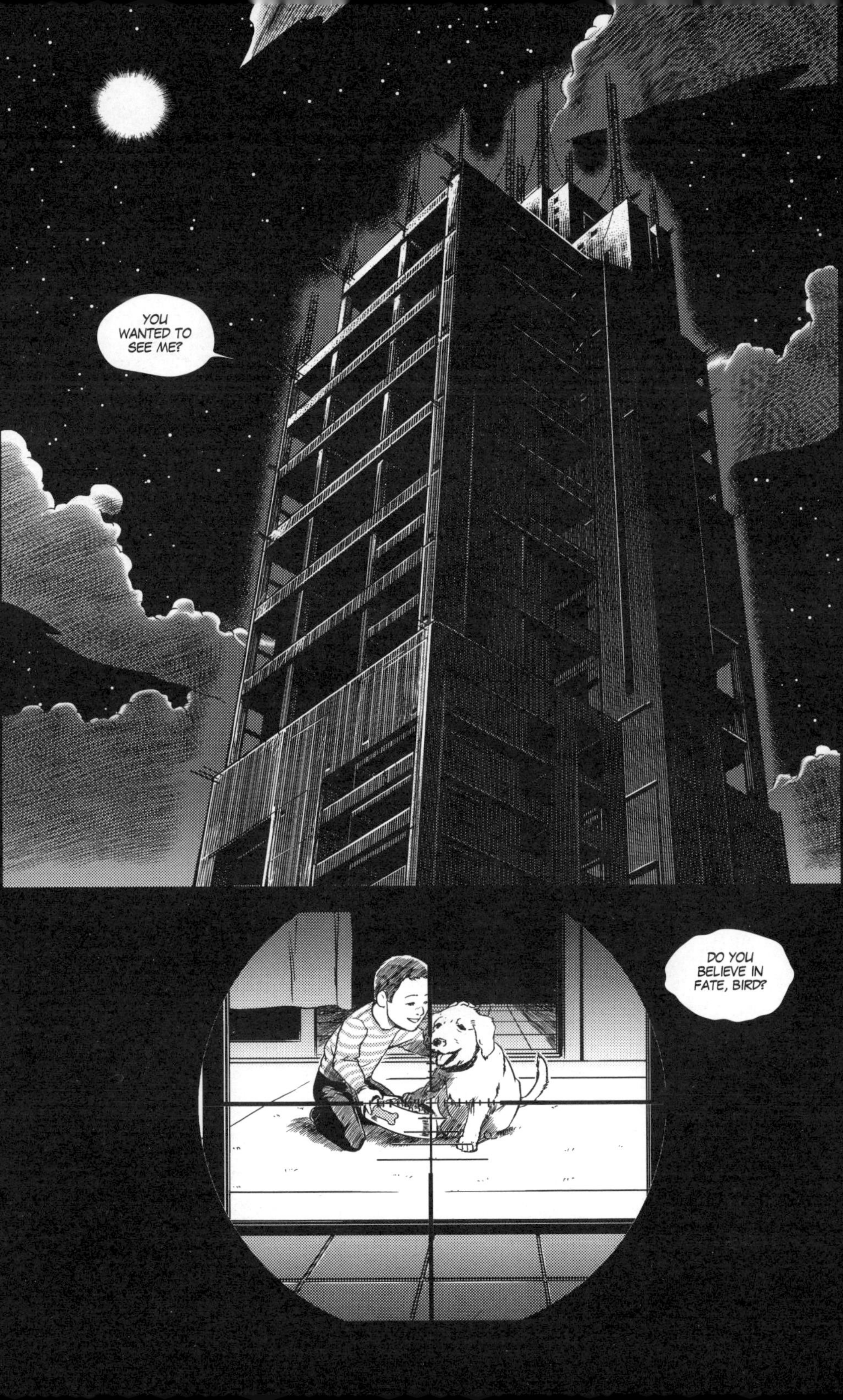
YOU WANTED TO SEE ME?
DO YOU BELIEVE IN FATE, BIRD?

YOU PROBABLY DO...
YOU ALWAYS WERE THE GULLIBLE TYPE
LAST TIME WE SAW EACH OTHER, I FELT THAT THERE WAS SOMETHING BIGGER AT PLAY...
WHAT'S YOUR POINT?
I ONLY BELIEVE IN COINCIDENCES...
YOU CALLED ME OVER FOR THIS CRAP?
SEE YA, CROW...

BEFORE YOU LEAVE, YOU MIGHT WANNA CHECK OUT WHAT'S BEEN FLOATING AROUND IN OUR CIRCLES.
DON'T TELL ME IT'S THAT KID'S DOG!
NO...
IT'S SOMETHING FAR MORE INTERESTING.
THAT'S YOUR GIRL, RIGHT?
THE ONLY THING I KNOW IS THAT SHE'S VERY VALUABLE.
THEY WANT HER CAPTURED ALIVE AT ANY COST!

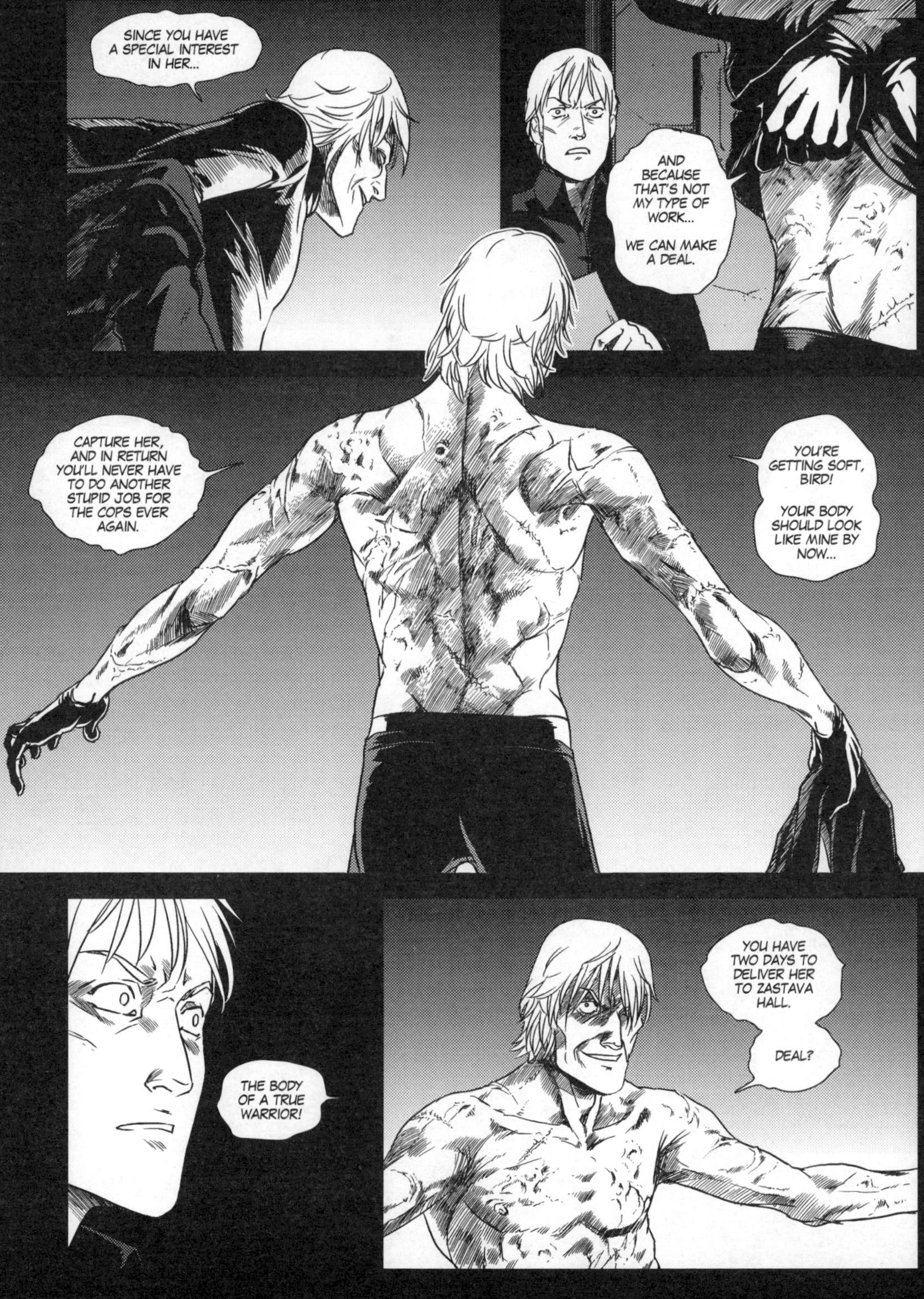
SINCE YOU HAVE A SPECIAL INTEREST IN HER...
AND BECAUSE THAT'S NOT MY TYPE OF WORK...
WE CAN MAKE A DEAL.
CAPTURE HER, AND IN RETURN YOU'LL NEVER HAVE TO DO ANOTHER STUPID JOB FOR THE COPS EVER AGAIN.
YOU'RE GETTING SOFT, BIRD!
YOUR BODY SHOULD LOOK LIKE MINE BY NOW...
THE BODY OF A TRUE WARRIOR!
YOU HAVE TWO DAYS TO DELIVER HER TO ZASTAVA HALL.
DEAL?

IF YOU TAKE LONGER THAN TWO DAYS, I'M GONNA HAVE TO KILL HER.
THAT'S THE PRICE FOR MY INFORMATION.
WORKING TOGETHER, JUST LIKE OLD TIMES!
HA!
BUSTER?

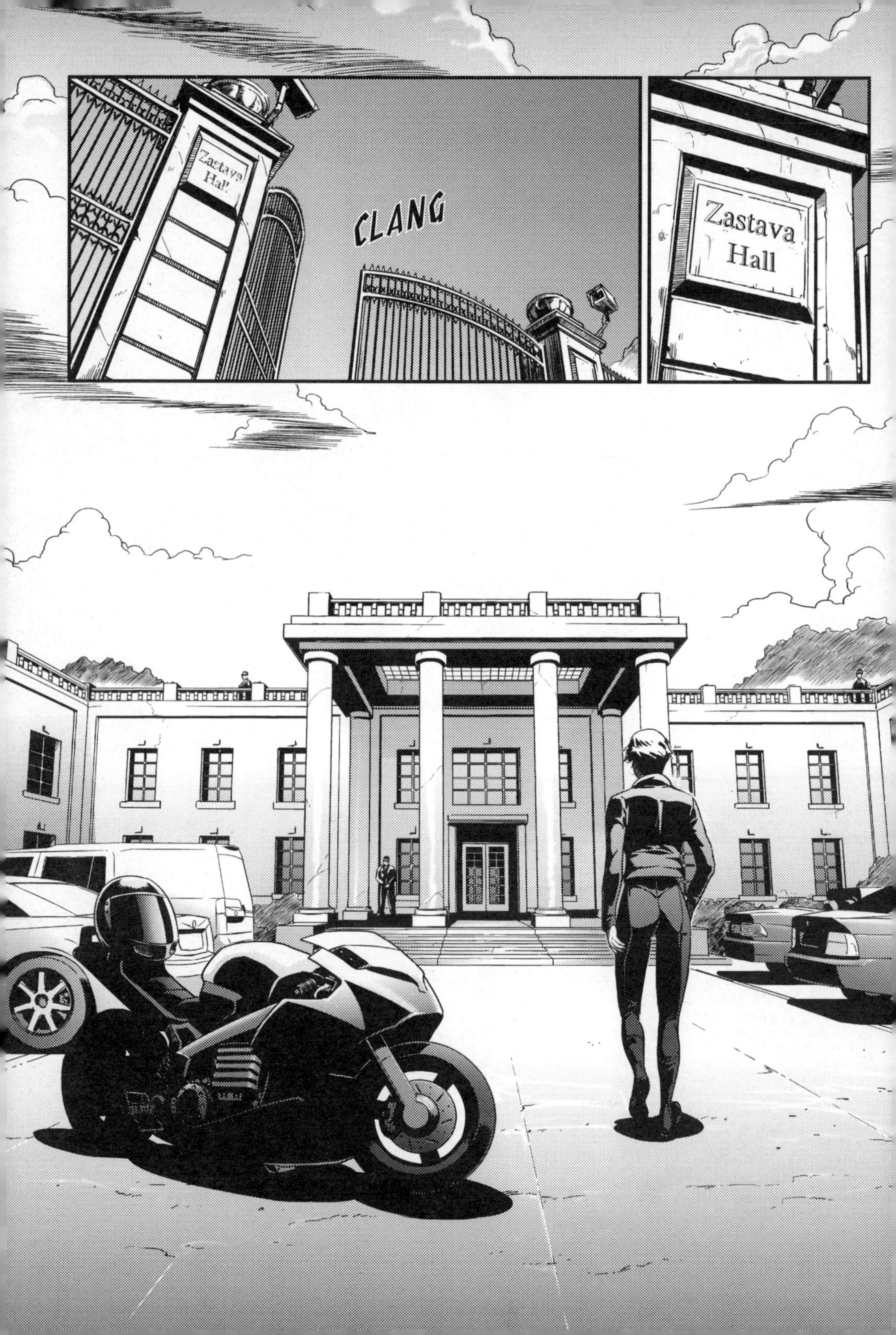
Zastava Hall
CLANG
Zastava Hall

04

WHUD

OOPS!

I'M SORRY! I GOT CARRIED AWAY...

ARE YOU OK, MR. SETH?

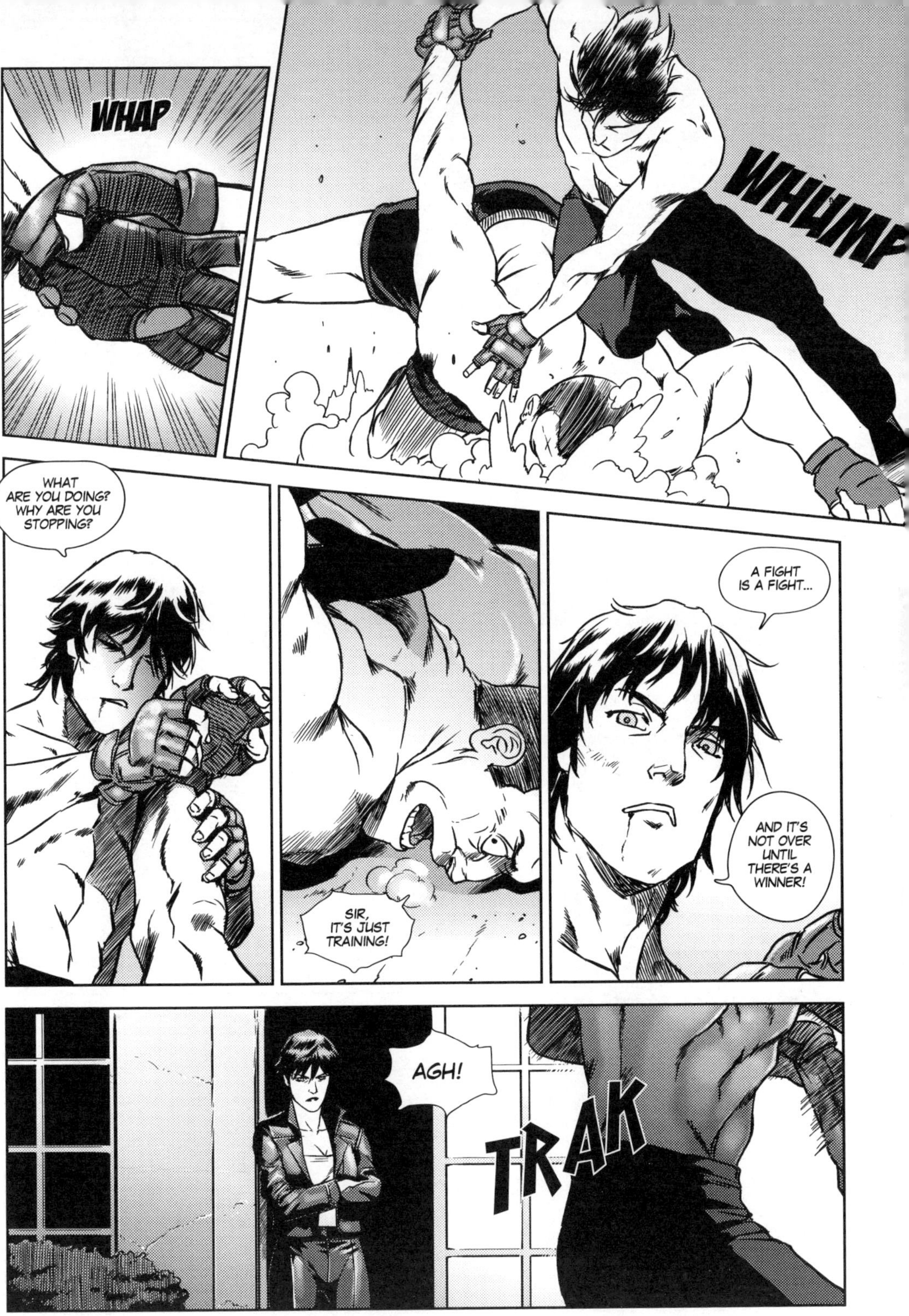
WHAP
WHUMP
WHAT ARE YOU DOING? WHY ARE YOU STOPPING?
SIR, IT'S JUST TRAINING!
A FIGHT IS A FIGHT...
AND IT'S NOT OVER UNTIL THERE'S A WINNER!
AGH!
TRAK

TAKE HIM AWAY AND PATCH HIM UP. NEXT TIME, GET ME A REAL FIGHTER!
ALWAYS THE SAME.
YOU DON'T LIKE TO LOSE.
SIS!
HOW ARE YOU?
LET'S CUT THE CHIT CHAT...
IT'S NOT OUR STYLE.
WHY WEREN'T YOU AT THE DINER?

I'M SO GLAD YOU'RE OK!
I GOT HELD UP WITH SOMETHING. BY THE TIME I GOT THERE, THE PLACE WAS TRASHED.
I'VE BEEN TRYING TO FIND YOU FOR A LONG TIME.
WHERE WERE YOU?
I WAS BUSY SURVIVING THE HIT'S AFTERMATH THANKS TO AN ASSASSIN THAT JUST SO HAPPENED TO BE THERE...
EVIDENTLY, THOSE ARE THE CONSEQUENCES FOR KILLING BOSS H. HALLER.
YOU DID THE RIGHT THING BY AVENGING OUR FATHER. NOW THEY KNOW.
ALTHOUGH HE'S NOT HERE ANYMORE, WE CAN STILL HOLD THIS FAMILY TOGETHER.
WHEN THINGS COOL OFF, YOU CAN TAKE YOUR PLACE AT MY SIDE.
AT YOUR SIDE?
AND SINCE WHEN WAS TAKING OVER THE FAMILY PART OF THE PLAN?
DO YOU SERIOUSLY THINK I BELIEVE ALL THIS BULLSHIT?
MS. KAT?

A FRIEND OF YOURS IS ASKING TO COME IN.
FRIEND?
THAT'S RIGHT. SHOULD I LET HIM IN?
EH, OK... I'LL BE RIGHT THERE...
WHEN I COME BACK, WE'RE GETTING TO THE BOTTOM OF THIS!
DON'T LET HER LEAVE. AND GET RID OF THE STRANGER.
COME IN!
CLANK

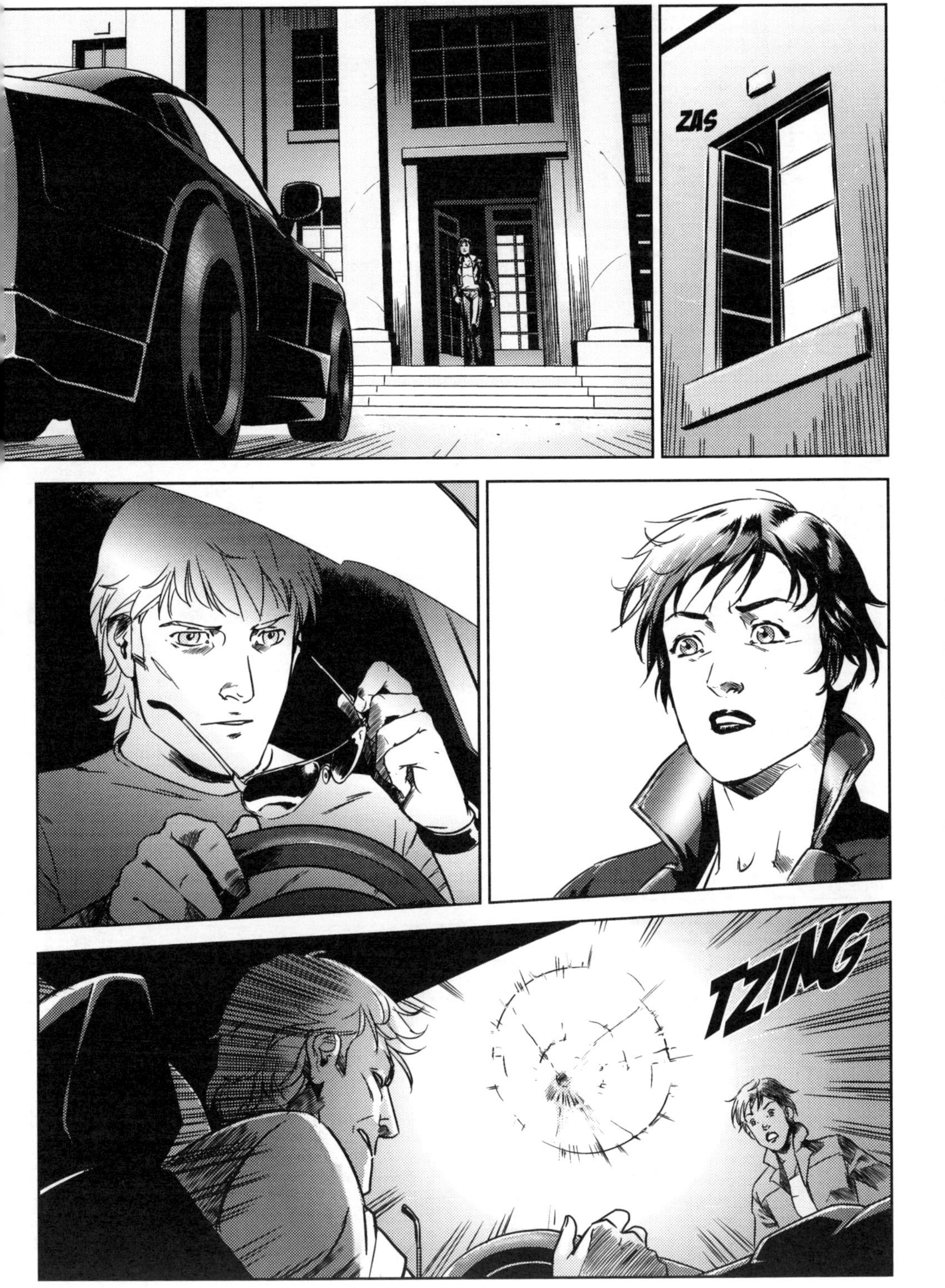
ZAS
TZING

SHIT! IT'S ARMORED!
GET ME THE .50 CALIBER!
MOTHER-FUCKERS...
MS. KAT?
PLEASE COME WITH US.
LET'S SEE IF YOU CAN HANDLE THIS!
SHIT!

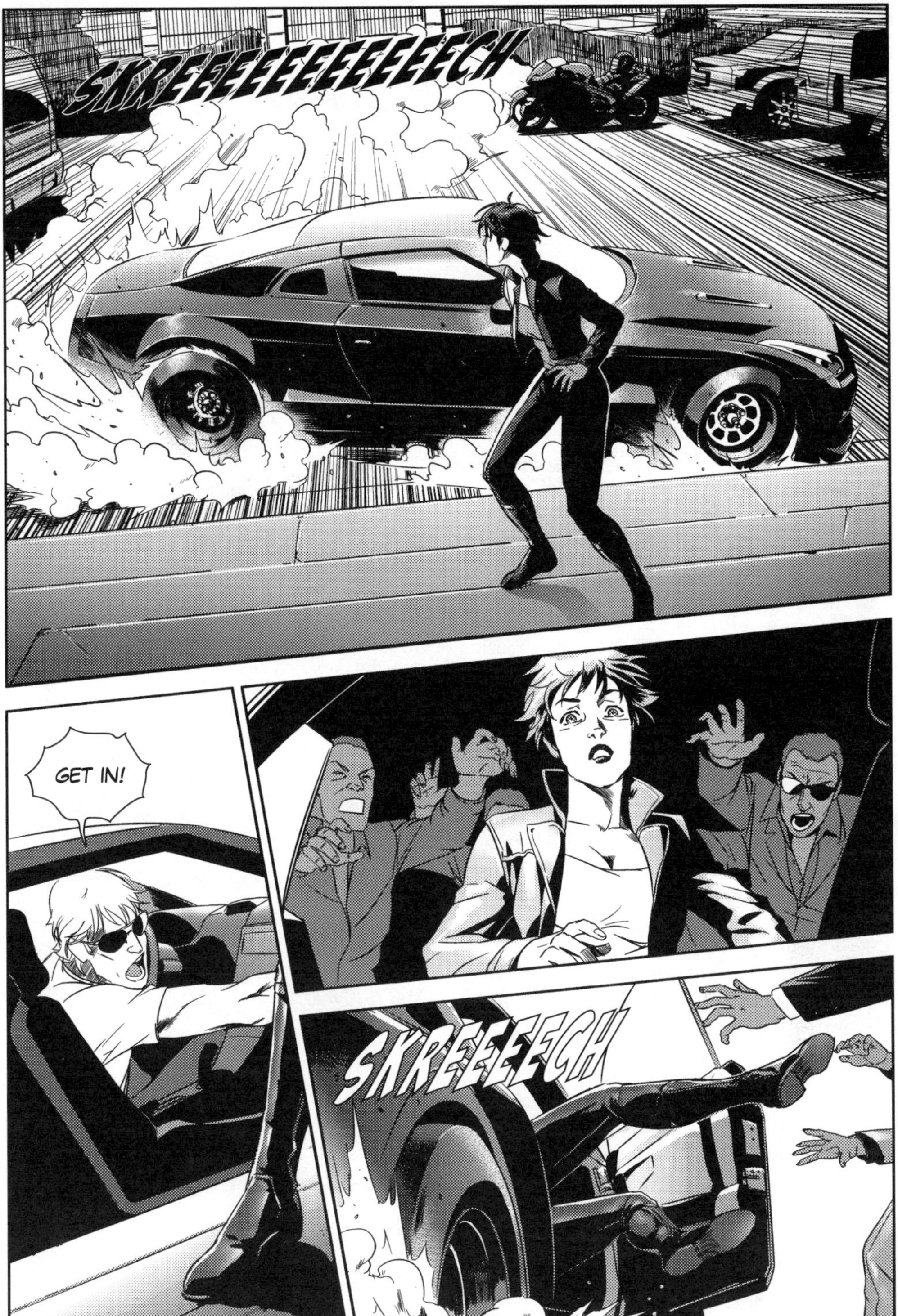
SKREEEEEEEEEEEECH
GET IN!
SKREEEECH

TZING
WROOOOOOOOOO
SPAK
WATCH IT, IDIOT!
TRÖK
I WANT HER ALIVE!
KILL HER FRIEND!
KRAAAAMM

WHAT ARE YOU DOING HERE?!?
IF IT MAKES YOU FEEL ANY BETTER, I DRAGGED YOU IN HERE SO THAT THEY WOULDN'T KILL ME STRAIGHT AWAY!
THESE GUYS ARE WELL TRAINED AND WON'T MAKE THE SAME MISTAKE TWICE!

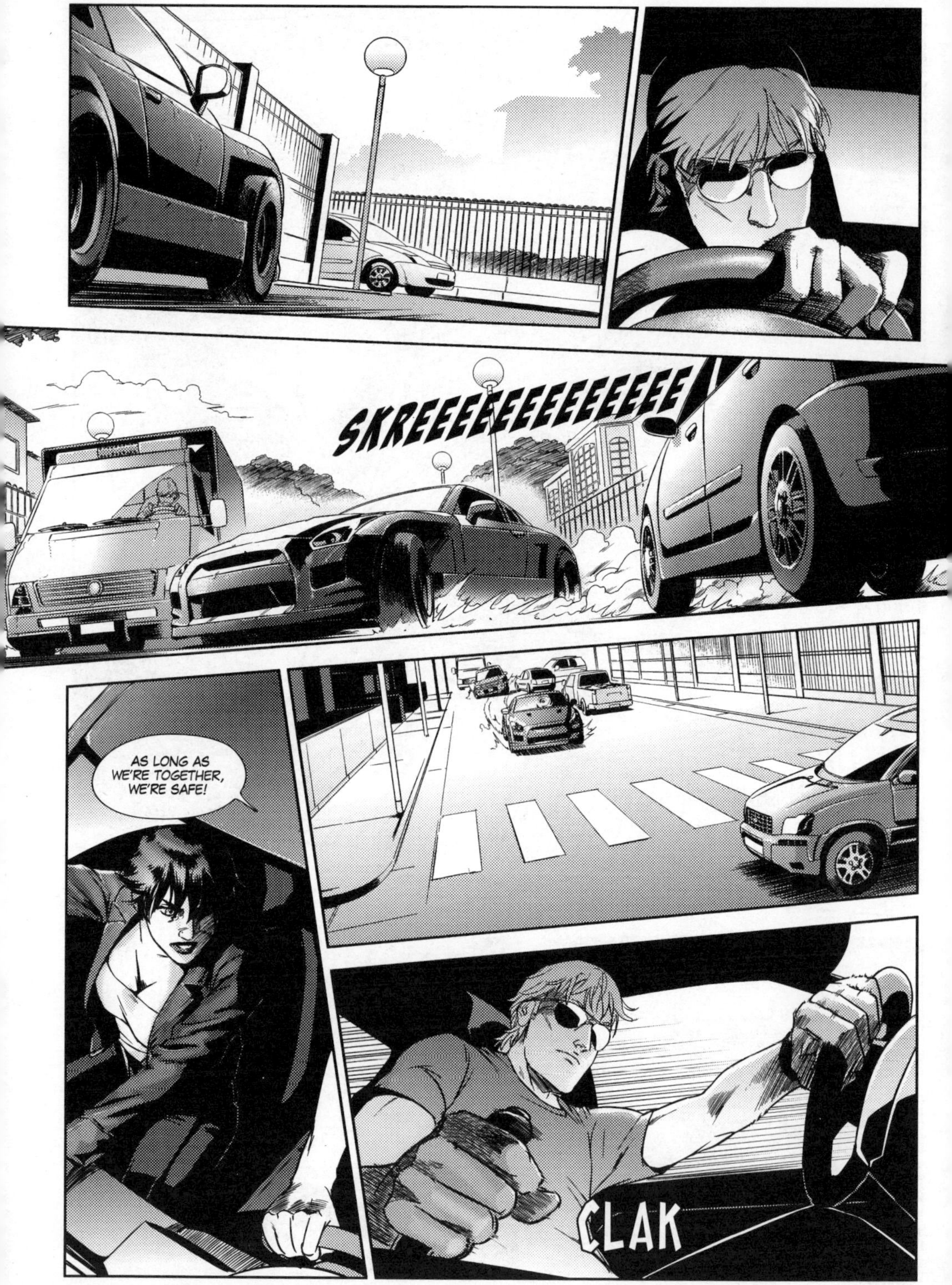
SKREEEEEEEEEEEEE
AS LONG AS WE'RE TOGETHER, WE'RE SAFE!
CLAK

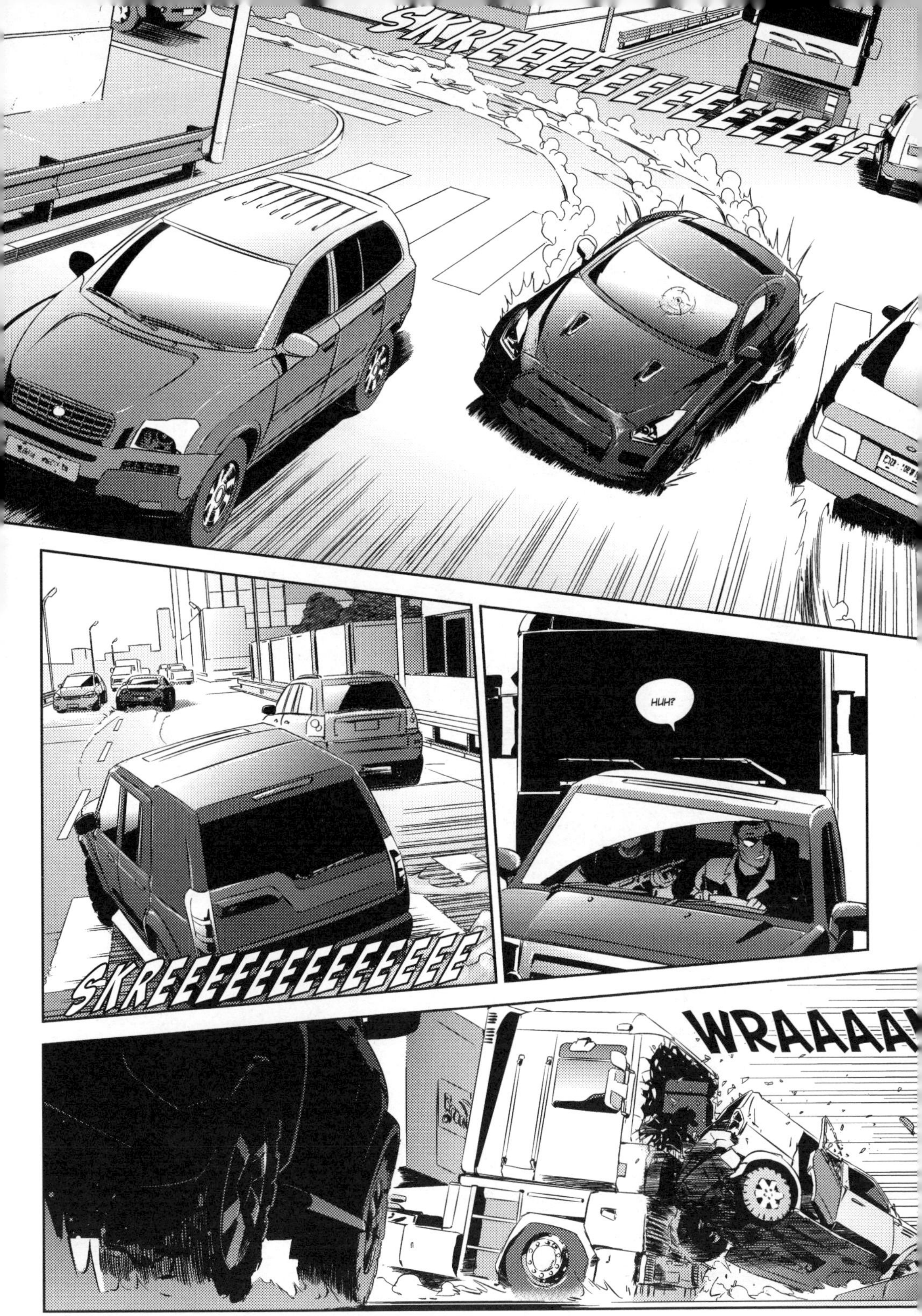
SKREEEEEEEEEEEEEEEEE
SKREEEEEEEEEEEEEE
HUH?
WRAAAA

JESUS!
FUCKER
DON'T HIT HER BY MISTAKE!
DON'T WORRY, MAN. I'M BETTER THAN A SURGEON WITH THIS THING.
EH?
BAAM

WHAT'S GOING ON HERE? STOP THE CAR!
YOUR FRIENDS ARE TOO PERSISTENT! I CAN'T STOP TILL WE'RE SAFE.
I'M SORRY TO INFORM YOU THAT, FOR SOME REASON, YOUR FAMILY WANTS YOU CAPTURED.
I'M SO STUPID...
KRISHH

THIS IS NOT A GOOD TIME TO GET SENTIMENTAL!
I TOLD YOU TO STOP THE CAR...
BAAM
100m
BAY BRIDGE
ONE WAY
I THOUGHT YOU MIGHT BE ABLE TO CLEAR SOME THINGS UP, BUT IT LOOKS LIKE I'M PRETTY EXPENDABLE HERE!
SKREEEEECH

STOP THE CAR OR I'LL BLOW YOUR HEAD OFF AND KILL US BOTH!
SKRECH
ARE YOU SURE ABOUT THIS?
SLAM
FUCK OFF!
WROOOOOOO

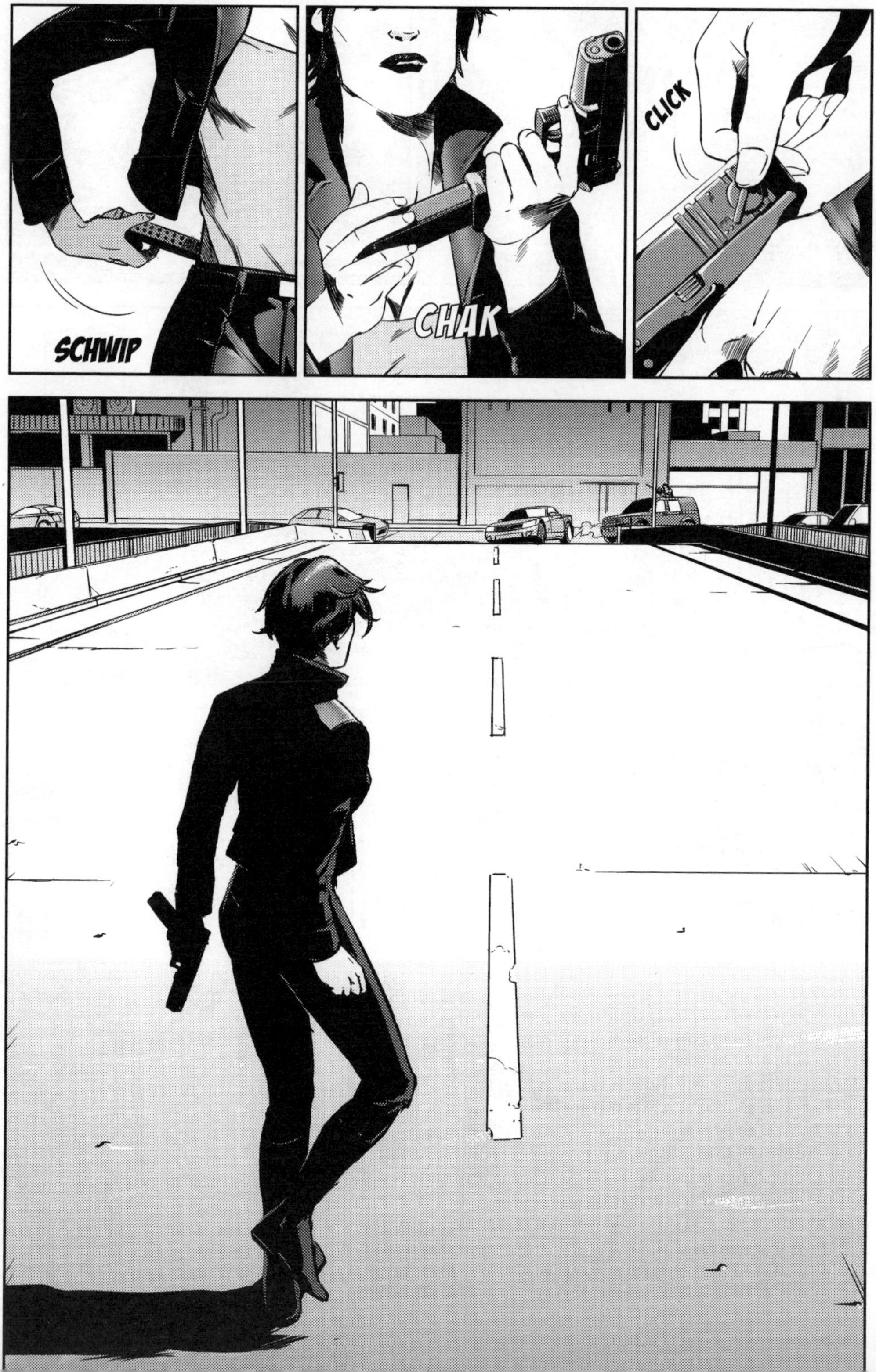
SCHWIP
CHAK
CLICK

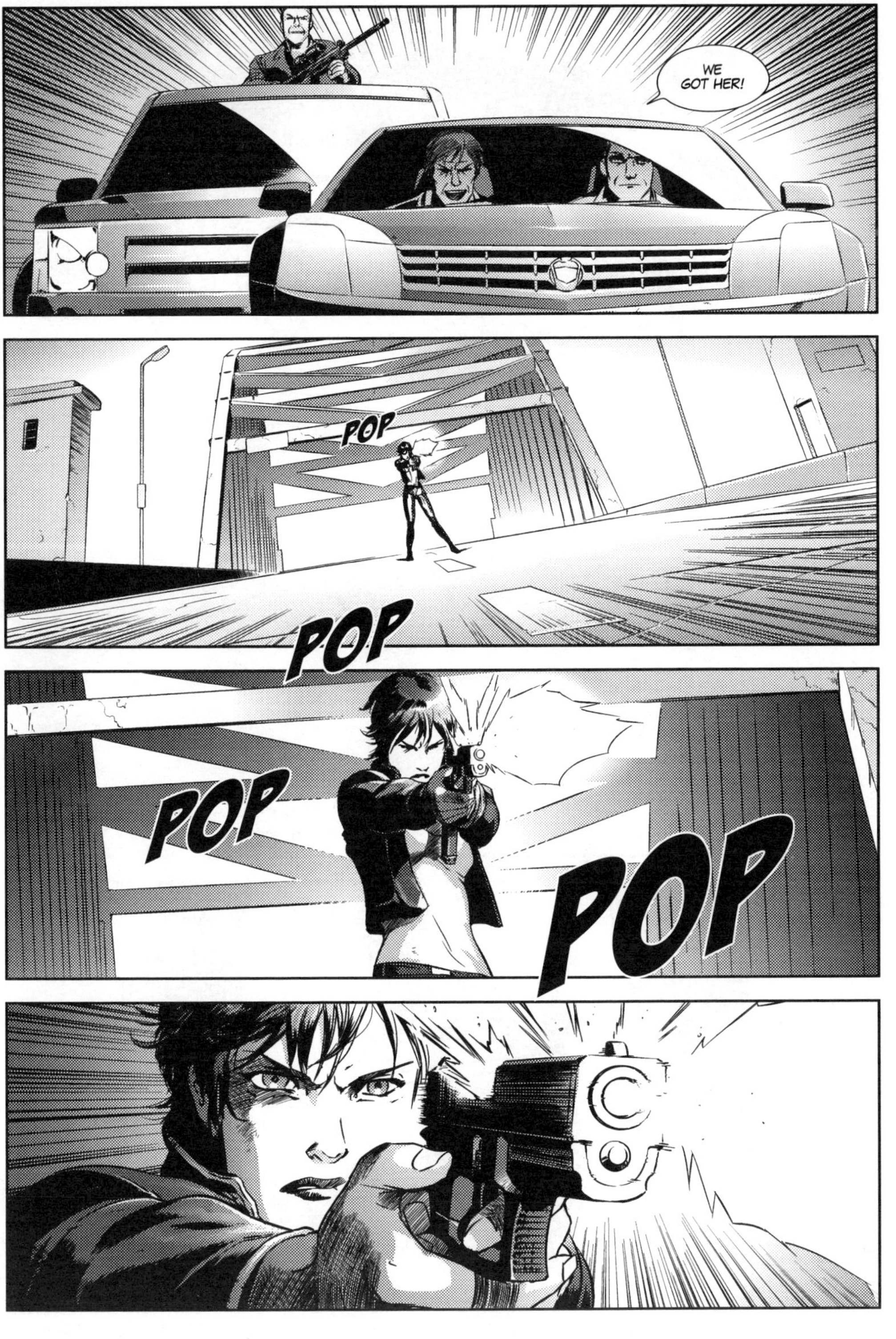
WE GOT HER!
POP
POP
POP
POP

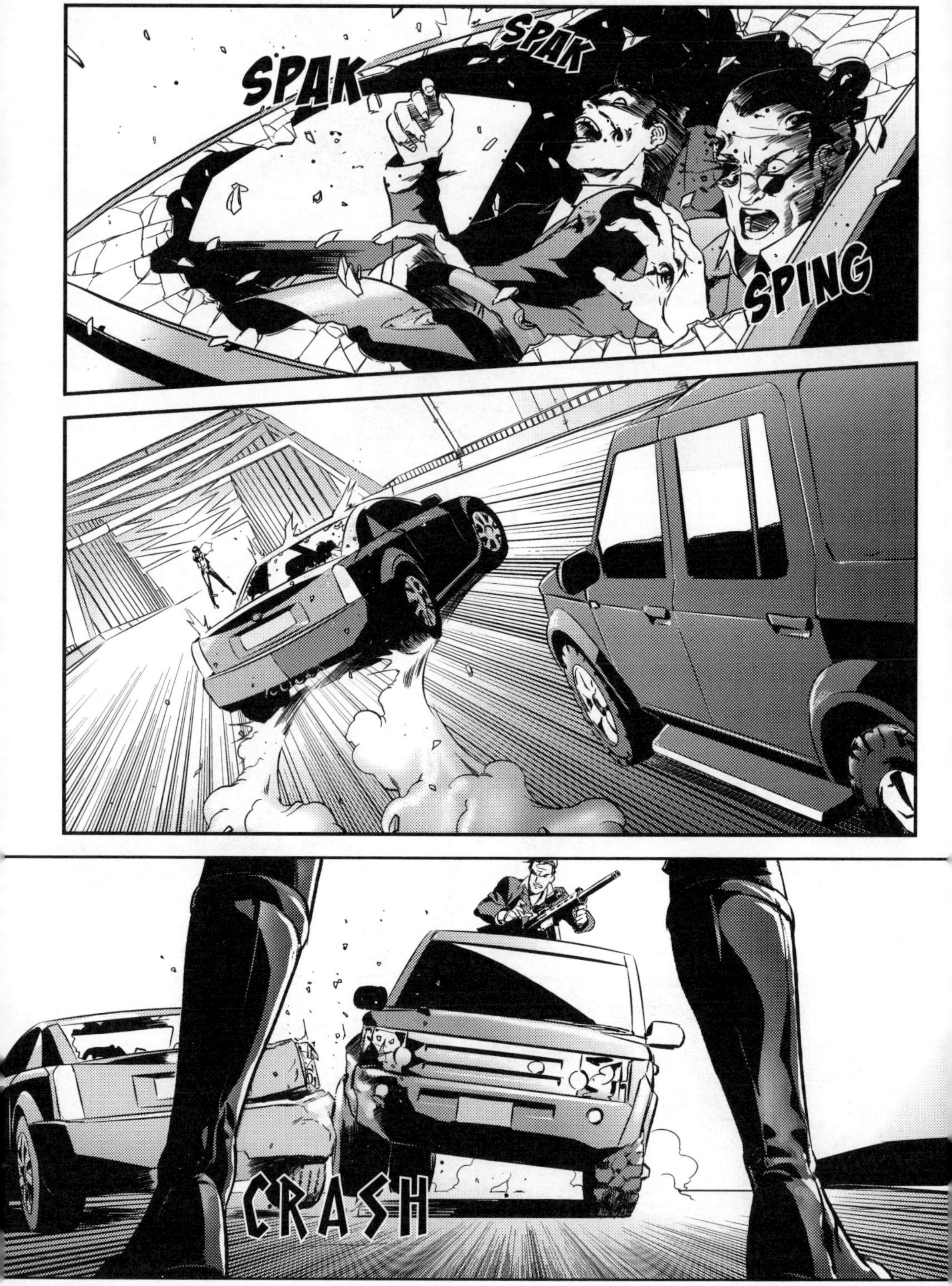
SPAK
SPAK
SPING
CRASH

RRRRRRRRRRRRRRRRRRRRRTTTT

CLIK

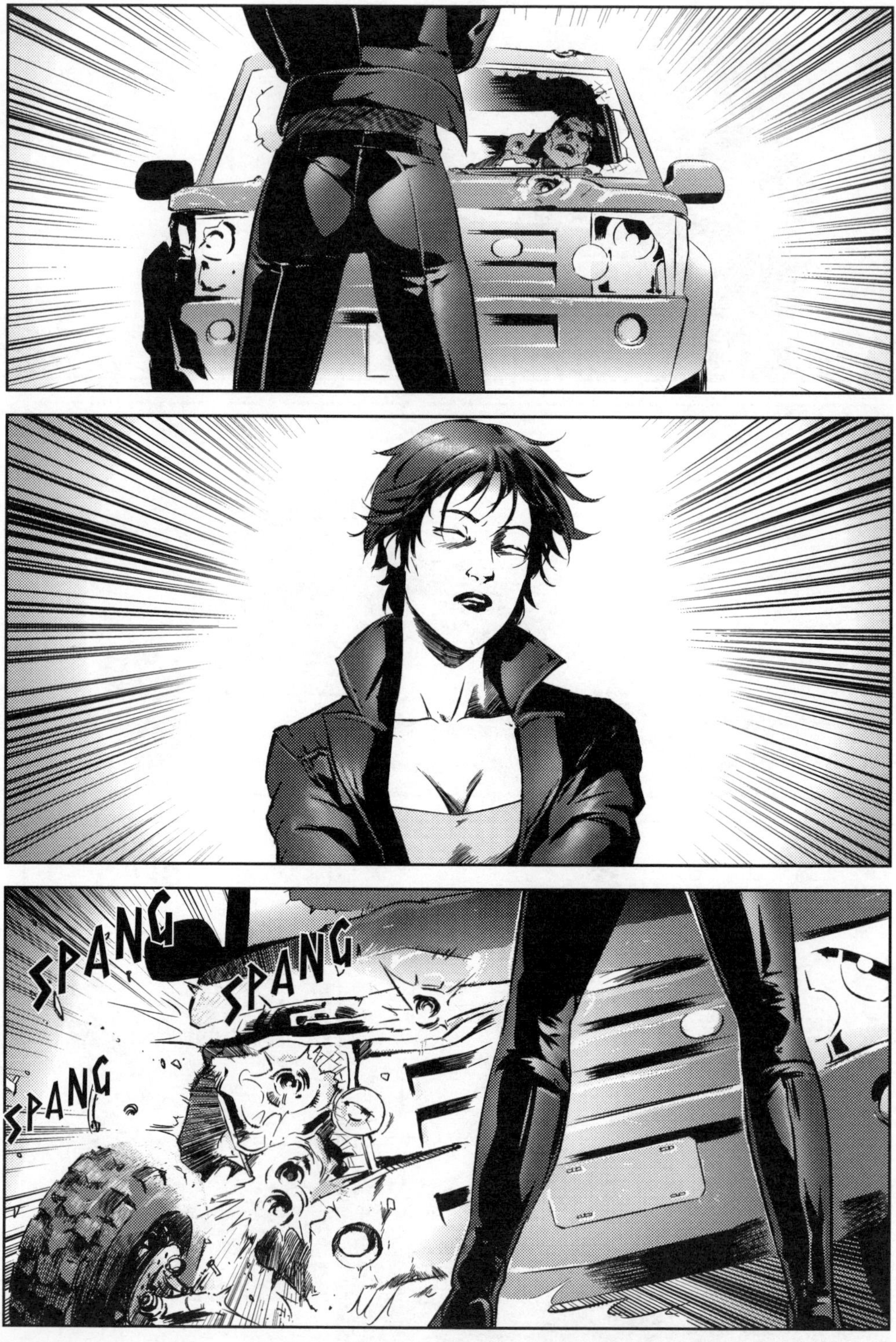
SPANG
SPANG
SPANG

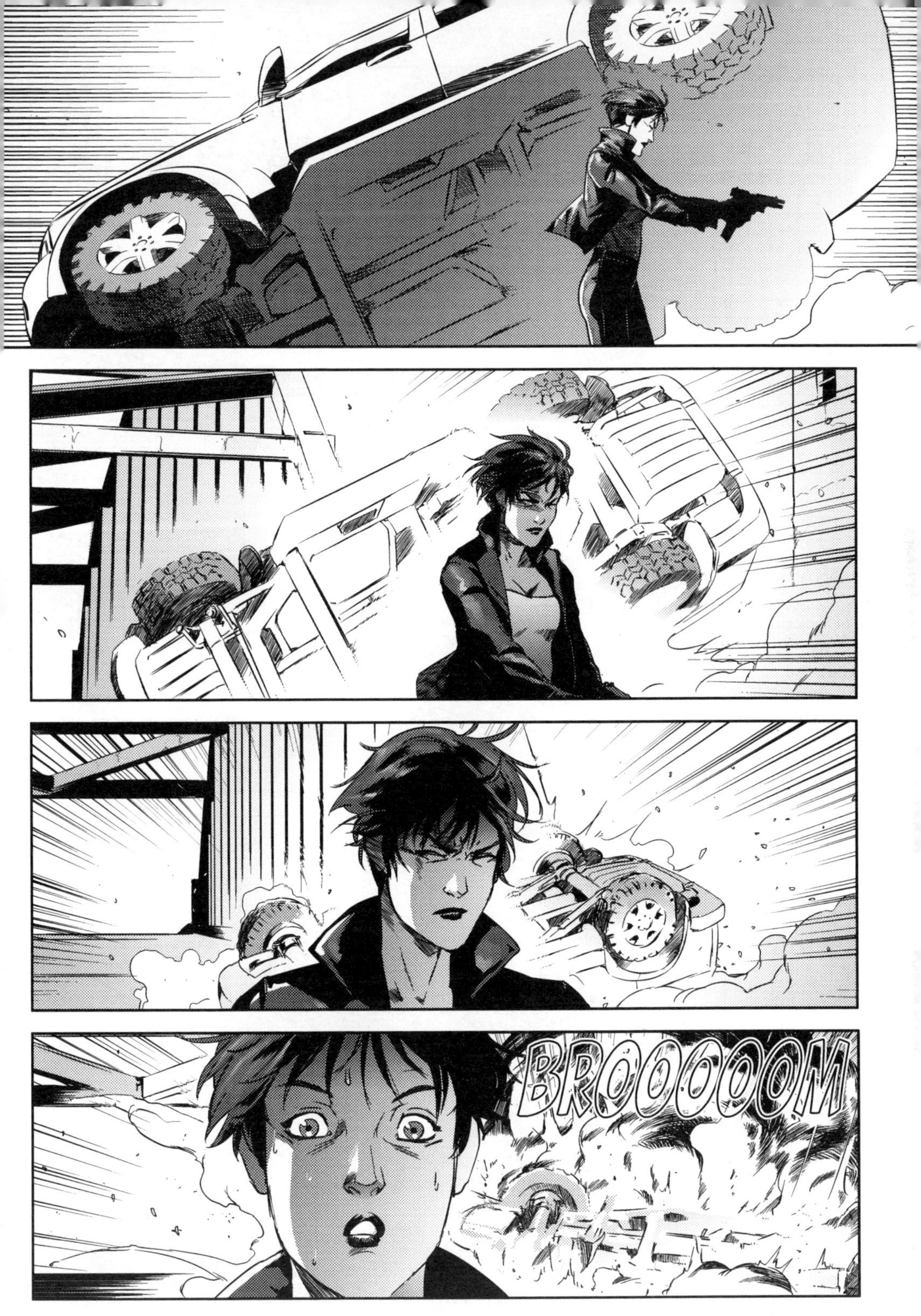
BROOOOOOM

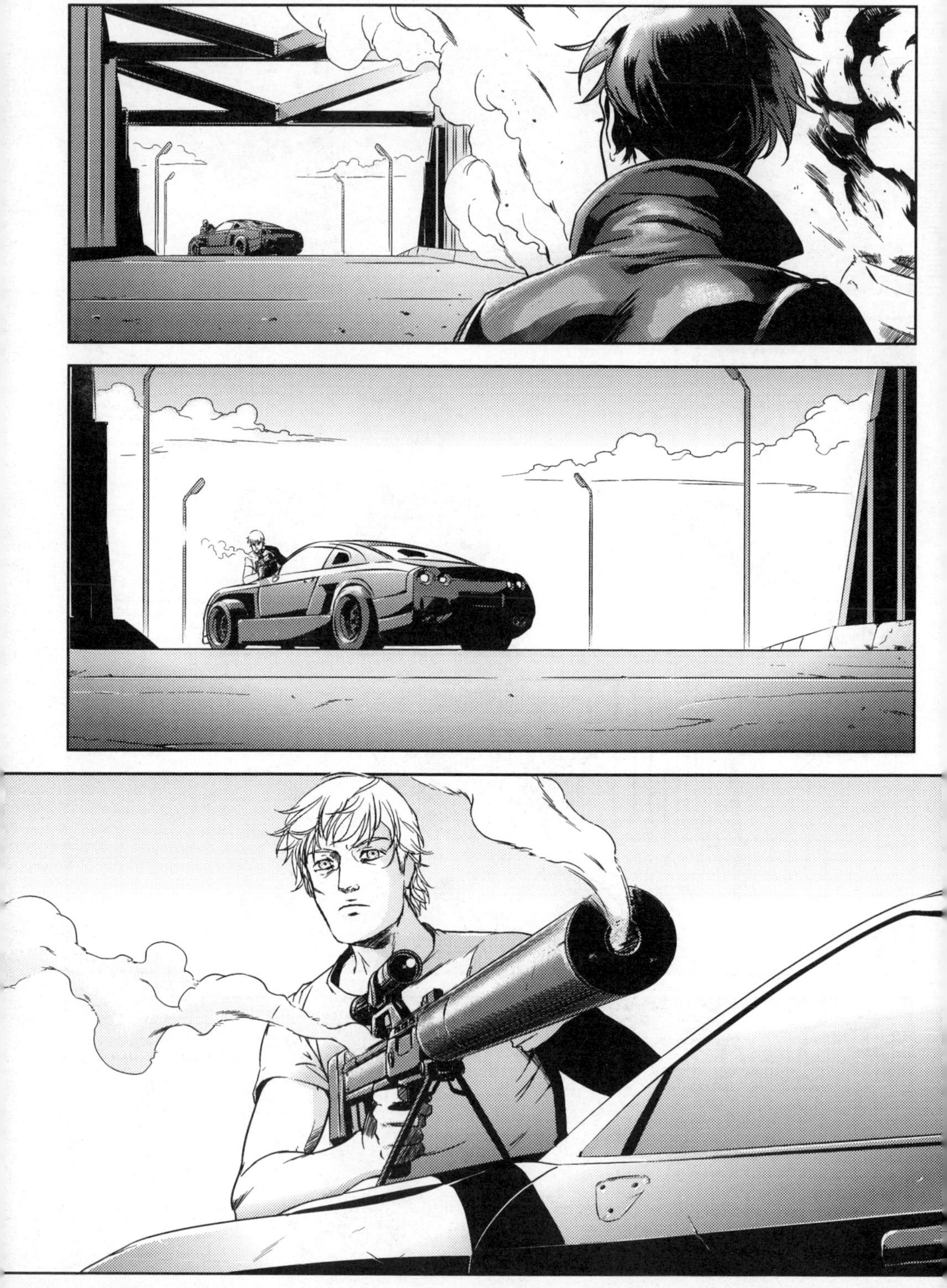

05

SOMETHING'S JUST NOT ADDING UP IN THIS STORY...

THE PEOPLE THAT ATTACKED US AT THE DINER WANTED US DEAD.

BUT TODAY THEY DID EVERYTHING POSSIBLE TO NOT HURT YOU.
IT LOOKS LIKE THINGS HAVE CHANGED SINCE THE DINER, AND THEY NEED YOU ALIVE NOW.
WEEEEEETTT

I GUESS THEY THOUGHT I'D KILL YOU WHEN I SAW YOU SITTING THERE IN THE DINER.
CLIK
BUT YOU WERE NOT MY TARGET, AND I DON'T WORK FOR FREE...
WHAT DO YOU THINK?
CRYING WON'T FIX ANYTHING.
I THINK YOU'RE IN TROUBLE, AND I WANT TO KNOW HOW TO GET OUT OF ALL THIS.

CRASH
WHY THE FUCK DO YOU KEEP HELPING ME?
GOD... HOW CAN SOMEONE BE THIS STUPID AND STUBBORN AT THE SAME TIME...
HAVE YOU LISTENED TO ANYTHING I'VE SAID?
HUH?
WHAM

WHO ARE YOU?!? WHAT DO YOU WANT?!? WHAT DO YOU GET OUT OF THIS?!?
BY NOW, YOU SHOULD'VE REALIZED THAT I'M ONE OF THE FEW PEOPLE THAT'S WILLING TO HELP YOU.
AND I THINK YOU'RE RUNNING OUT OF FRIENDS!
I DON'T NEED YOUR PITY! WHAT DO YOU WANT? ANSWER ME!
OK.
CRASH

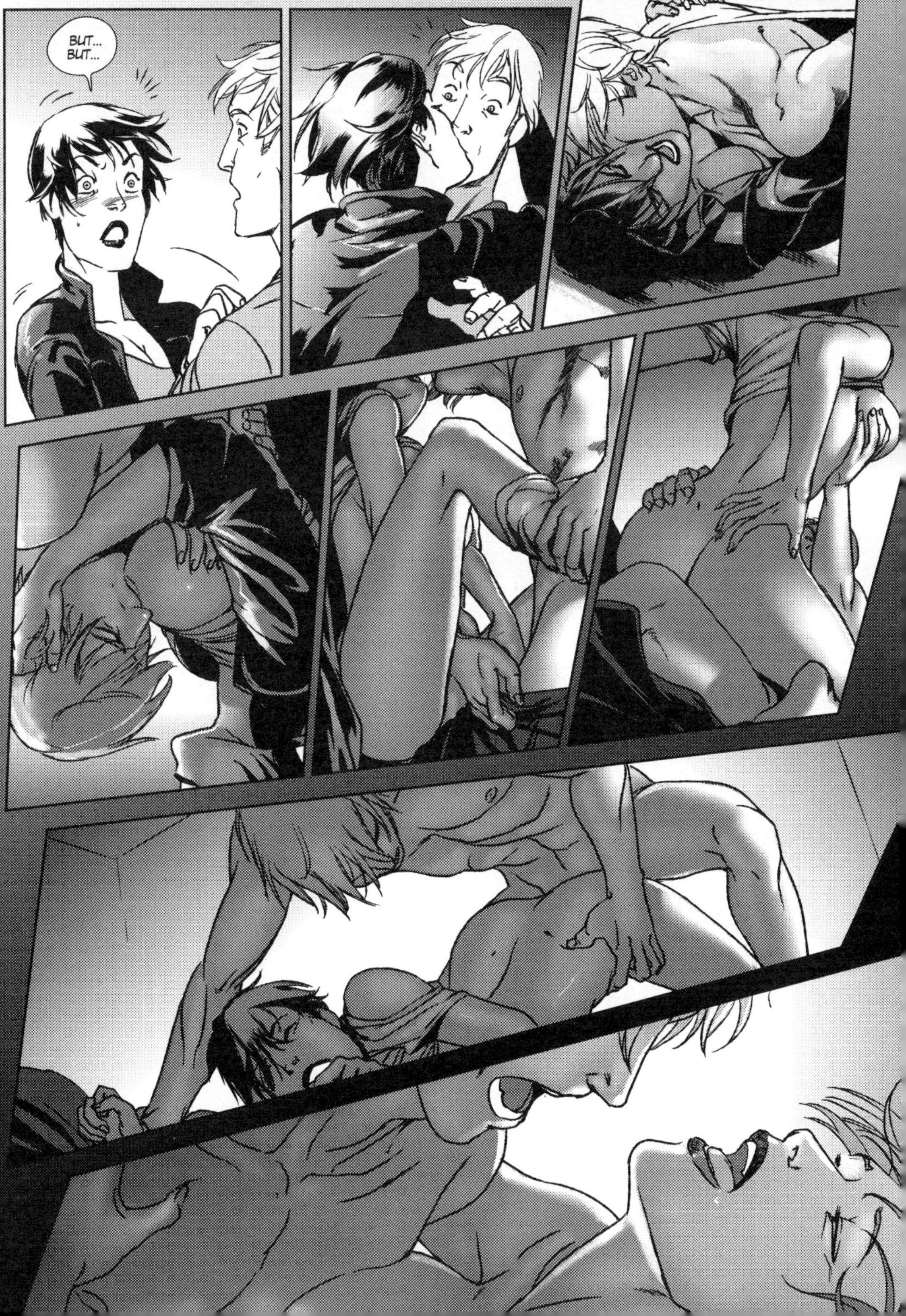
BUT...
BUT...

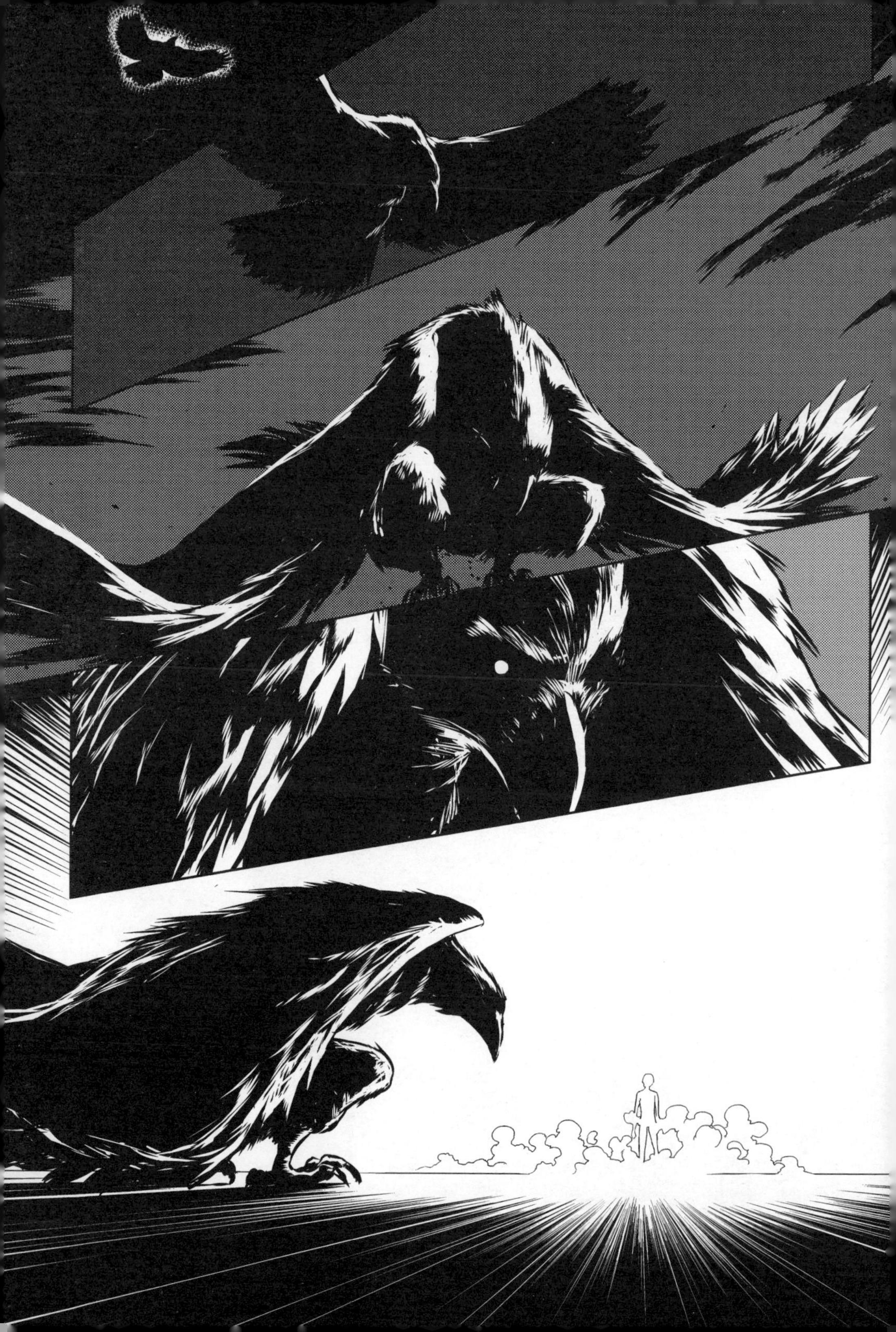

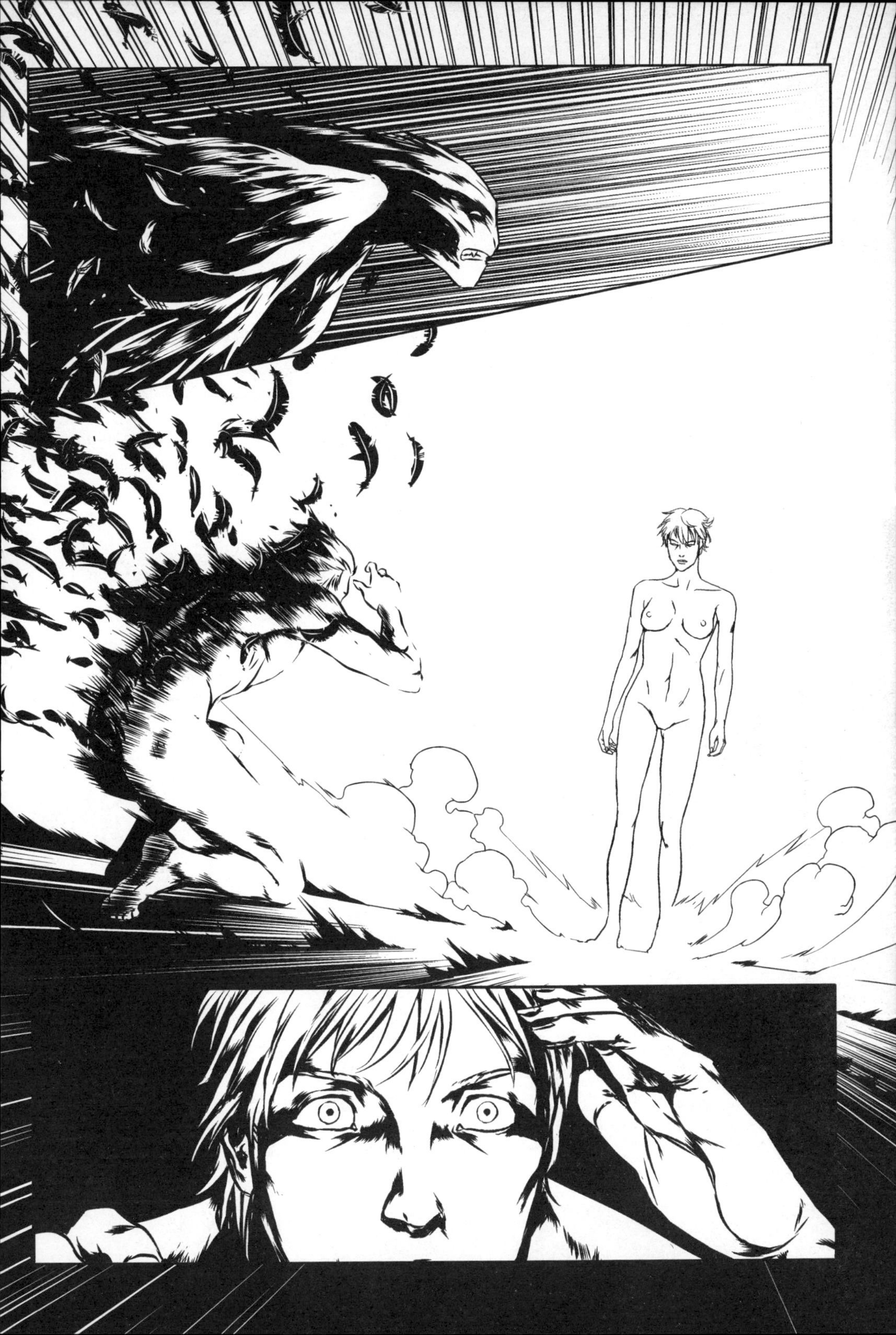

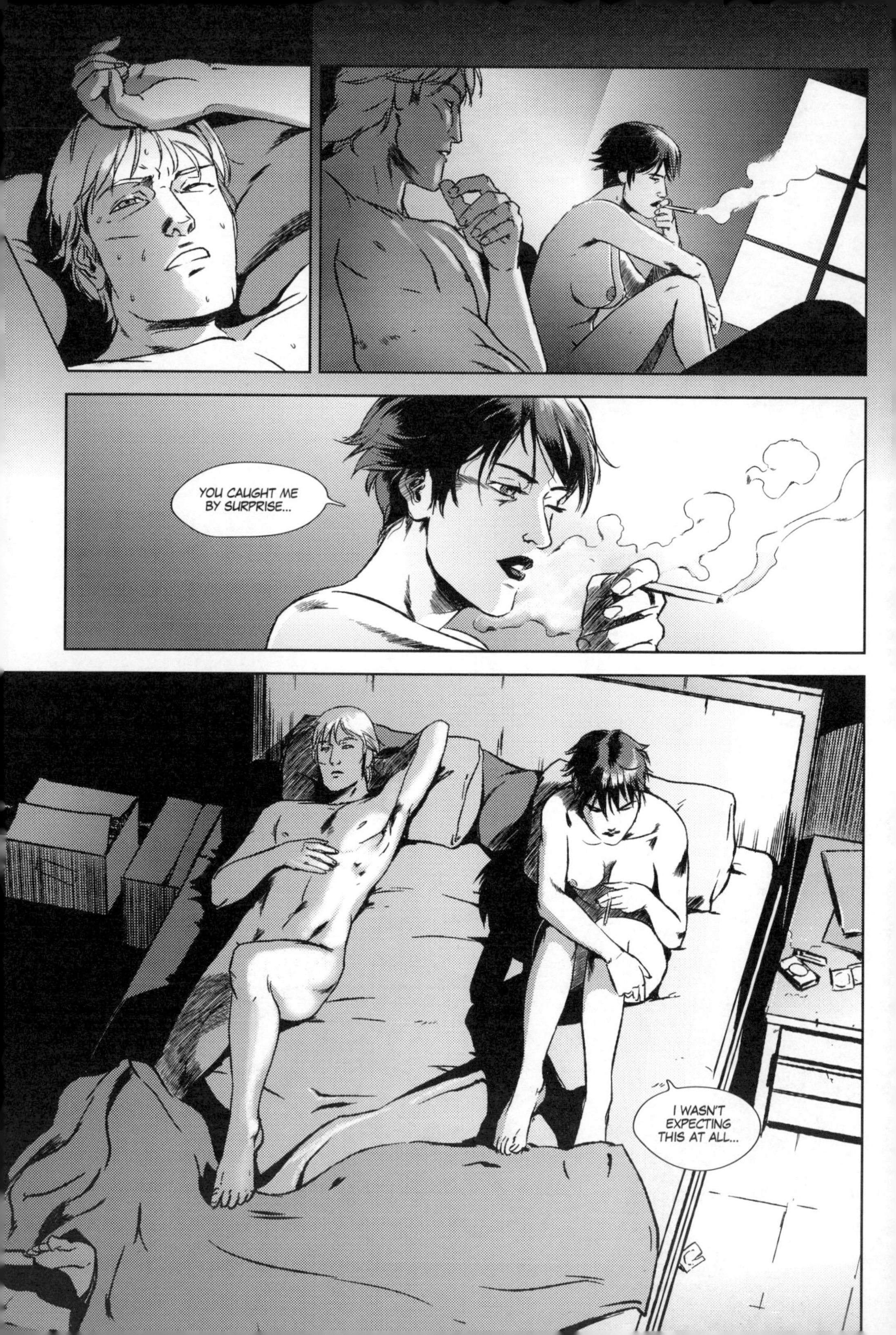
YOU CAUGHT ME BY SURPRISE...
I WASN'T EXPECTING THIS AT ALL...

ACTUALLY...
I'VE BEEN WANTING TO DO THAT EVER SINCE I SAW YOU AT TONY'S PLACE...
OR MAYBE I'M MORE SINCERE THAN YOU ARE.
HEY! A KITTY!
WHAT'S ITS NAME?
I DON'T KNOW. IT'S NOT MINE
AND LIKE MANY THINGS AROUND HERE, I CAN'T SEEM TO MAKE IT GO AWAY.
OH, YOU HAVE NO HEART! IS IT A STRAY?

IT'S BEEN AROUND FOR A FEW MONTHS, SO I THINK IT IS.
MONTHS? AND IT STILL DOESN'T HAVE A NAME?
I CALL IT "CAT."
"CAT"? THAT'S NOT A NAME!
LET'S GIVE YOU A CUTE NAME.
HOW ABOUT "RUDOLPH" OR "LEOPOLD"?
I ALWAYS LIKED "RUFO". ALTHOUGH I THINK IT'S MORE OF A DOG'S NAME...
ARE THOSE EVEN CAT NAMES?!?
OH! SOMEONE'S NOT VERY CAREFUL! WHAT HAPPENED TO YOUR BACK?
YOU DON'T WANT TO KNOW...
LET'S MAKE IT A GAME! YOU ASK A QUESTION, THEN I ASK A QUESTION... OK?
THIS IS NOT A GOOD IDEA...
DON'T BE LIKE THAT!

THEY'RE SCARS FROM MY PAST JOBS...
SOME IN MY LINE OF WORK VALUE THEM LIKE TROPHIES.
OK...
LADIES FIRST!
WELL, WHAT HAPPENED TO YOUR BACK?
SOMEHOW, EVERY TARGET I'VE ELIMINATED HAS LEFT A MARK ON ME
BULLSHIT!
I GUESS I'M THE EXCEPTION TO THE RULE. I'VE LEFT A SCAR ON YOUR FACE AND I'M STILL ALIVE!
HAHAHA!
WELL, WE'LL SEE ABOUT THAT...
JUST KIDDING!
MY TURN!
WHAT WAS THE CONNECTION BETWEEN THE MAN AT THE IMPERIAL HOTEL AND YOUR FATHER?
MY FATHER WAS A POWERFUL CRIME BOSS. HE WAS ALWAYS VERY SEVERE WITH ME...
NOTHING WAS EVER GOOD ENOUGH FOR HIM.
I TRIED TO JOIN THE FAMILY BUSINESS MANY TIMES, BUT HE NEVER LET ME.
HE DID LET MY BROTHER SETH JOIN, THOUGH.

HE WAS ALWAYS HIS FAVORITE, AND NOW HE'S THE ONE RUNNING THE FAMILY.
A FEW DAYS AGO HE CONTACTED ME AND TOLD ME THAT H. HALLER, THE MAN AT THE HOTEL, HAD KILLED OUR FATHER. HE SAID HE WAS WILLING TO LET ME JOIN THE FAMILY BUSINES IF I HELPED HIM AVENGE OUR FATHER.
I ALWAYS WANTED OUR FATHER TO BE PROUD OF ME, SO I DID WHAT SETH ASKED ME TO DO.
REVENGE IS POINTLESS.
KILLING SOMEONE NEVER REALLY MAKES THINGS RIGHT AGAIN.
MY TURN!
WHAT'S THE STORY WITH ALL THOSE BOXES?
BOOKS
I LIKE TO HAVE EVERYTHING READY JUST IN CASE I NEED TO LEAVE IN A HURRY.
I'M CLOSE TO ACHIEVING MY DREAM, SO THAT'S WHY ALL MY THINGS ARE PACKED UP.
OOKS
KITCHEN
MEDS
PHOTOS
PAPERS
BATHROOM
DON'T TELL ME YOU'RE SAVING UP TO ESCAPE TO SOME PARADISE AND LEAVE ALL YOUR PROBLEMS BEHIND!

OOPS...
SORRY, BUT BY THIS POINT YOU SHOULD DEFINITELY KNOW THAT'S IMPOSSIBLE.
RIGHT?
CHANGING THE SUBJECT...
SO, NOW WHAT?
NOW, I'M SLEEPY.
AND LATER, I'LL PROBABLY BE HUNGRY.
SO YOU BETTER HAVE A PLAN TO DEAL WITH THAT.
OK.
WHO WOULD HAVE THOUGHT...
THAT YOU'D END UP BEING THE AFFECTIONATE TYPE...

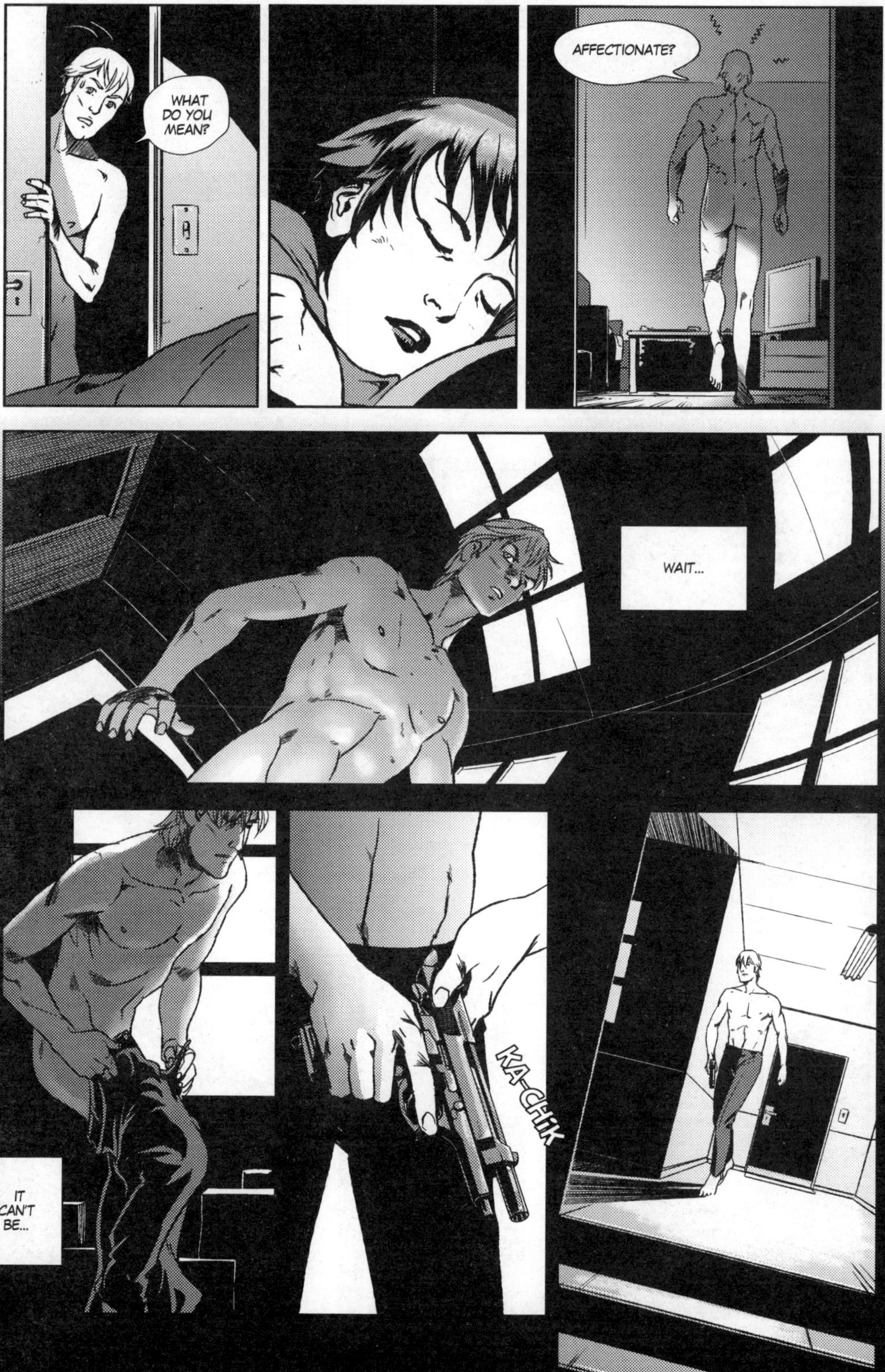
WHAT DO YOU MEAN?
AFFECTIONATE?
WAIT...
IT CAN'T BE...
KA-CHIK

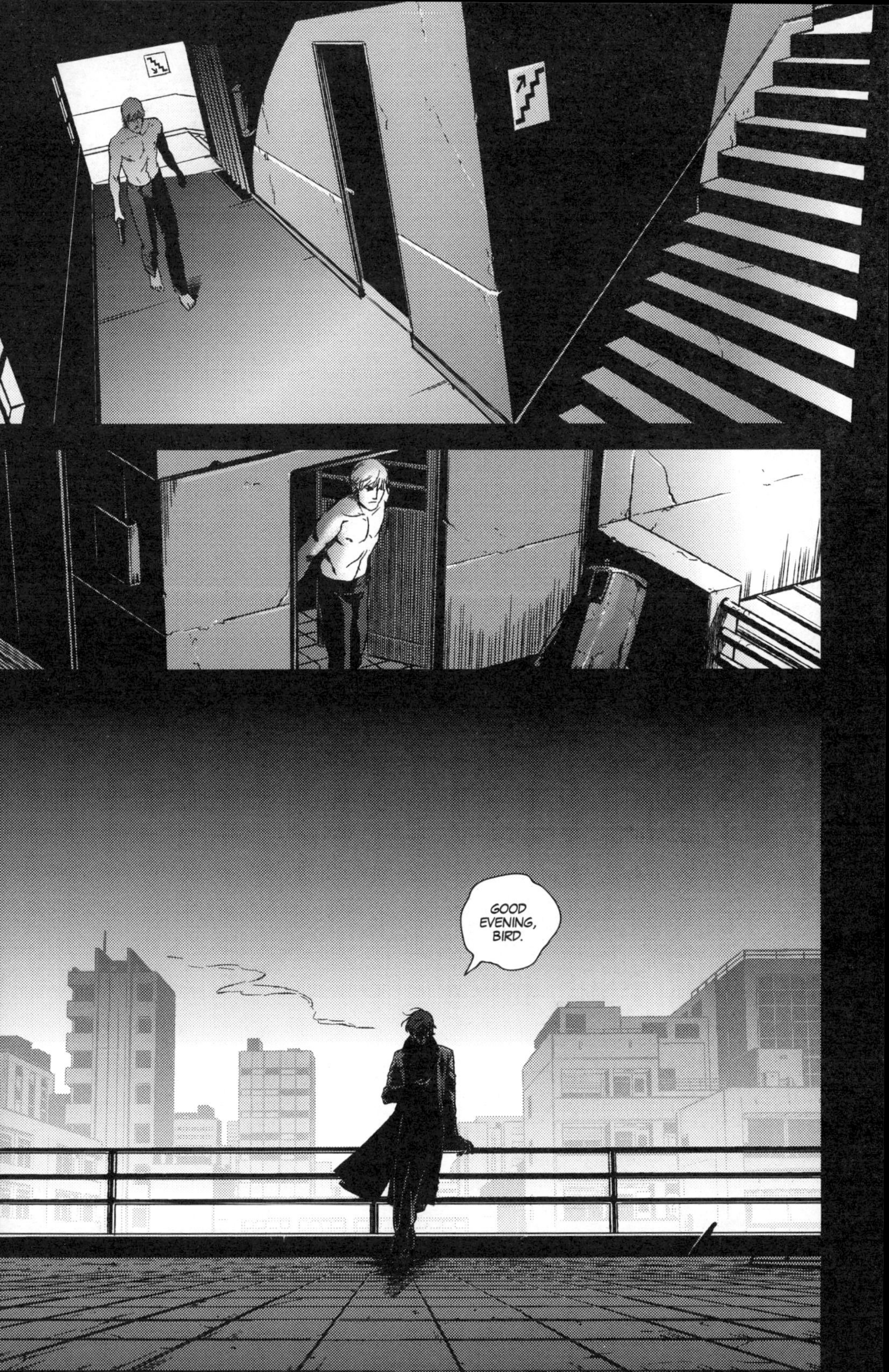
GOOD EVENING, BIRD.

DO I HAVE TO SPELL OUT HOW WRONG THIS IS?
WHAT ARE YOU DOING HERE?
OR IS SLEEPING WITH THE PREY A NEW FETISH OF YOURS?
OUR DEAL IS OVER.
I'M GONNA HELP HER GET OUT OF THE MESS SHE'S IN.
HAHAHA!
DON'T TELL ME THAT SLEEPING WITH HER MADE YOU LOSE YOUR MIND!
ARE YOU PLANNING ON TAKING HER TO YOUR TROPICAL ISLAND?

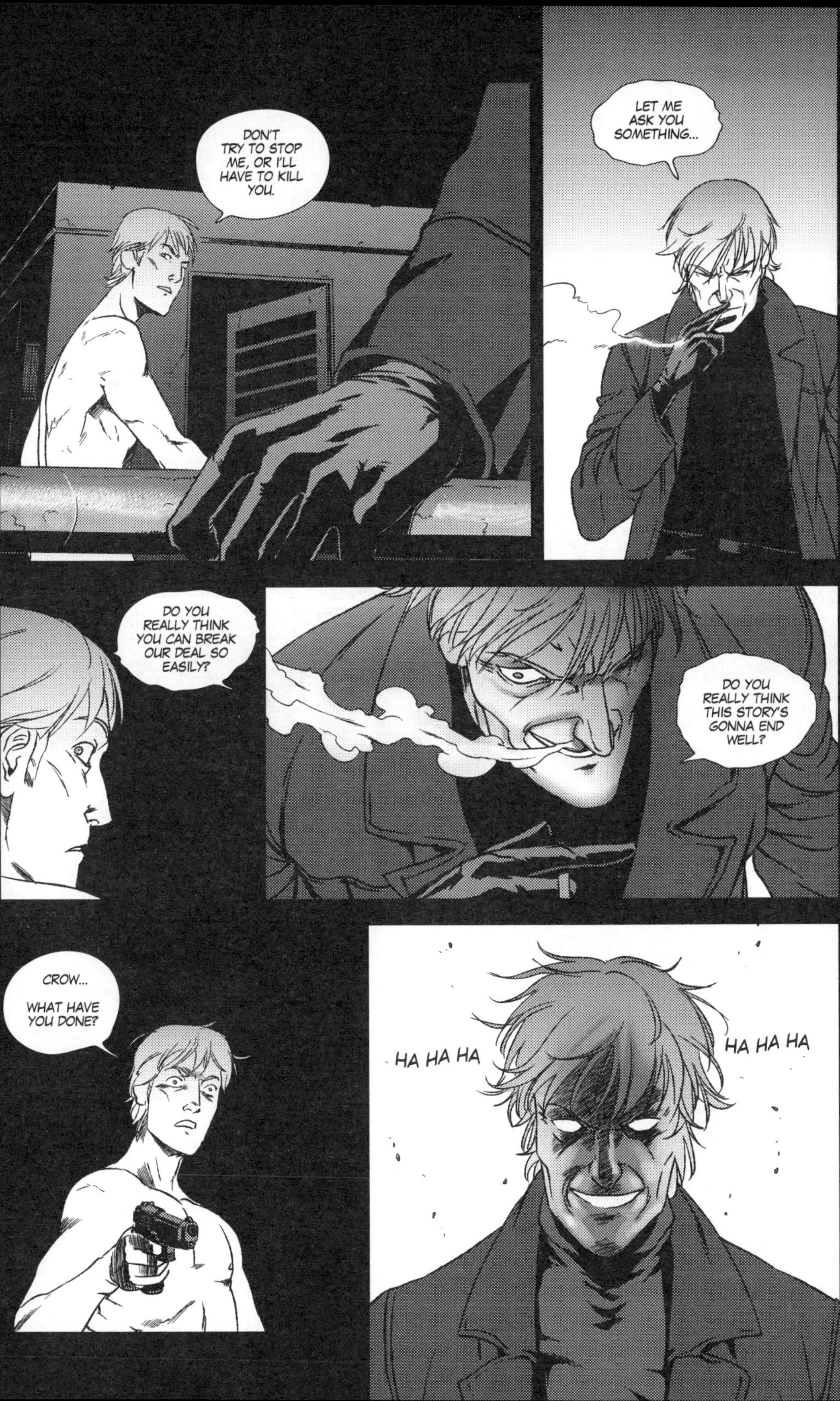
DON'T TRY TO STOP ME, OR I'LL HAVE TO KILL YOU.
LET ME ASK YOU SOMETHING...
DO YOU REALLY THINK YOU CAN BREAK OUR DEAL SO EASILY?
DO YOU REALLY THINK THIS STORY'S GONNA END WELL?
CROW...
WHAT HAVE YOU DONE?
HA HA HA
HA HA HA

A WOLF IN SHEEP'S CLOTHING IS STILL A WOLF!
HA HA HA HA
FLASH
WHAT?!?

CHOPPER HERE.
WE HAVE A VISUAL ON THE SECONDARY TARGET.
IT'S MOVING DOWNSTAIRS.
OVER.
THIS IS 01.
WE'RE MOVING THE PRIMARY TARGET.
HOLD POSITION.
OVER.
TAKE HER DOWNSTAIRS. WE'LL DEAL WITH THE GUY.
SWAT

TEAM 02, THE TARGET IS HEADING YOUR WAY. DO YOU HAVE A VISUAL? OVER.
THIS IS 02. NEGATIVE.
ARE YOU SURE THE TARGET'S GOING DOWNSTAIRS? OVER.
WHAM
EH?
TAP
02? DO YOU READ ME? OVER.

CRASH
WHAT?
DON'T SHOOT...
LET HER GO OR KISS YOUR FRIEND GOODBYE.
A TOUGH GUY, JUST LIKE THEY SAID.
BRING HER OVER HERE...
WE ARE NOT HERE TO KILL YOU OR THIS GIRL.
WE JUST WANT THE WOMAN.
THIS IS A GIFT FROM A MUTUAL FRIEND.
HE HOPES THAT IT CAN SETTLE THIS MISUNDERS-TANDING.
WHUMP

IT'S UP TO YOU HOW BLOODY THIS ALL GETS.
WELL?
LET HER GO.
THAP
BIRDIE!
CALM DOWN. IT'S OVER NOW...

06

YOU'VE TOLD ME NOT TO PRY INTO HOW YOU MAKE A LIVING PLENTY OF TIMES, SO LET'S NOT CHANGE THAT NOW!
AFTER SO MANY YEARS BEHIND THE COUNTER, I'VE GOTTEN PRETTY GOOD AT READING PEOPLE.
AND I'VE BEEN OBSERVING YOU FOR SEVERAL YEARS NOW.
IF YOU ASK ME, IT LOOKS LIKE YOU HAVE A BROKEN HEART, MY FRIEND.
IT'S NOT HARD TO PIECE TOGETHER THAT YOU HAVE THAT LOOK ON YOUR FACE BECAUSE OF YOUR "GIRLFRIEND."
DO YOU NOW KNOW WHAT IT FEELS LIKE TO BE A HUMAN BEING?
WELL, IT'S NOT JUST THAT, TONY...
SOMEHOW I'LL MAKE MY DREAM COME TRUE. BUT, ONLY IF I CAN FORGET ABOUT HER...

I HAVE SOME GOOD ADVICE ABOUT DREAMS, BIRD. THEY'RE JUST THAT. DREAMS.
FOR EXAMPLE, THIS DINER'S BEEN MY DREAM MY ENTIRE LIFE, TO THE POINT THAT I DIDN'T BUILD ANYTHIING ELSE, LIKE A FAMILY...
TODAY, IT'S GONE! I'M ALMOST 70 YEARS OLD AND I HAVE TO START FROM SCRATCH AGAIN. AT THIS POINT IN MY LIFE, IT'S HIGLY UNLIKELY THAT I'LL EVER HAVE EITHER OF THOSE TWO. NO BAR, AND NO FAMILY.
I'M NOT LASHING OUT AT YOU, BIRD. THE TRUTH IS, BECAUSE OF YOU I'M NOW ABLE TO SEE THAT MY DREAM WAS SOMETHING ELSE.
REGARDING YOUR GIRLFRIEND, LEMME TELL YOU THAT IN LIFE THE ODDS OF FINDING THE RIGHT PERSON ARE MUCH WORSE THAN YOU CAN TELL AT YOUR AGE.
THERE ARE PEOPLE THAT, DEEP DOWN, YOU KNOW AREN'T RIGHT FOR YOU. BUT THERE ARE OTHERS THAT MIGHT MAKE YOU START TO ASK YOURSELF SOME QUESTIONS.
DON'T MAKE THE SAME MISTAKES I MADE, BIRD. DON'T BE AFRAID TO OPEN UP TO OTHER PEOPLE...
THANKS FOR THE COFFEE AND THE PEP TALK.
I NEED YOU TO TAKE CARE OF HANNA TILL THIS IS ALL OVER.
SURE.

AND I WANT YOU TO HOLD ON TO THIS FOR ME. IF I DON'T COME BACK FOR IT, IT'S YOURS.
WHUD
SO LONG, BIRD!
GOODBYE, TONY.

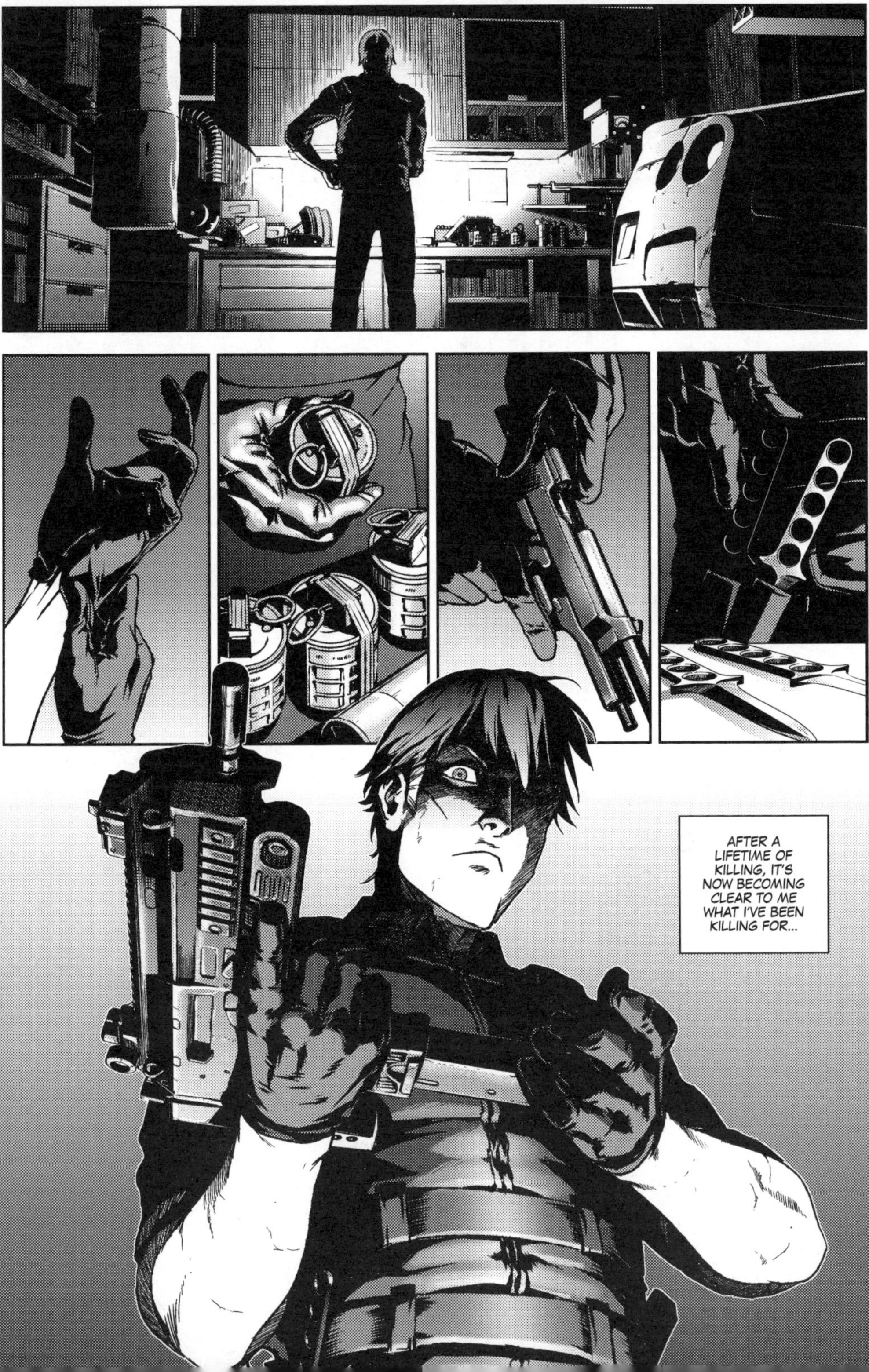
AFTER A LIFETIME OF KILLING, IT'S NOW BECOMING CLEAR TO ME WHAT I'VE BEEN KILLING FOR...

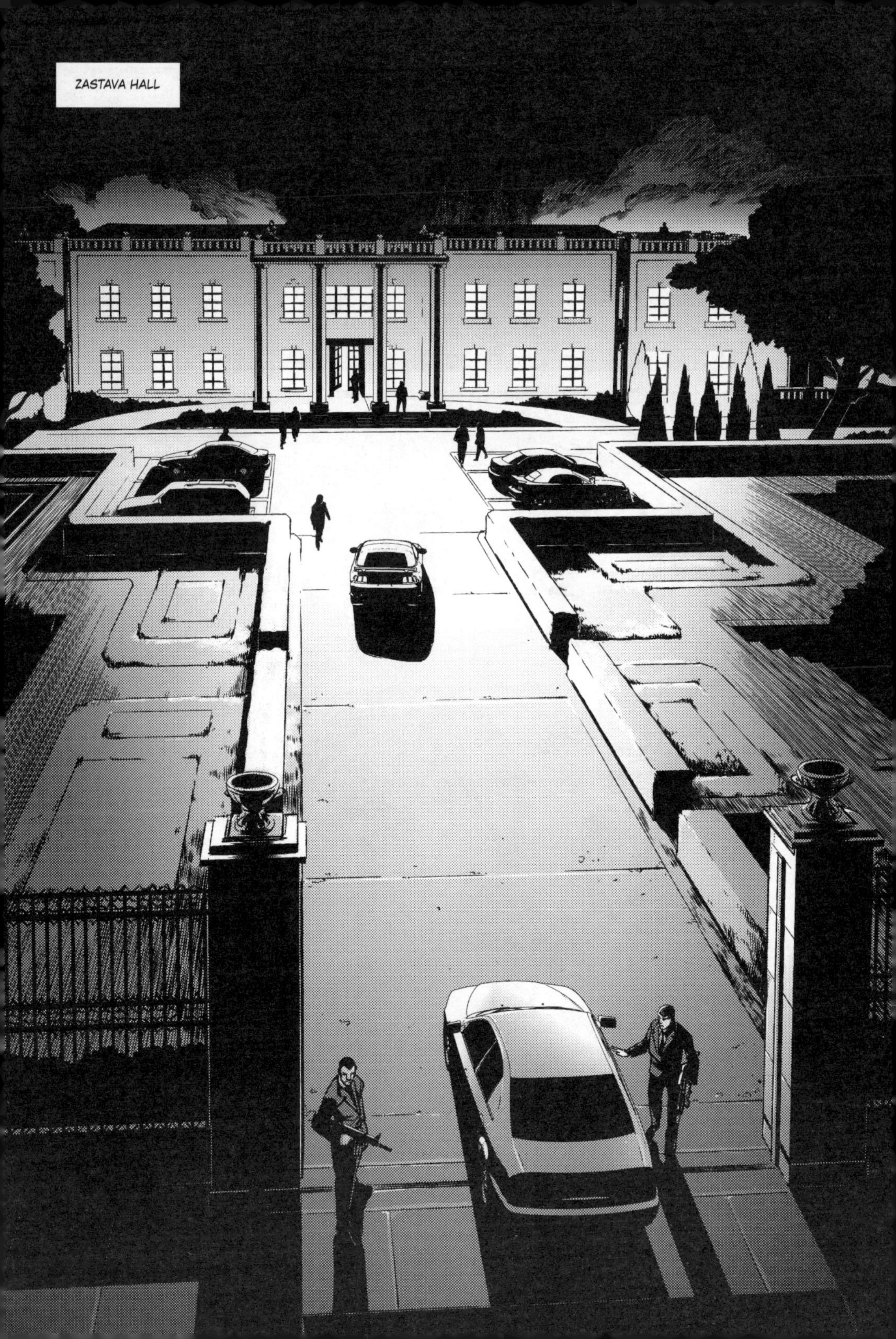
ZASTAVA HALL

THANK YOU ALL FOR BEING HERE TONIGHT, GENTLEMEN.
MY LATE FATHER'S WISH WAS TO CREATE A STRONG UNION BETWEEN THE HALLER AND ZASTAVA FAMILIES.
IN ORDER TO HONOR THAT, ANY TYPE OF VIOLENT ACT WILL NOT BE TOLERATED.

AND I HAVE NO REGRETS ABOUT OFFERING MY OWN SISTER AS A GUARANTEE...

IF THAT'S WHAT IT TAKES TO BRING ABOUT PEACE, SO BE IT.

FOR THE SAKE OF THAT PEACE, I HAVE HERE A SERIES OF DOCUMENTS THAT WILL MAKE THE MERGER BETWEEN OUR FAMILIES OFFICIAL.

THIS IS UNIT 5.

ALL CLEAR.

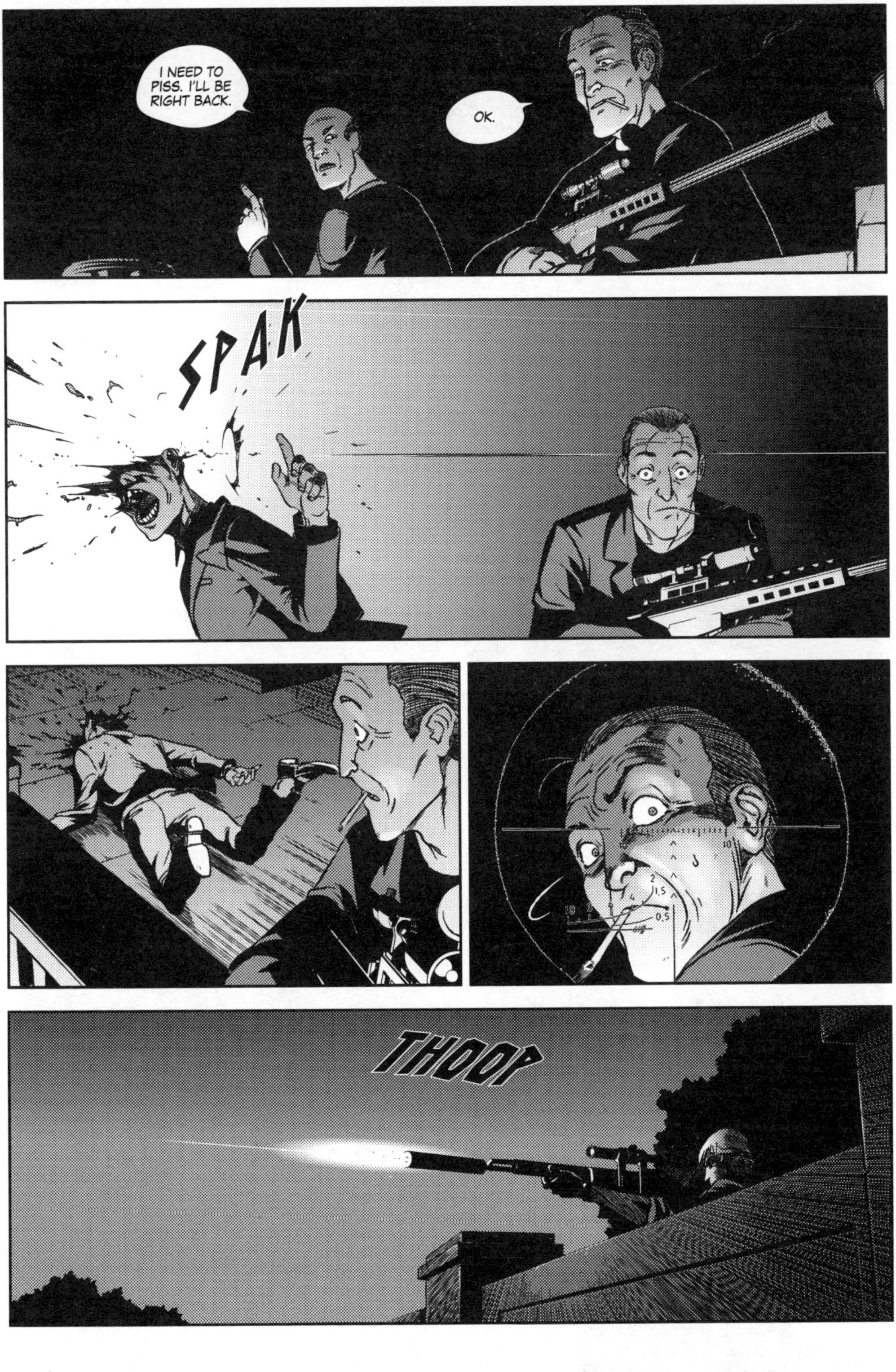
I NEED TO PISS. I'LL BE RIGHT BACK.
OK.
SPAK
THOOP

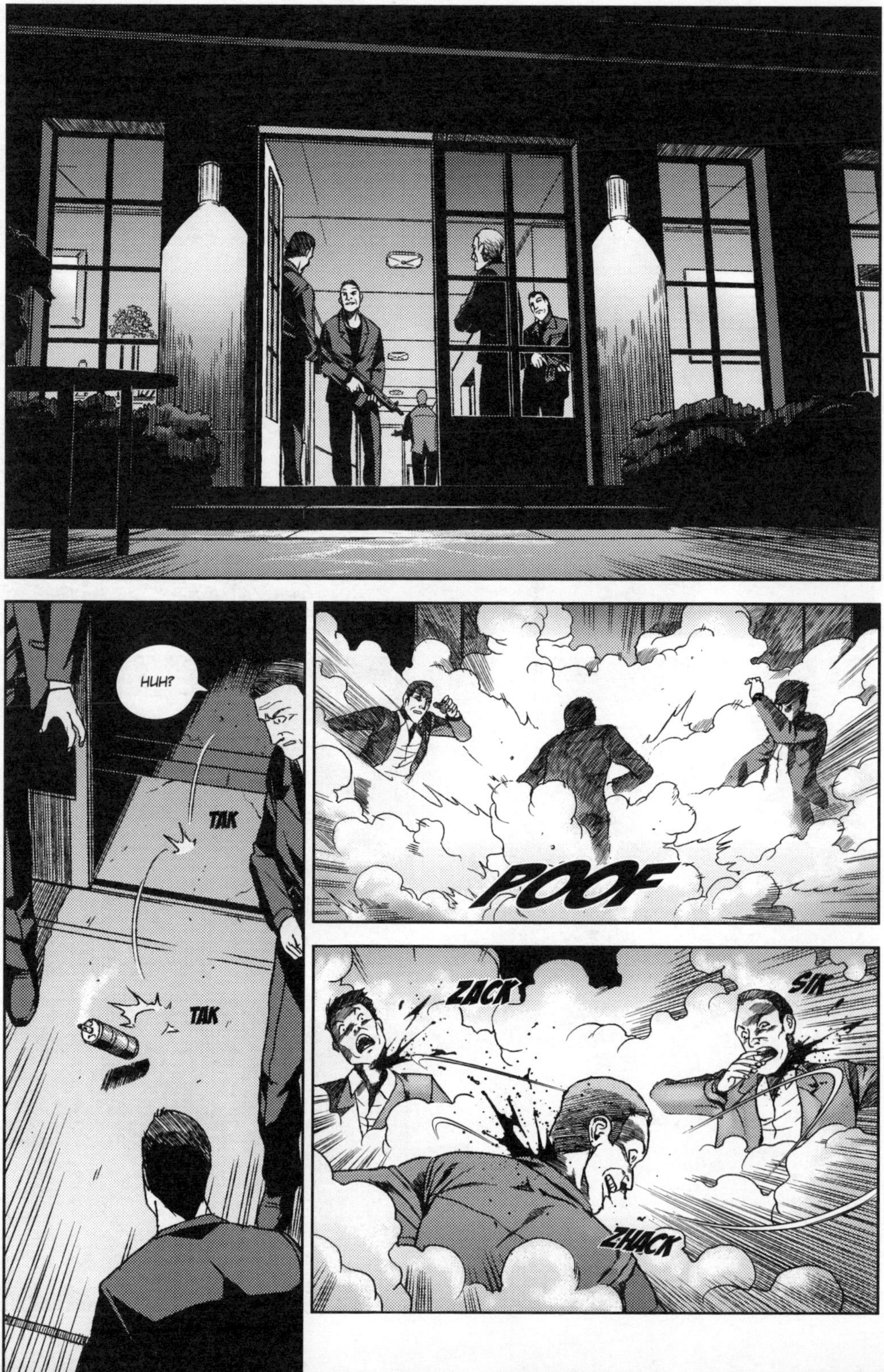
HUH?
TAK
TAK
POOF
ZACK
SIK
ZHACK

COFF! COFF!

THIS IS UNIT 3! WE'RE UNDER ATTACK!

THOOP

SHIT... THERE'S MORE THAN I THOUGHT. IT'S TIME TO END THIS...

BOSS! WE'RE BEING ATTACKED!
FOR YOUR SAFETY, DON'T LEAVE THE LIBRARY UNTIL FURTHER NOTICE!
HOW?
WHO'S ATTACKING US?!?
WHAT?!?
THIS WAS SUPPOSED TO BE A PEACEFUL MEETING!
WE KNEW YOU WOULDN'T LIVE UP TO THOSE WORDS!
IT'S CLEAR WHY YOUR FATHER NEVER WANTED YOU INVOLVED WITH THE FAMILIES!
YOU'RE NOT READY FOR THIS LEVEL OF RESPONSIBILITY!
SNAP
THIS MEETING IS OVER. WE WON'T AGREE TO ANYTHING UNDER THESE CIRCUM-STANCES.

CLAK
KA-CHAK
GENTLEMEN, NOBODY IS LEAVING THIS ROOM UNTIL EVERY ONE OF YOU HAS SIGNED EACH AND EVERY DOCUMENT.

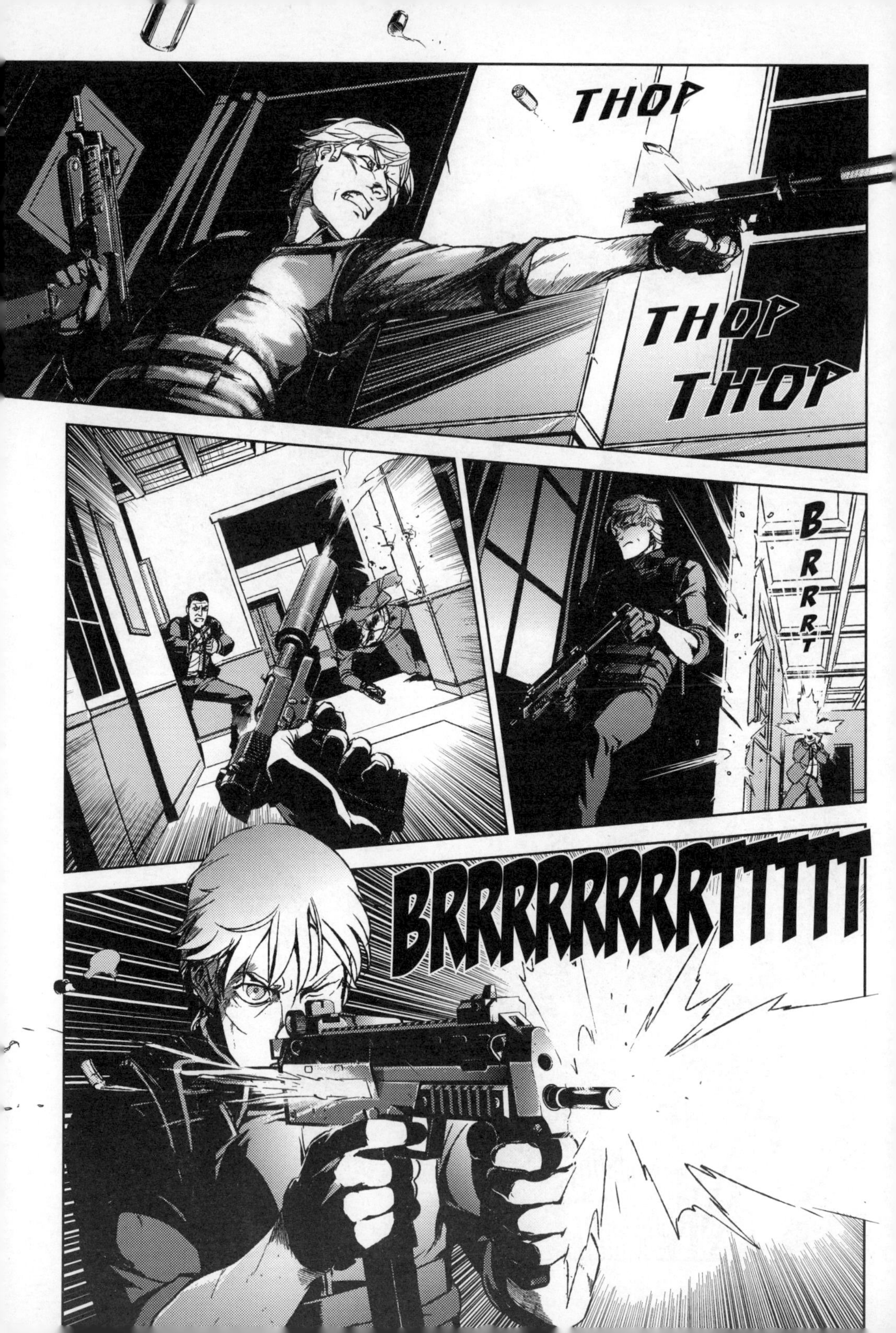
THOP
THOP
THOP
BRRRT
BRRRRRRRRRTTTTT

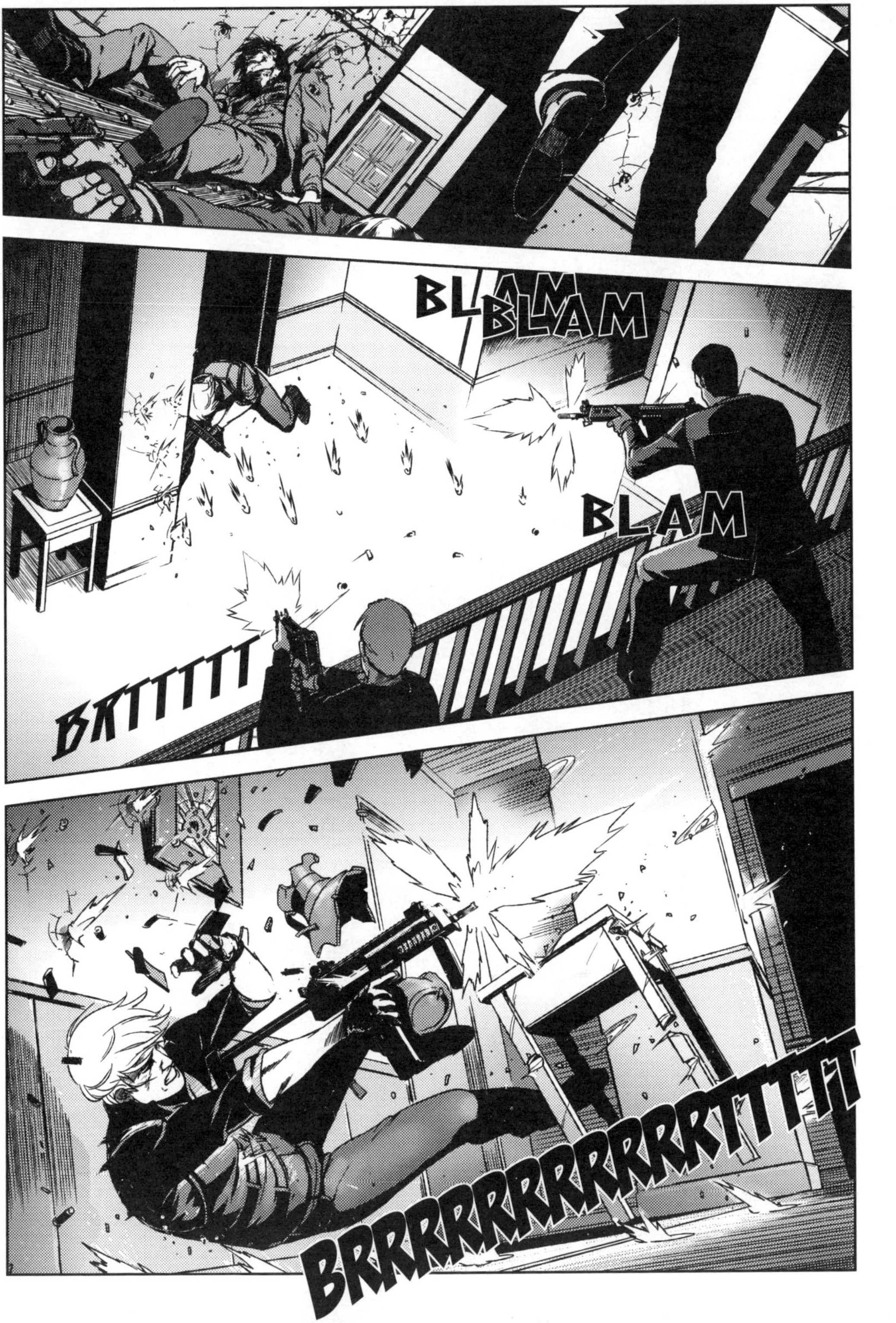
BLAM
BLAM
BLAM
BRTTTTT
BRRRRRRRRRRRTTTTT

SPACK
SPACK
SPACK
BLAMM
BLAMM
BLAM
UGH...
JUST A LITTLE MORE...
QUICK!
COVER THE ENTRANCE TO THE LIBRARY!

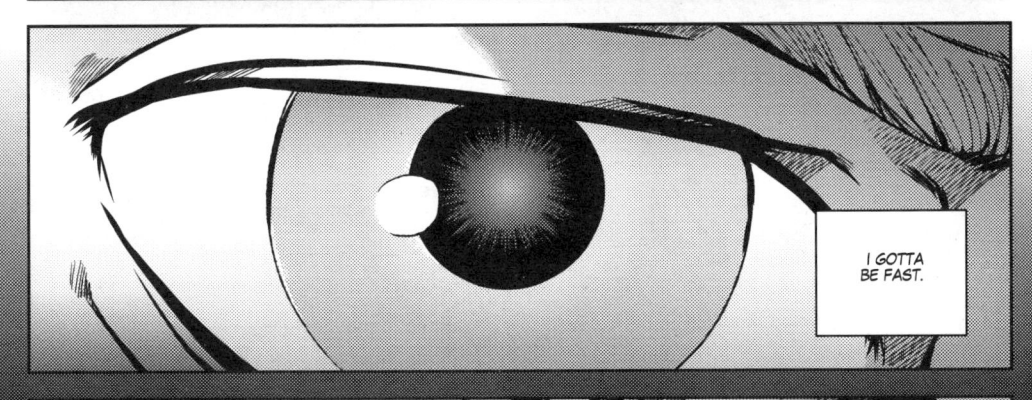

THE LIBRARY. THAT MUST BE WHERE THEY'RE KEEPING HER...

ONE DOWN HERE, ONE ON THE UPPER RIGHT, TWO ON THE STAIRS, AND THREE IN THE UPSTAIRS HALLWAY.

THIS IS GONNA BE TOUGH...

I GOTTA BE FAST.

CHA-CHUKK

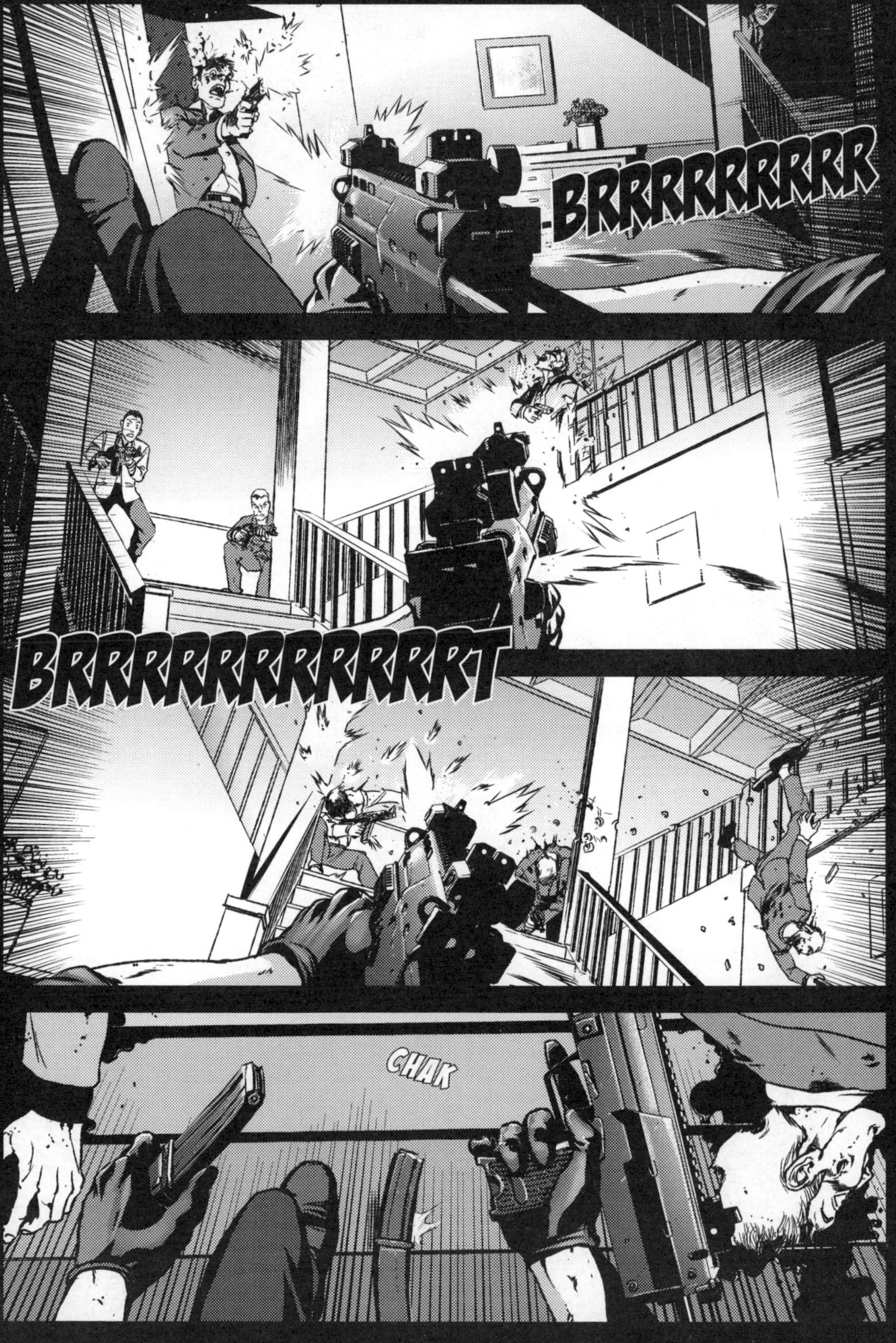
BRRRRRRRRRR
BRRRRRRRRRRRRRT
CHAK

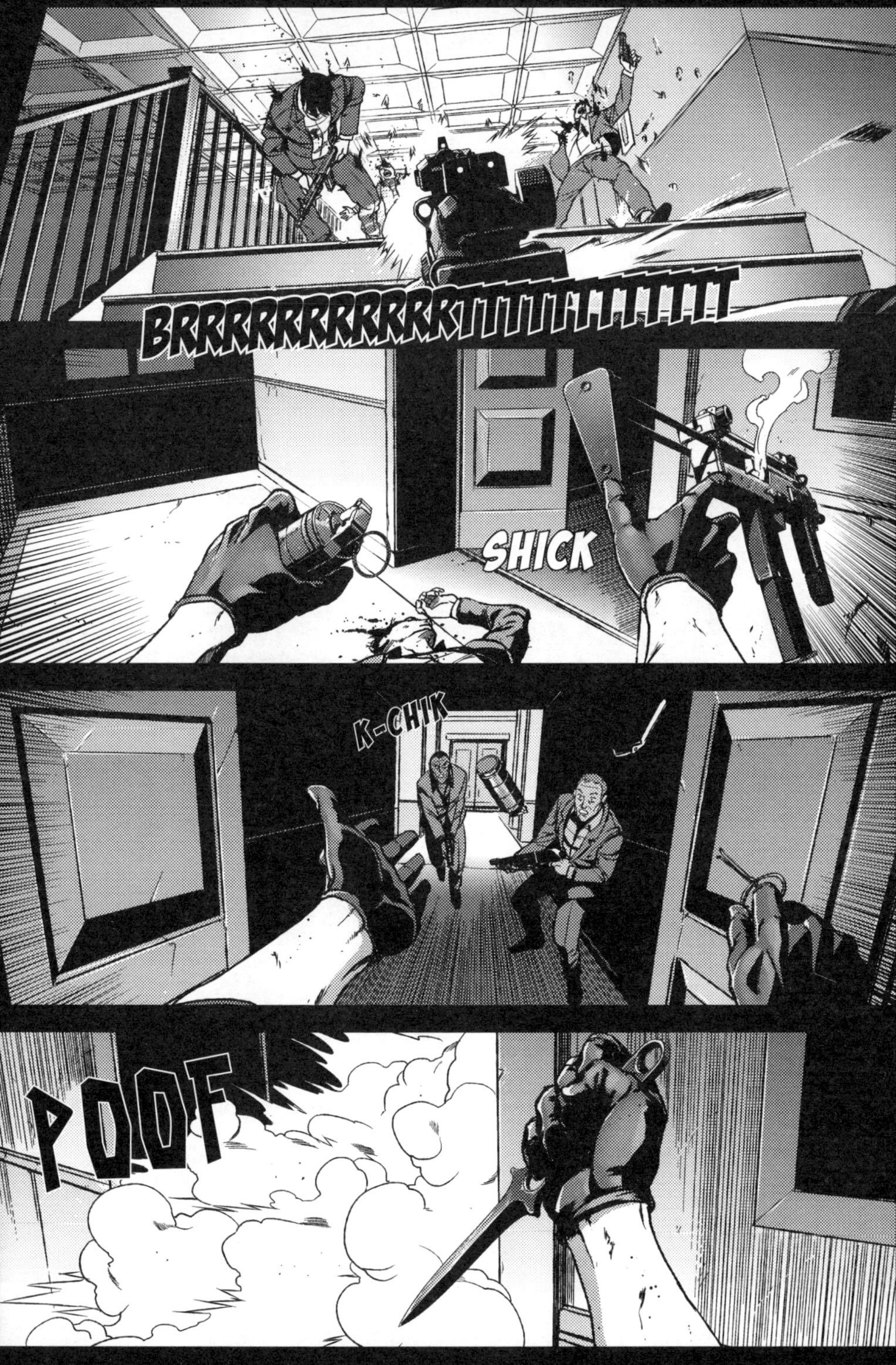
BRRRRRRRRRRRRTTTTTTTTTTTT
SHICK
K-CHIK
POOF

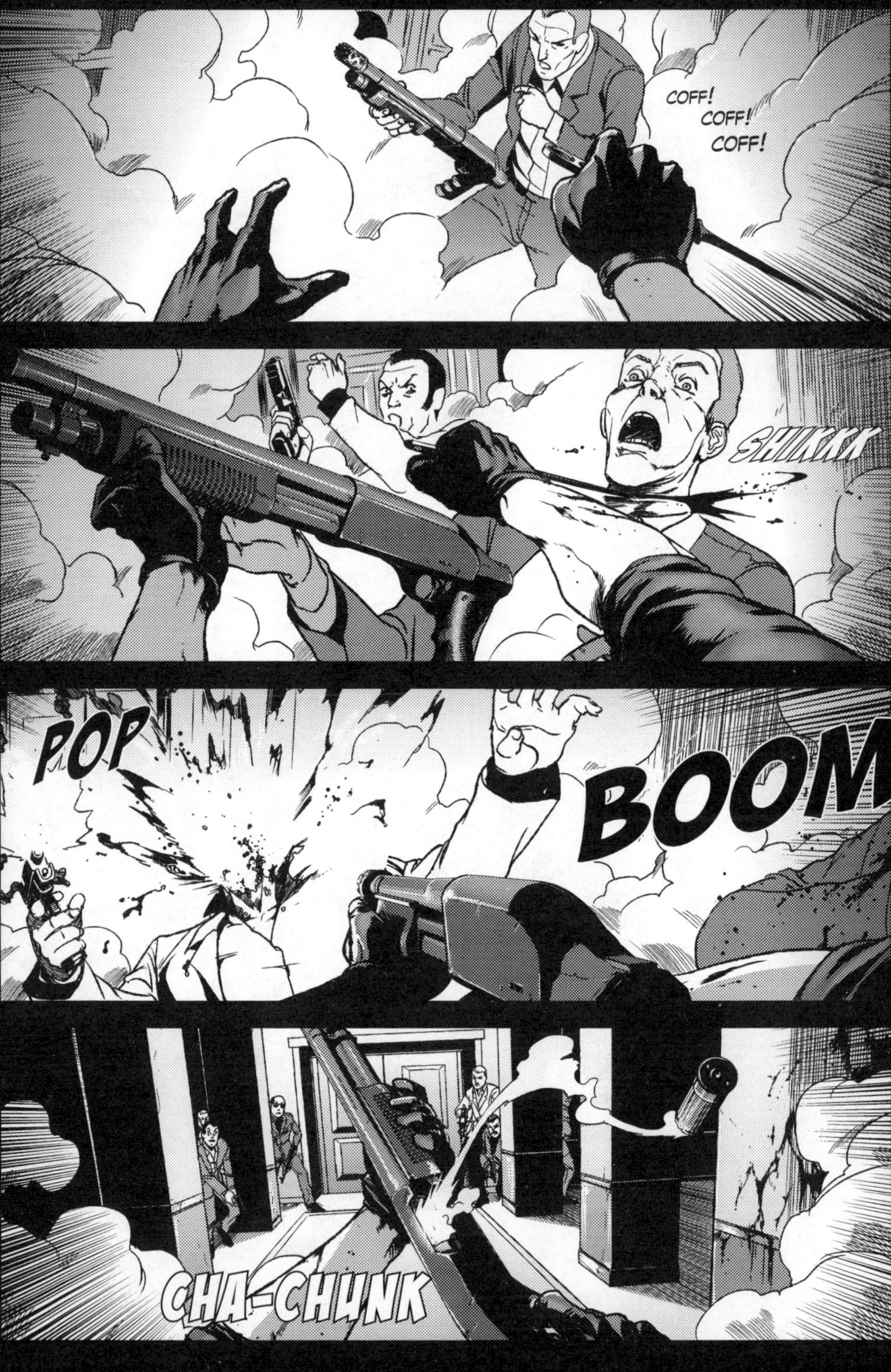
COFF!
COFF!
COFF!
SHIKKK
POP
BOOM
CHA-CHUNK

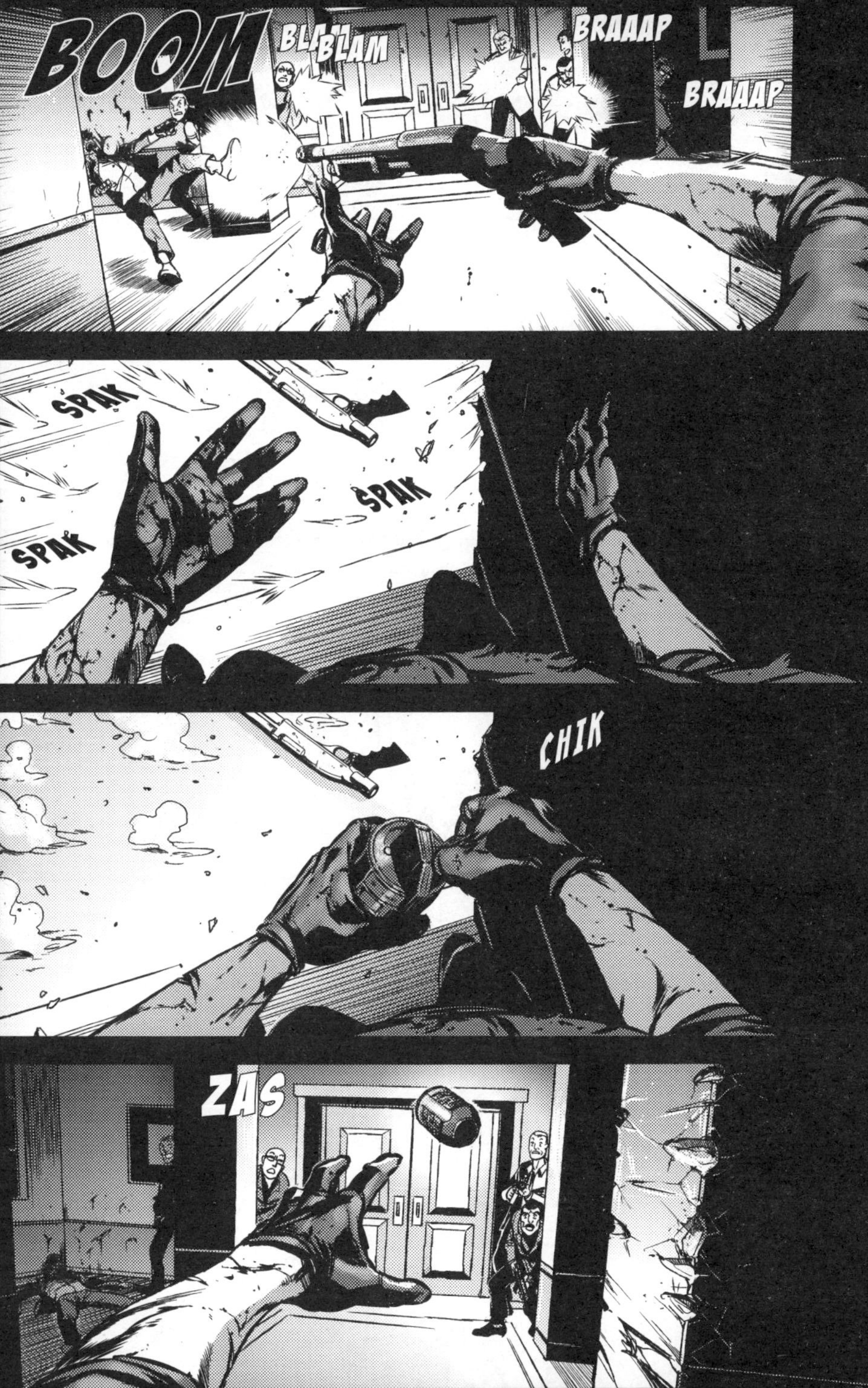
BOOM
BLAM BLAM
BRAAAP
BRAAAP
SPAK
SPAK
SPAK
CHIK
ZAS

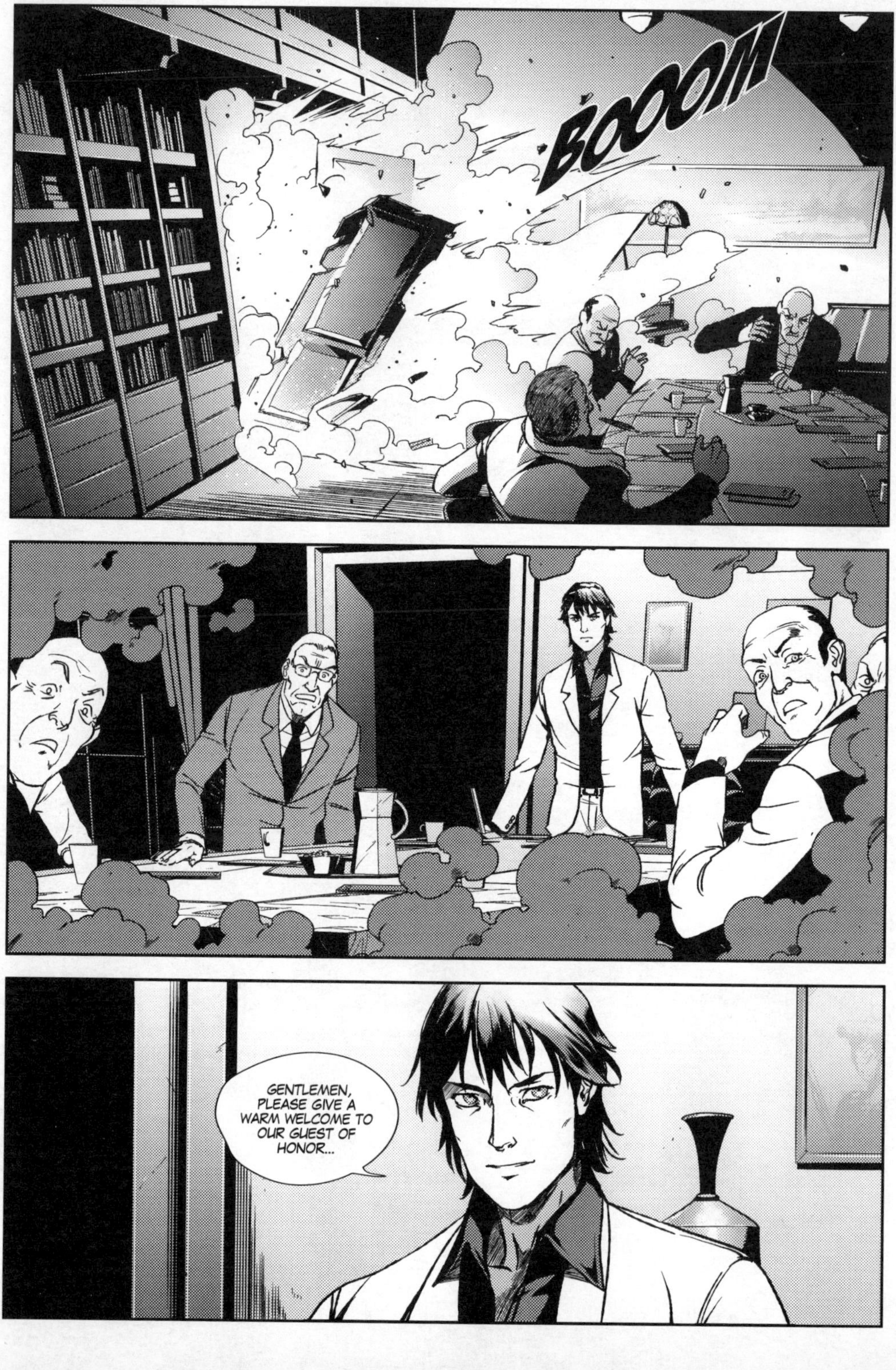
BOOOM
GENTLEMEN, PLEASE GIVE A WARM WELCOME TO OUR GUEST OF HONOR...

CHIK

EVERYBODY OUT!

YOU'RE A DEAD MAN!

THIS IS WAR!

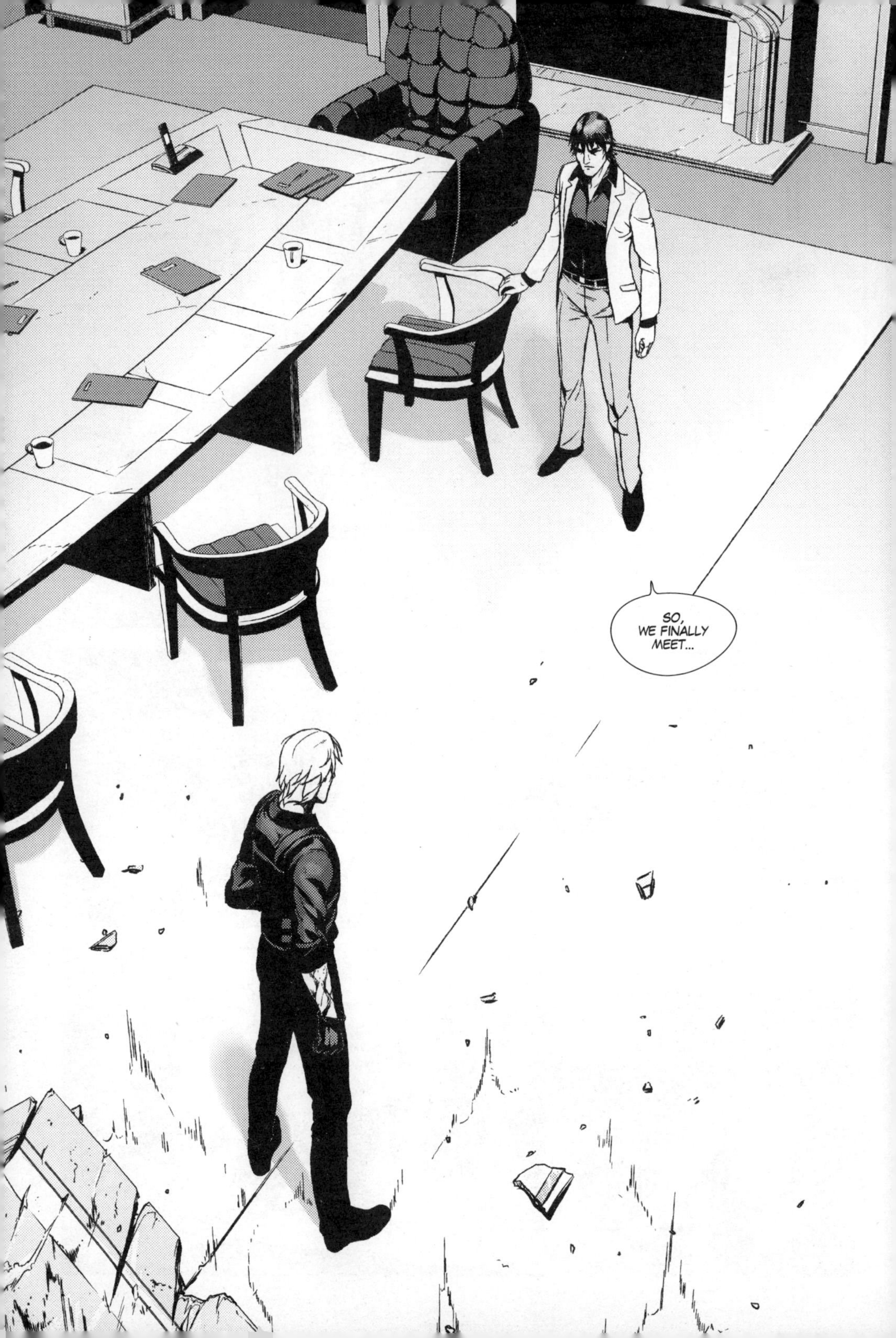
SO, WE FINALLY MEET...

07

WHERE IS SHE?
YOU ARE HERE FOR HER AFTER ALL...
IT'S A SHAME YOU GOT HERE IN SUCH BAD SHAPE...
SNAP
BRING HER OUT HERE!

I THINK YOU TWO HAVE MET BEFORE.

THIS TYPE OF SITUATION'S TURNING INTO A BAD HABIT...

DON'T WORRY...

SHE'S SO DRUGGED UP SHE CAN'T EVEN REMEMBER HER OWN NAME.

GIVE UP, AND I WON'T HAVE TO KILL HER.

ZAS

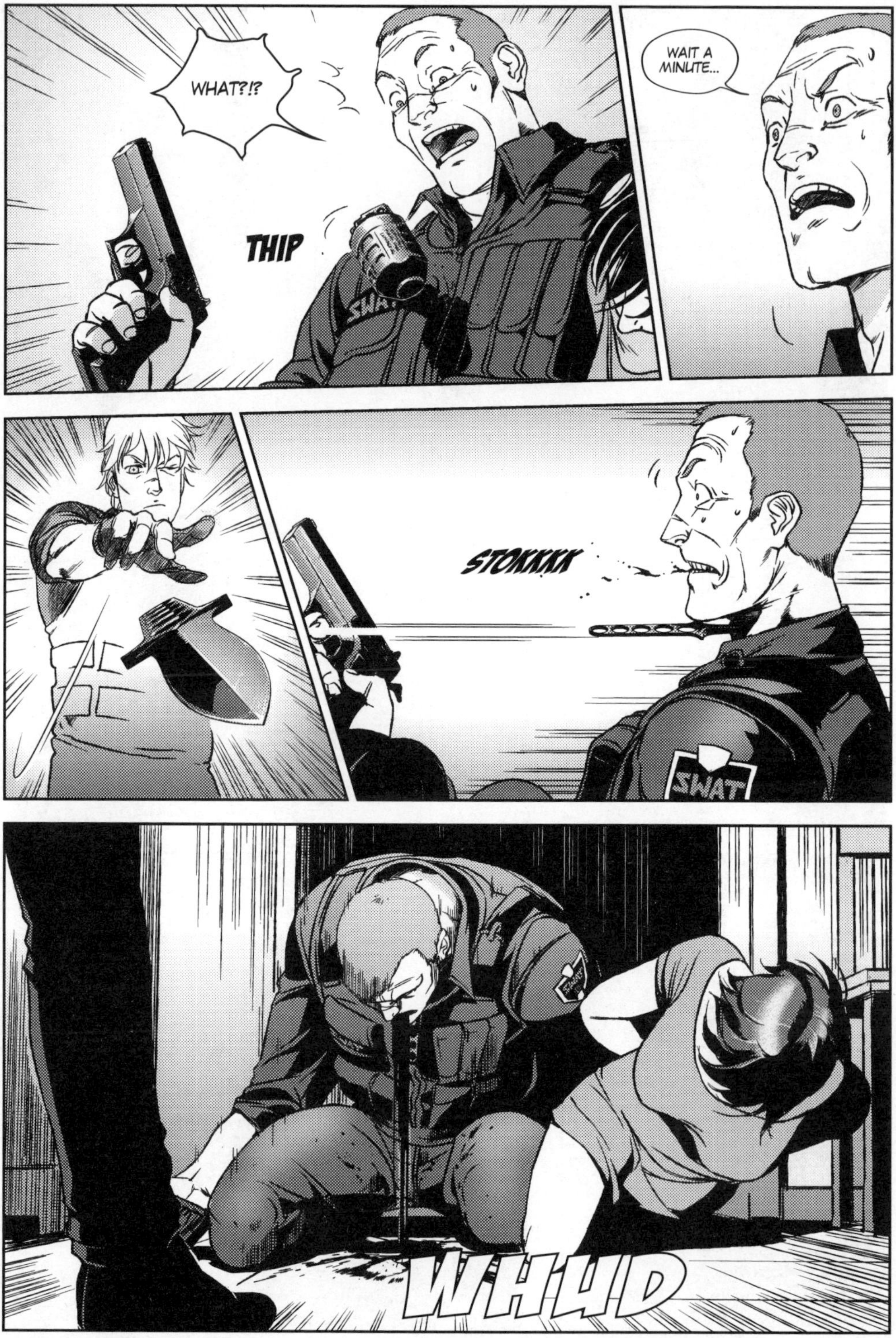
WHAT?!?
THIP
WAIT A MINUTE...
SWAT
STOKKKK
SWAT
WHUD

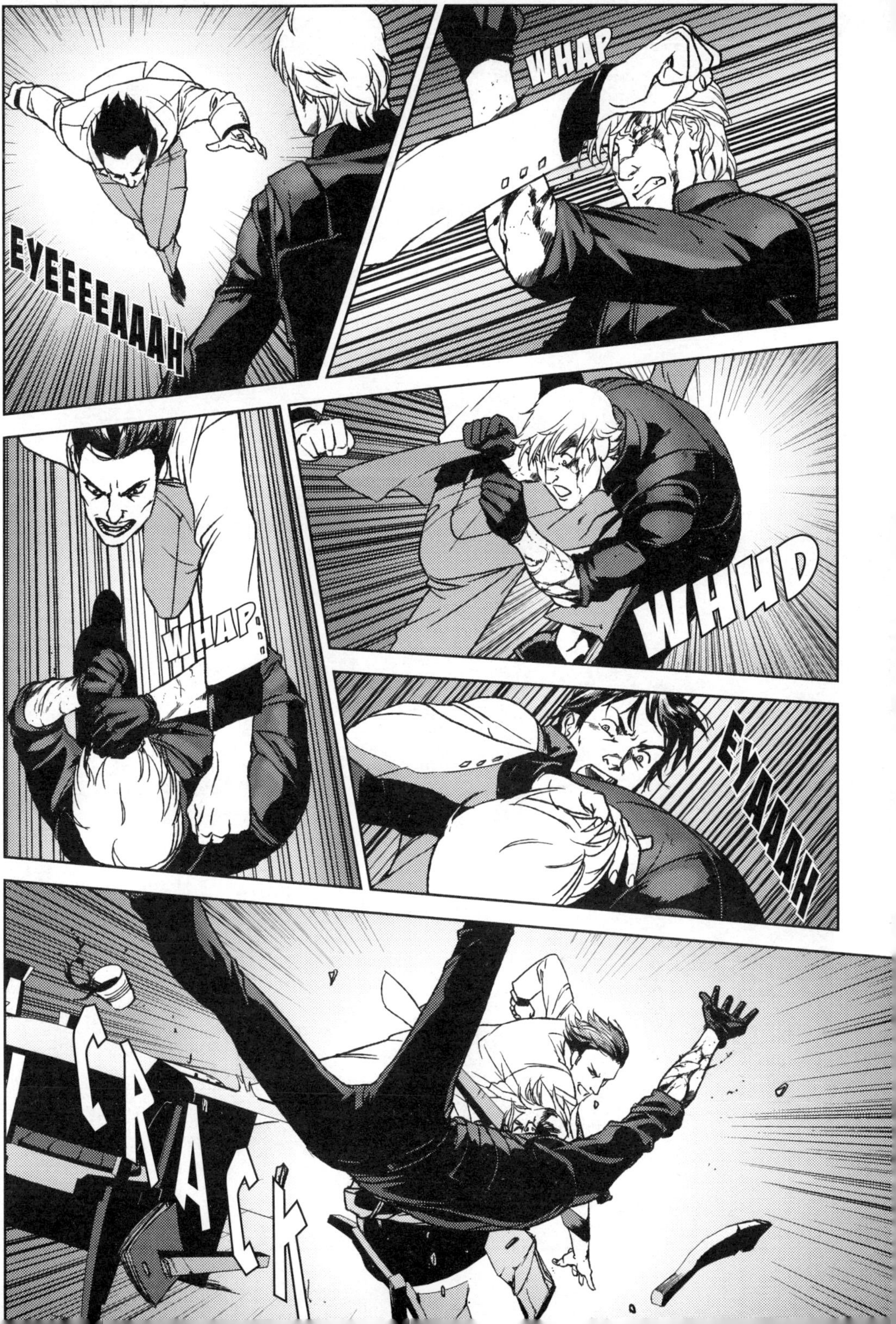
WHAP
EYEEEEAAAH
WHUD
WHAP
EYAAAH
CRACK

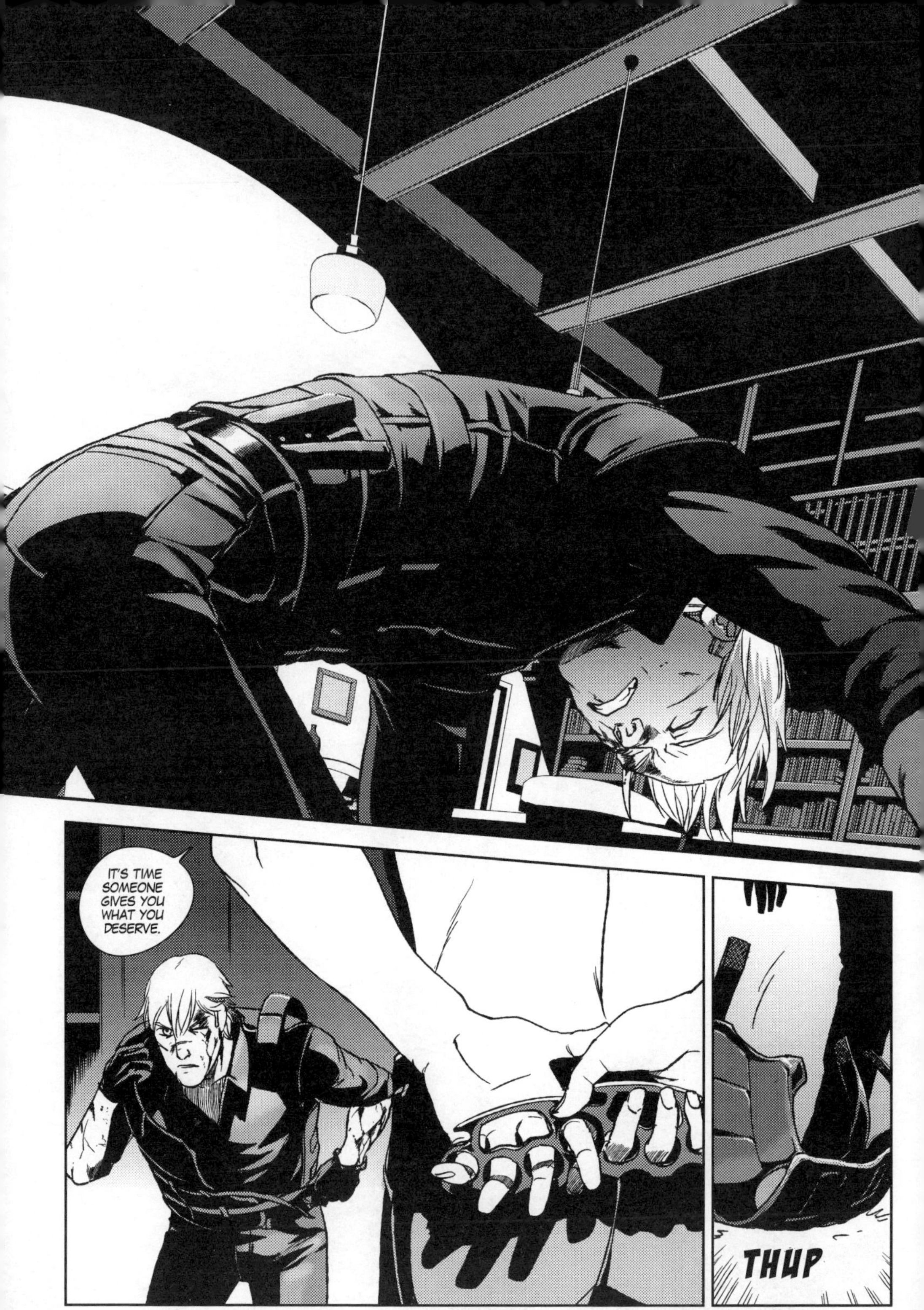
IT'S TIME SOMEONE GIVES YOU WHAT YOU DESERVE.
THUP

IS THIS THE INFAMOUS HITMAN THAT'S CAUSED ME SO MUCH TROUBLE?
TAP
WHUD

FUCKER!
WHUD
WHAMM
I CAN SEE WHY MY SISTER LIKES YOU.
IT'S A SHAME THERE WON'T BE MUCH LEFT TO LIKE AFTER I'M THROUGH WITH YOU!

WHUD
ARE THESE YOUR TOOLS OF THE TRADE?
TRAK
AGH!!!
I MUST CONFESS, I'M A BIT DISAPPOINTED...
BASED ON YOUR REPUTATION, I WAS EXPECTING MUCH MORE OUT OF YOU!

THE ONLY THING YOU HAD TO DO WAS TAKE THE MONEY!
BUT NO...
YOU HAD TO COME AND TRY TO RESCUE HER...
AND RUIN MY PARTY!
KA-CHUK
I GUESS IN THE END YOU WERE BOTH FATED TO MEET, HUH?
BUT GOOD THINGS DON'T LAST FOREVER.
ON THE PLUS SIDE, SHE'LL HAVE THE PRIVILEGE OF WATCHING ME KILL YOU.
AND THEN SHE'LL BE NEXT.
TIME TO DIE!

PLIK
PLIK

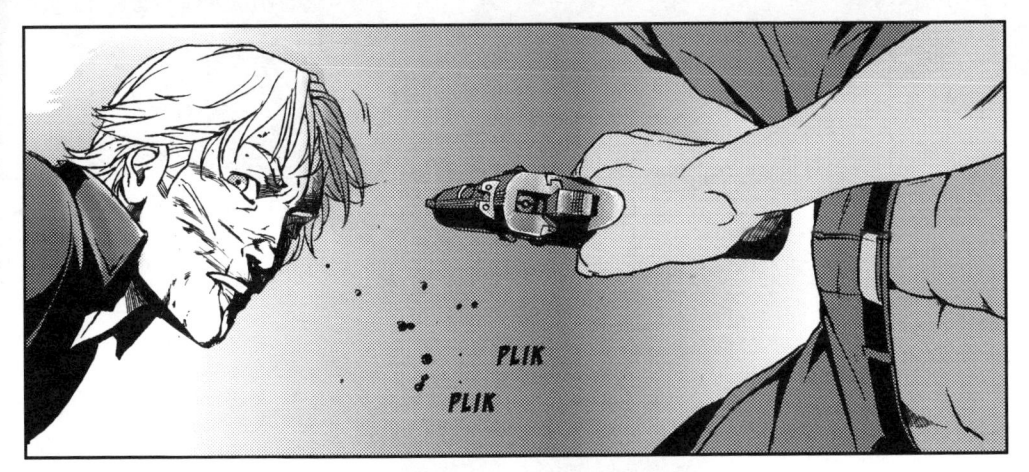

HUCK...

COFF
COFF

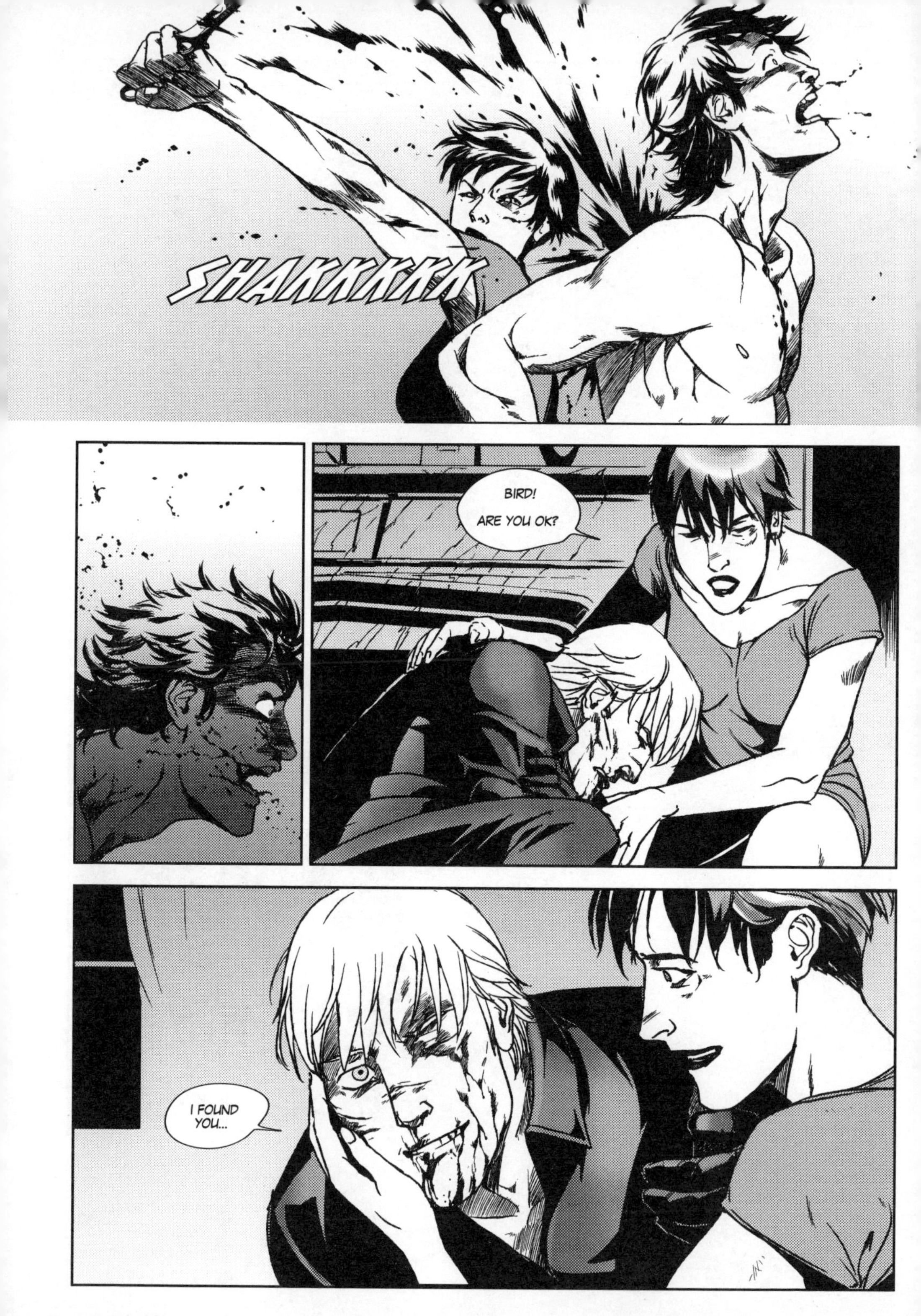
SHAKKKKKK
BIRD!
ARE YOU OK?
I FOUND YOU...

HAHAHA! THE TWO LOVEBIRDS!

UNFORTUNATELY, THIS STORY DOESN'T HAVE A HAPPY ENDING...

THERE'S ONE LAST THING YOU SHOULD KNOW, SIS...

HE WAS THE ONE THAT KILLED OUR FATHER...

DAD WAS PAYING OFF COPS AND POLITICIANS TO TURN THE FAMILY BUSINESS INTO SOMETHING LEGITIMATE...
AND I WASN'T GOING TO LET THAT HAPPEN...
A DIRTY COP WE GAVE JOBS TO HIRED YOUR FRIEND...
I GUESS IT'S NOT HIS FAULT. HE DIDN'T KNOW WHO THE TARGET WAS, AFTER ALL...
HAHAHA...
ANYWAY...
GOODBYE, SIS...
COFF, COFF...
UGH...

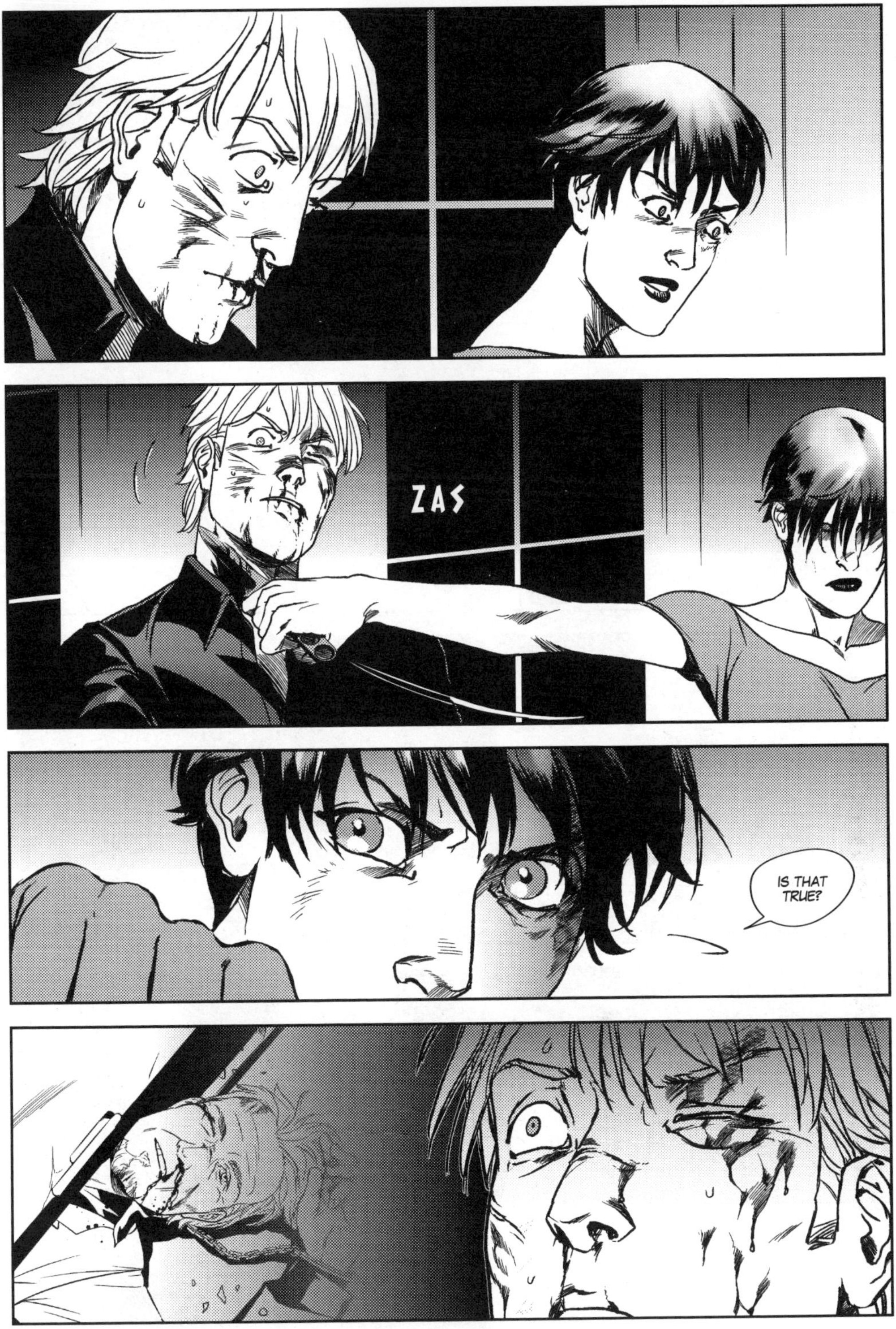
ZAS
IS THAT TRUE?

I'M SORRY...

TAK

WHAT COULD I EXPECT FROM SOMEONE LIKE YOU...

YOU'VE TAKEN MY FAMILY, MY HONOR...

AND I WAS STUPID ENOUGH TO ALMOST GIVE YOU MORE THAN JUST MY BODY...

I HOPE THAT YOU AT LEAST GOT PAID ENOUGH TO MAKE THAT STUPID DREAM OF YOURS COME TRUE...

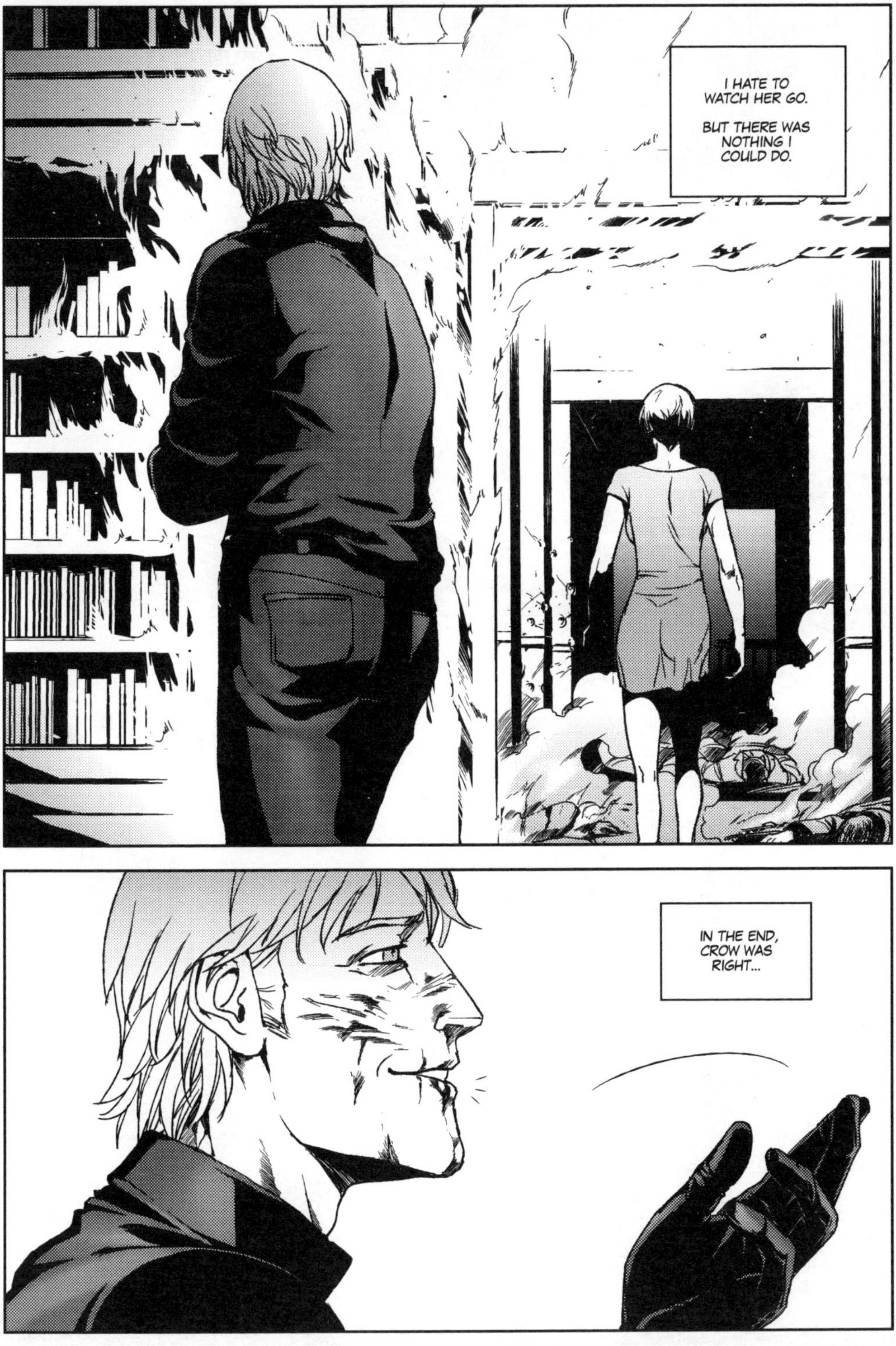
I HATE TO WATCH HER GO.
BUT THERE WAS NOTHING I COULD DO.
IN THE END, CROW WAS RIGHT...

COFF COFF

...THIS IS THE END OF THE JOURNEY.

CLAP CLAP CLAP

CLAP CLAP CLAP

BRAVO!

I'M SO PROUD OF YOU!

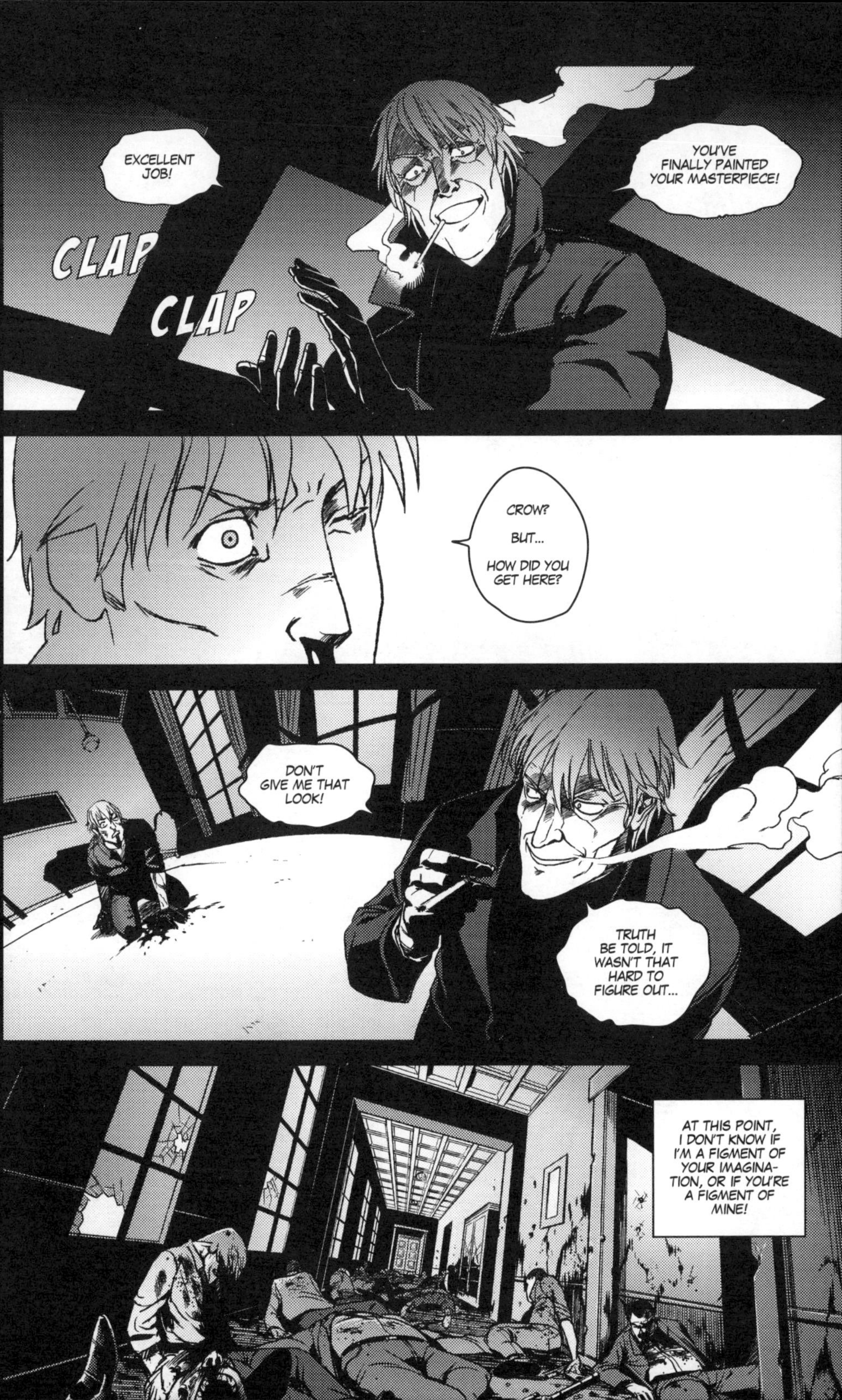
EXCELLENT JOB!
YOU'VE FINALLY PAINTED YOUR MASTERPIECE!
CLAP
CLAP
CROW?
BUT...
HOW DID YOU GET HERE?
DON'T GIVE ME THAT LOOK!
TRUTH BE TOLD, IT WASN'T THAT HARD TO FIGURE OUT...
AT THIS POINT, I DON'T KNOW IF I'M A FIGMENT OF YOUR IMAGINATION, OR IF YOU'RE A FIGMENT OF MINE!

I'M SURE THAT YOU FELT A WONDERFUL PLEASURE AS YOU MOWED DOWN ALL THESE PEOPLE.
YOU'RE WRONG! I DID THIS FOR HER!
ARE YOU STILL CONFUSED?
WE ARE THE WOLF, NOT THE SHEEP, BIRD!
I SHOULD PROBABLY ALSO TAKE OUT TONY AND HANNA...
WILL YOU JUST FORGET ABOUT HER?
OR DO I HAVE TO KEEP ON PLAYING THE ROLE OF YOUR MALEVOLENT ALTER-EGO FOREVER?
YOU'RE LEAVING ME NO CHOICE BUT TO KILL HER SO THAT SHE CAN FINALLY BE OUT OF OUR LIVES FOR GOOD!
DON'T YOU DARE!!!
I'M WARNING YOU, CROW...
BIRD...
WE ARE NOT NORMAL PEOPLE...
OUR ACTIONS WILL ALWAYS AFFECT REGULAR FOLKS.

WHAT DO YOU HAVE THERE?
IT'S A DETONATOR...
I'VE PUT CHARGES ALL OVER THE MANOR...
EVEN HERE...
IF WE ARE BOTH THE SAME PERSON...
I GUESS THE ONE THAT SURVIVES IS THE REAL BIRD...
IF SOMEONE SURVIVES, THAT IS!
I LIKE YOUR STYLE!
OR MAYBE YOU'RE FINALLY GOING INSANE!

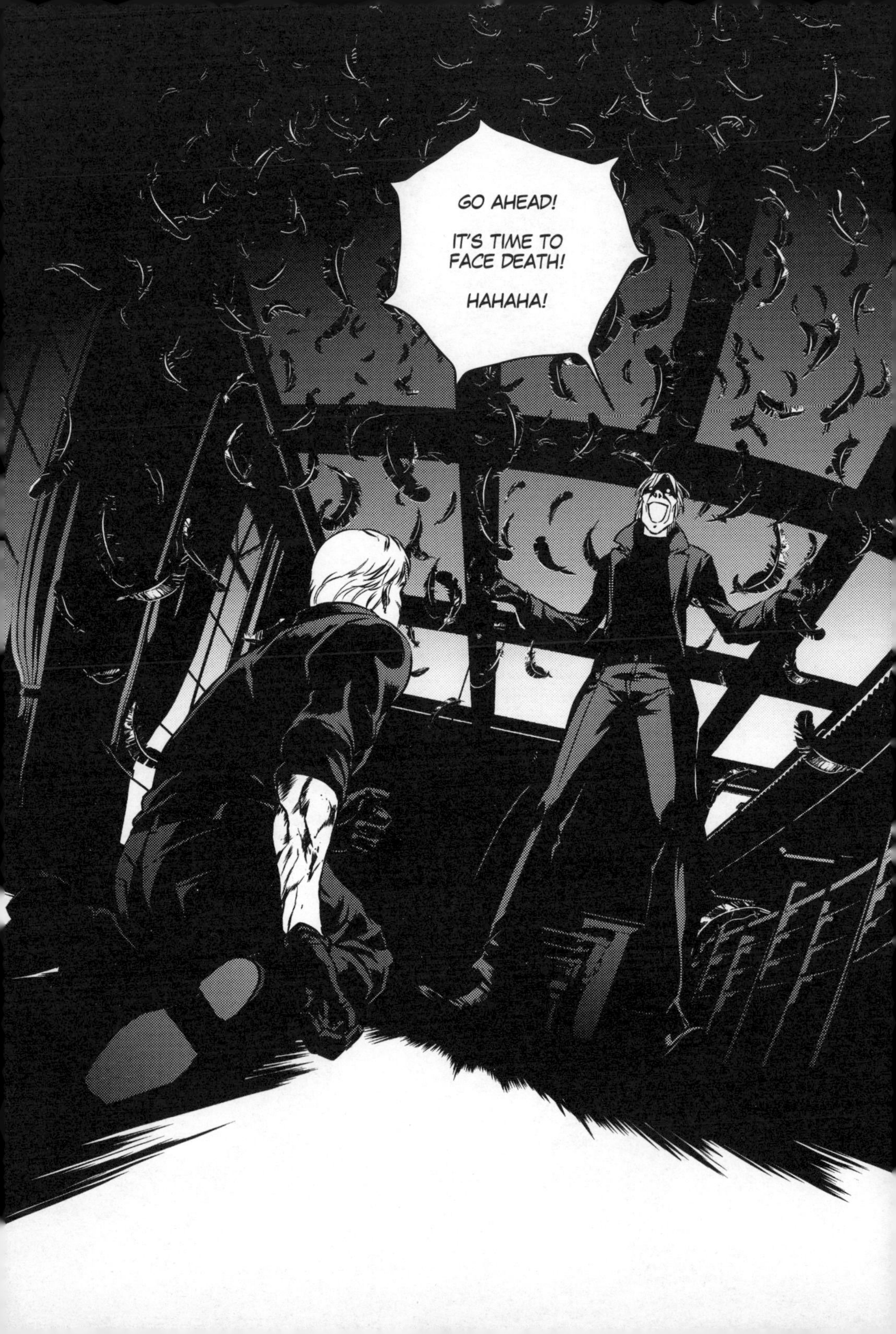
GO AHEAD!
IT'S TIME TO FACE DEATH!
HAHAHA!

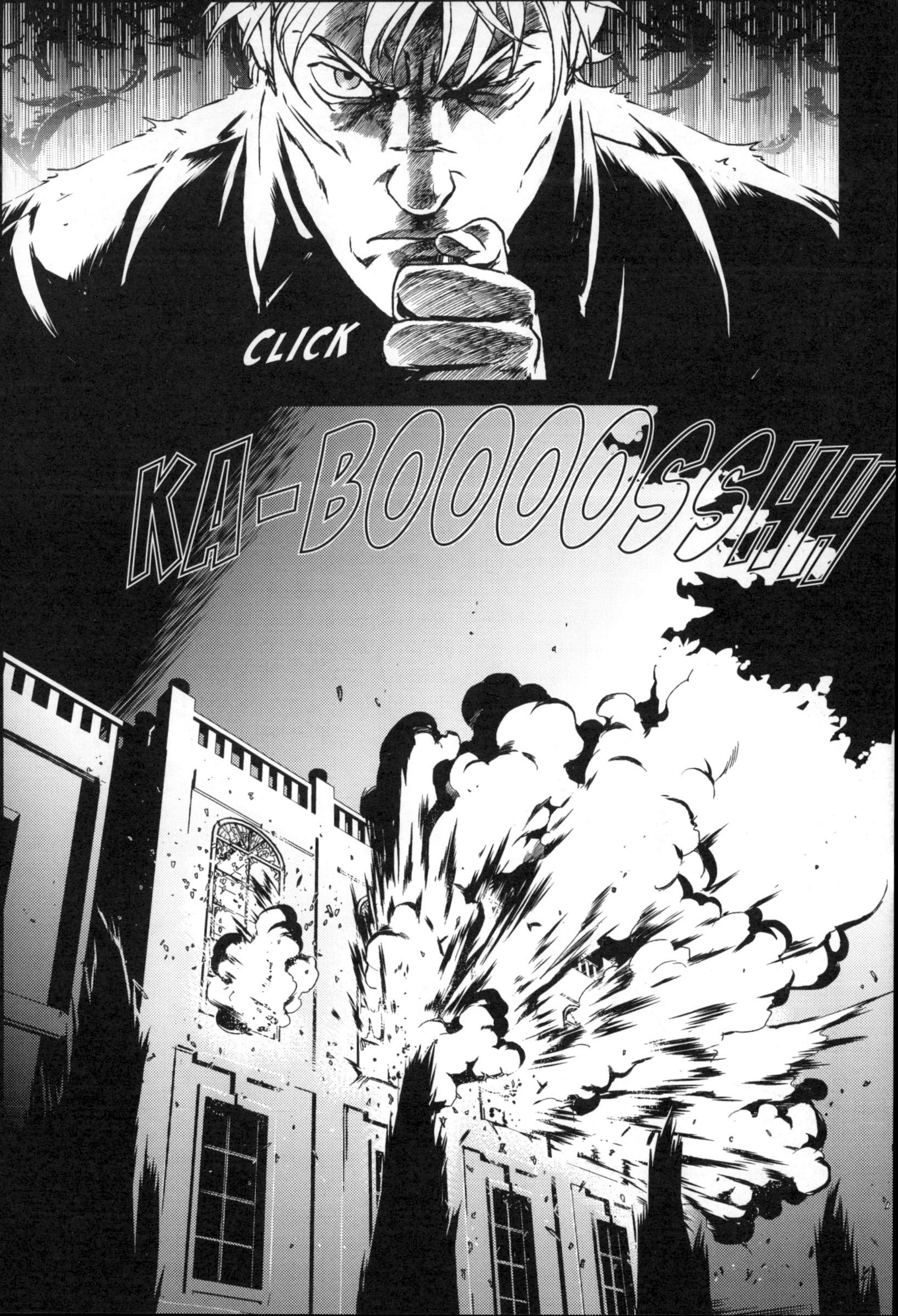
CLICK
KA-BOOOOOSSHH

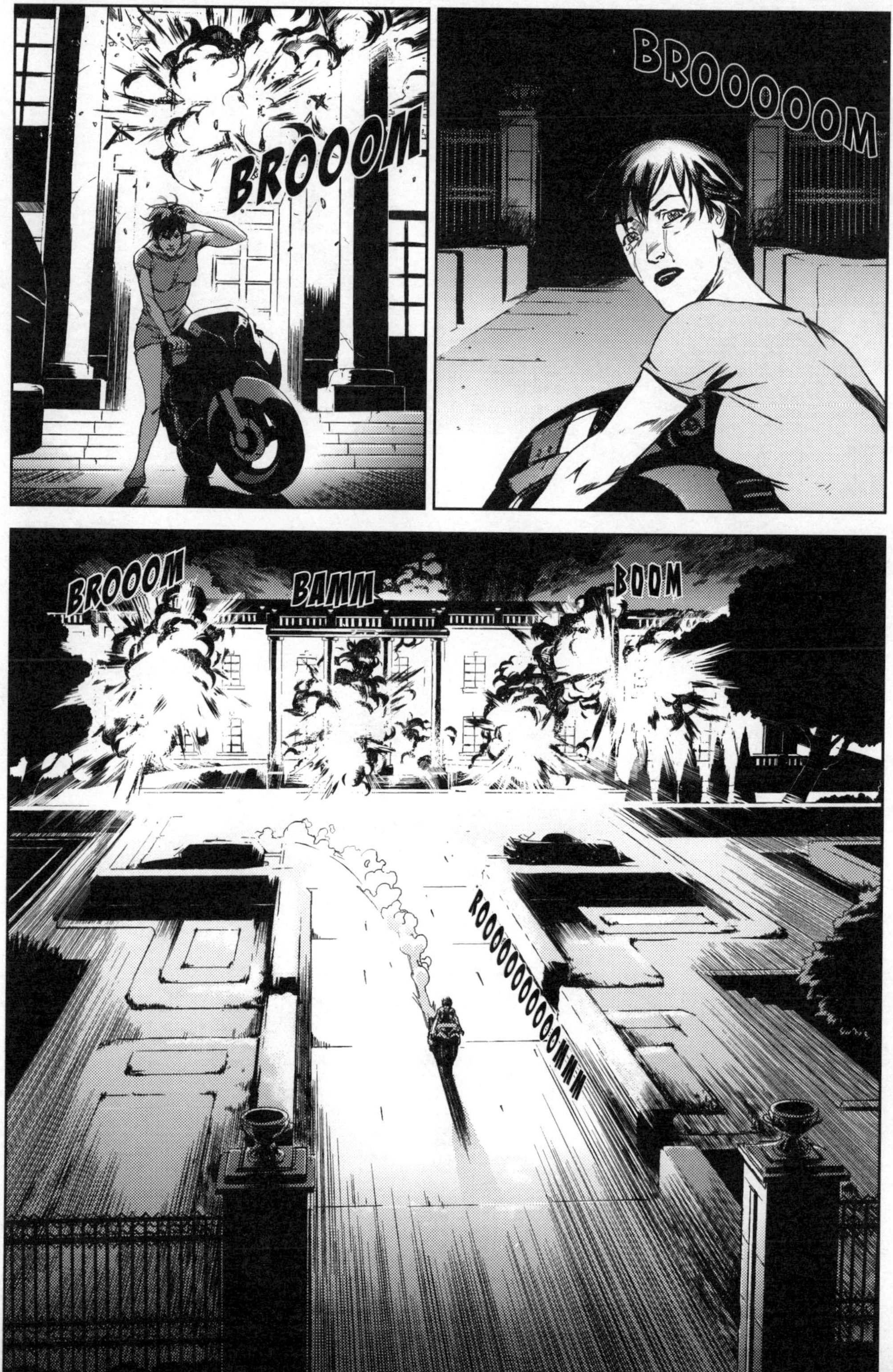
BROOOM
BROOOOOM
BROOOM
BAMM
BOOM
ROOOOOOOOOOOMMM

EPILOGUE

Panel 1:

"THAT'S RIGHT. AFTER A LONG INVESTIGATION, WE WERE ABLE TO BREAK UP A CRIMINAL ORGANIZATION THAT LED ALL THE WAY TO THE TOP OF THE LOCAL POLICE FORCE."

"THANK YOU FOR YOUR TIME, MR. MIKERS! WE WOULD ALSO LIKE TO CONGRATULATE YOU ON YOUR PROMOTION TO CHIEF COMMISSIONER!"

"OH? AH! THANKS!"

Panel 2:

"HEY TONY!"

"HEY! EVENING, McMILLAN! LOOK! YOUR FORMER PARTNER'S ON TV!"

Panel 3:

"LOOKS LIKE ALL THAT TIME I SPENT BABYSITTING HIM PAID OFF. IT REALLY SEEMS LIKE IT CAME UP ROSES FOR EVERYONE BUT ME!"

"I WAS WONDERING IF YOU HAD ANY NEWS ABOUT YOUR FRIEND..."

"I HAVE MANY FRIENDS, LIEUTENANT."

"I'M SORRY, BUT I DON'T THINK I CAN HELP YOU WITH THAT."

Panel 4:

CRASH

"C'MON, TONY. I JUST WANNA THANK HIM."

"HUH?"

"WHAT? NOT AGAIN!"

DON'T LOOK AT ME LIKE THAT! IT'S ALWAYS THE SAME WITH YOU! I'M OVER HERE WORKING MY ASS OFF, AND YOU'RE FLIRTING WITH A COUGAR!
THE NEXT GLASS YOU BREAK IS COMING OUT OF YOUR FUTURE SALARY!
?
SORRY I CAN'T HELP YOU, LIEU-TENANT.
I HAVE ENOUGH PROBLEMS AS IT IS!
OK, I UNDERSTAND.
BUT ONE DAY YOU'RE GONNA HAVE TO EXPLAIN TO ME HOW YOU REBUILT THIS JOINT IN JUST FOUR MONTHS!
Tony's Restaurant
ALL OF MY PAPERWORK IS IN ORDER.
YOU'RE WELCOME TO JOIN US AT THE OFFICIAL GRAND OPENING, MAJOR.
THANK YOU, BUT I'M ON DUTY. MAYBE NEXT TIME. GOODBYE, TONY!

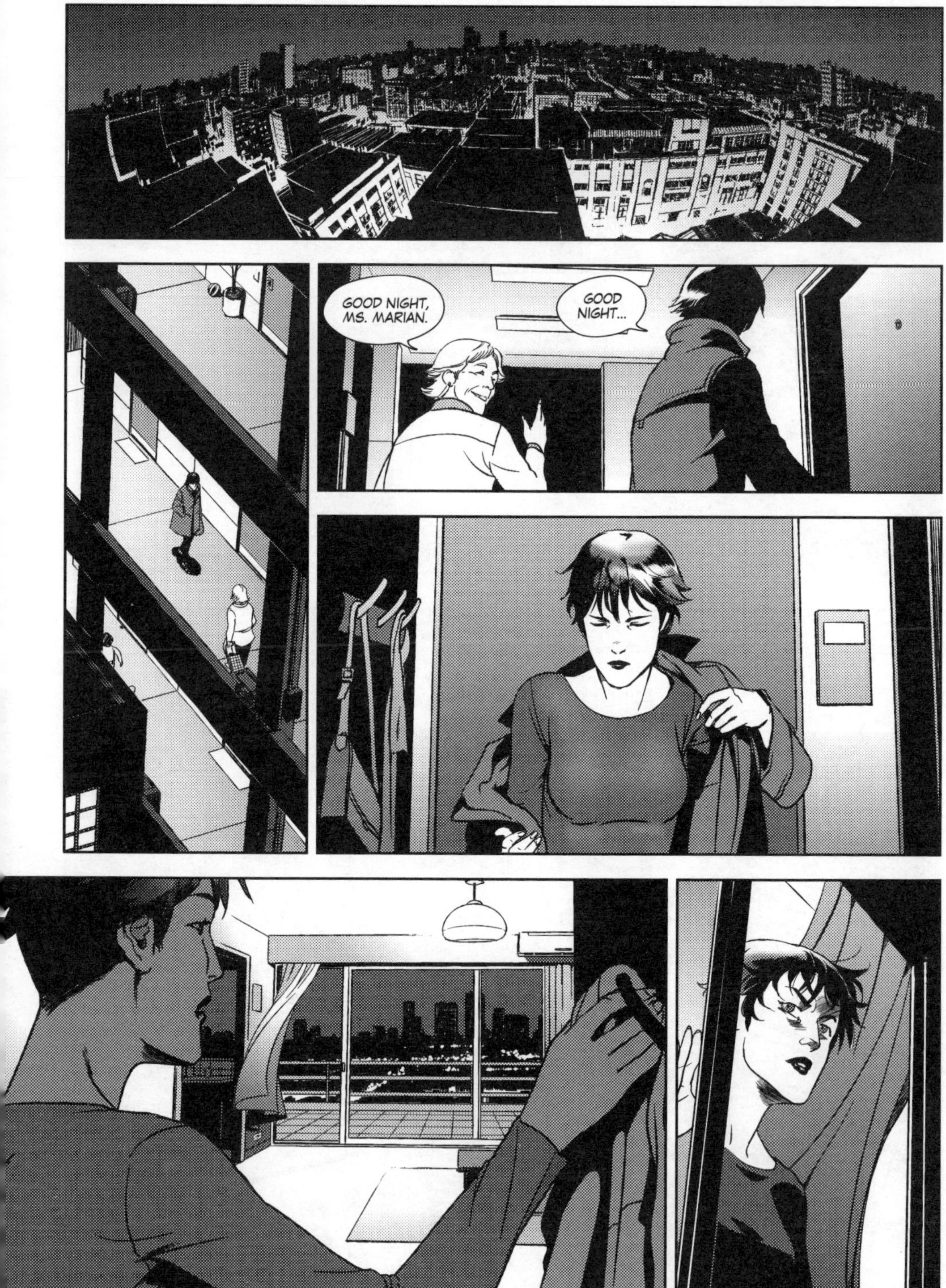
GOOD NIGHT, MS. MARIAN.
GOOD NIGHT...

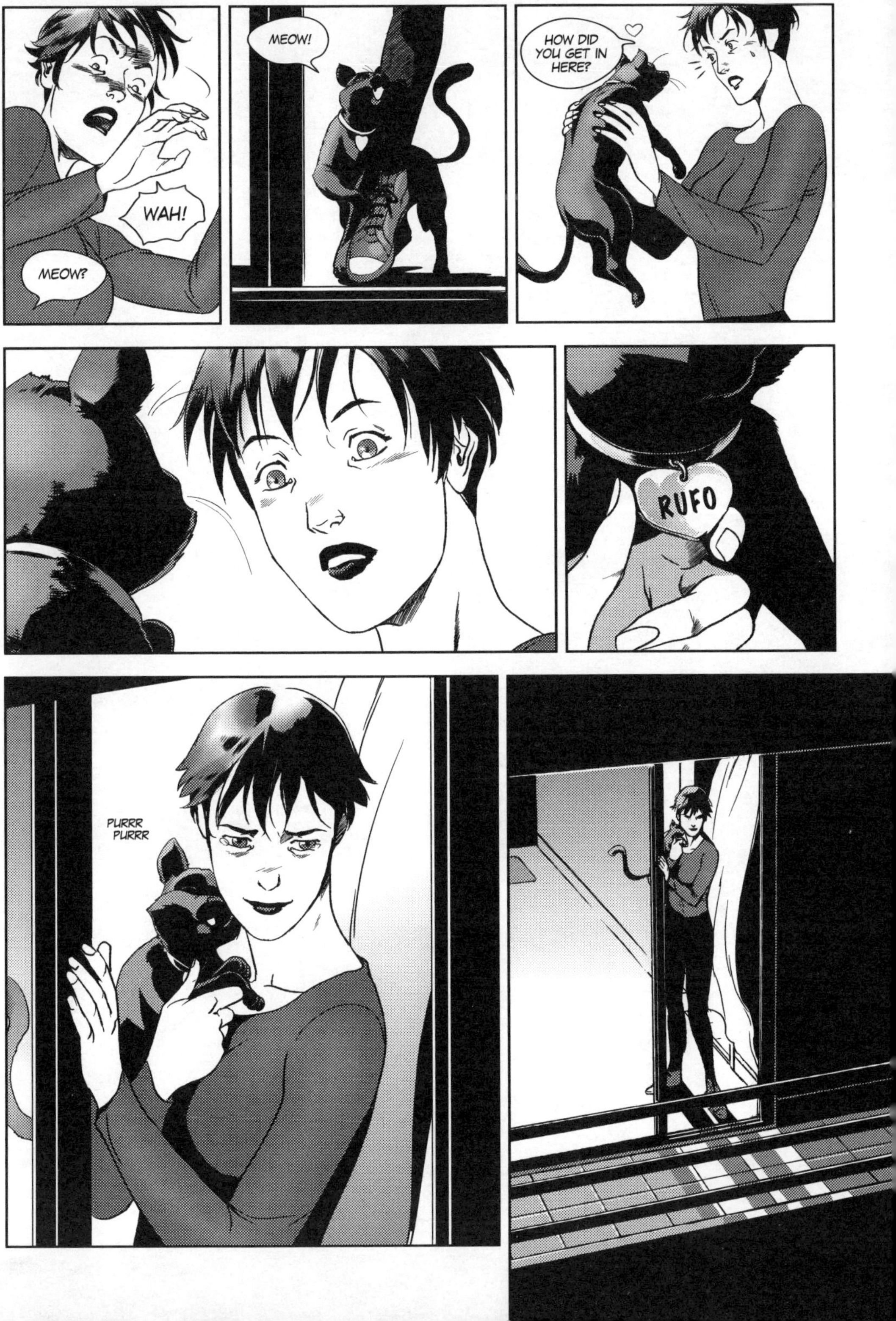
WAH!
MEOW?
MEOW!
HOW DID YOU GET IN HERE?
RUFO
PURRR PURRR

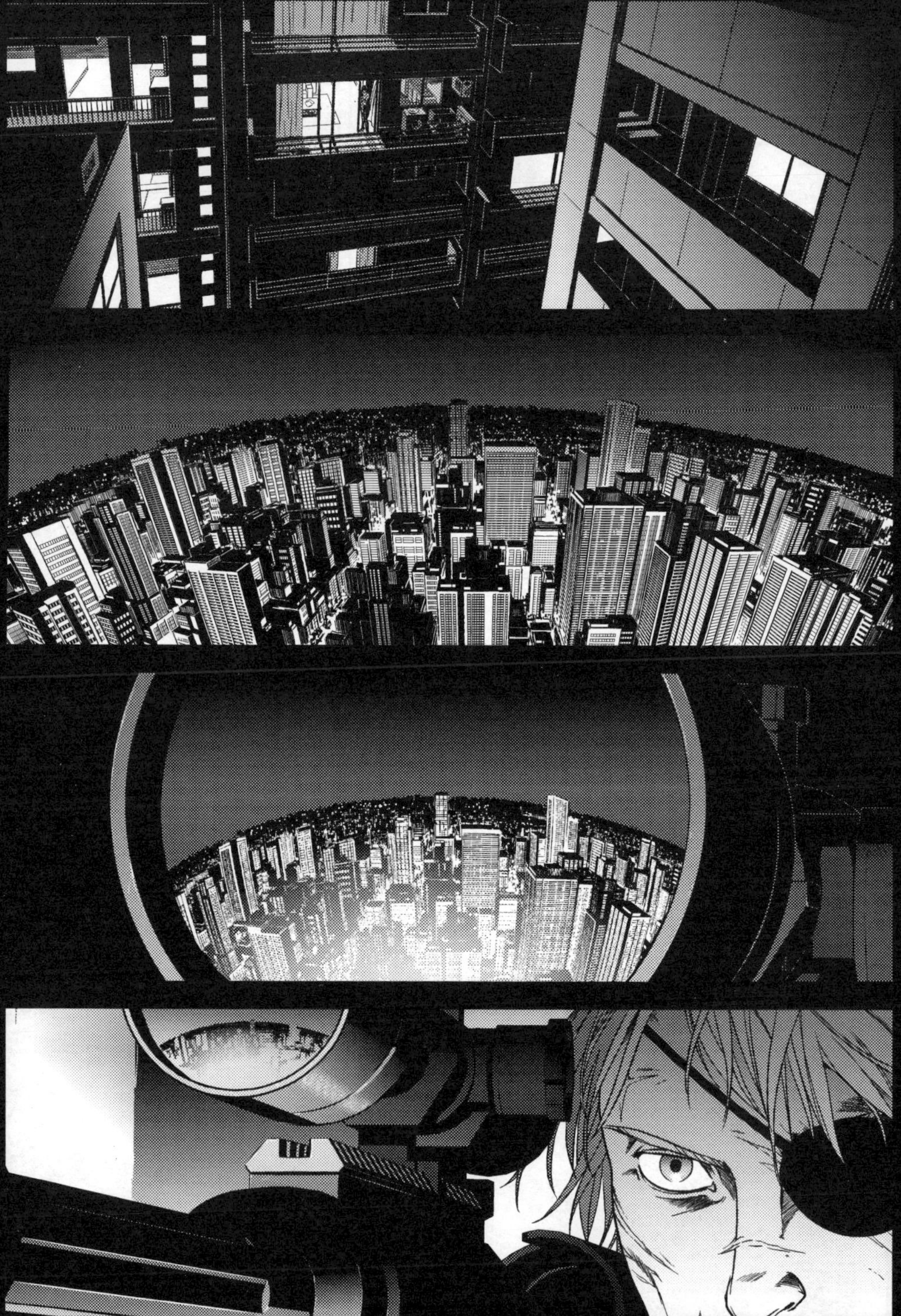

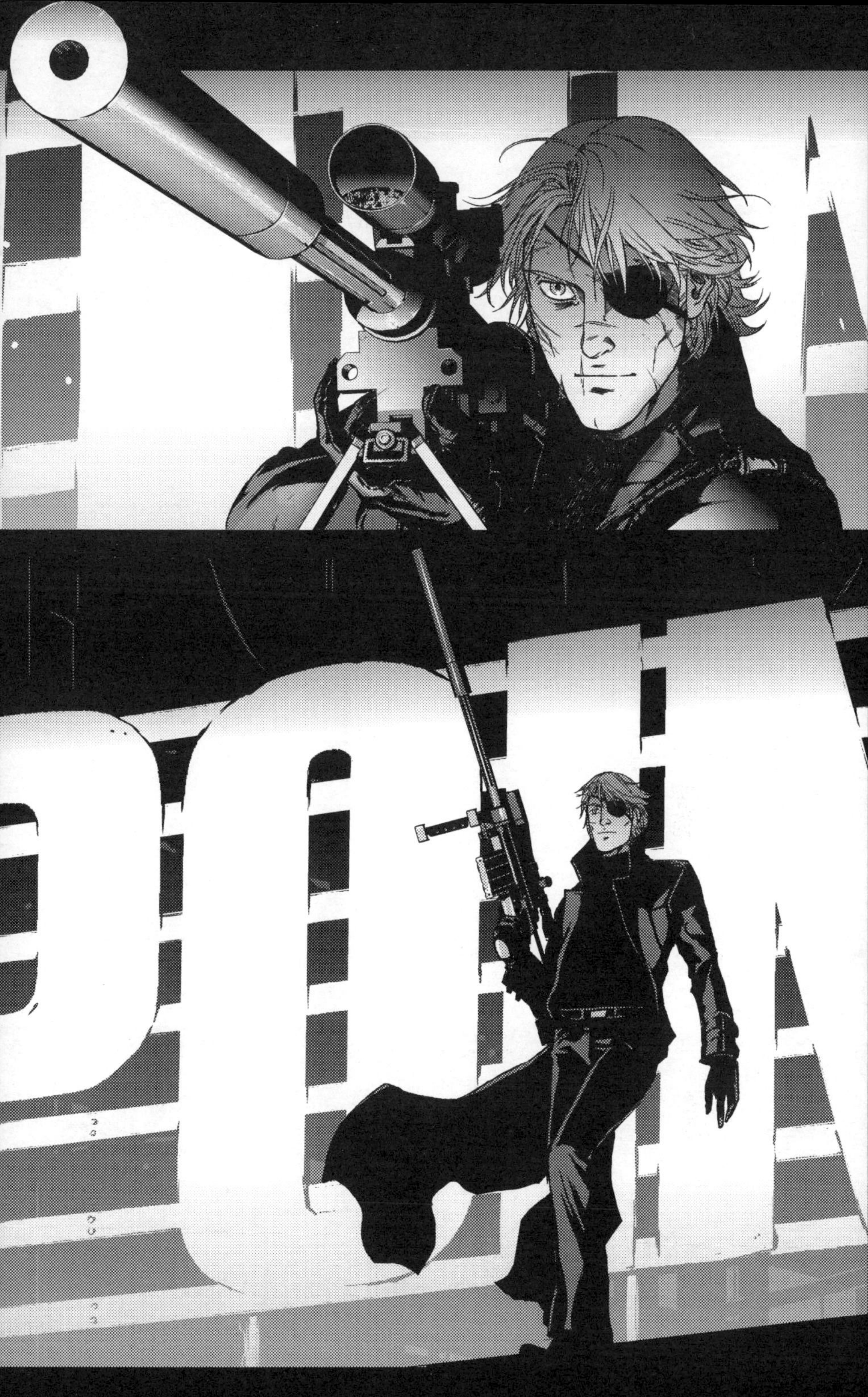

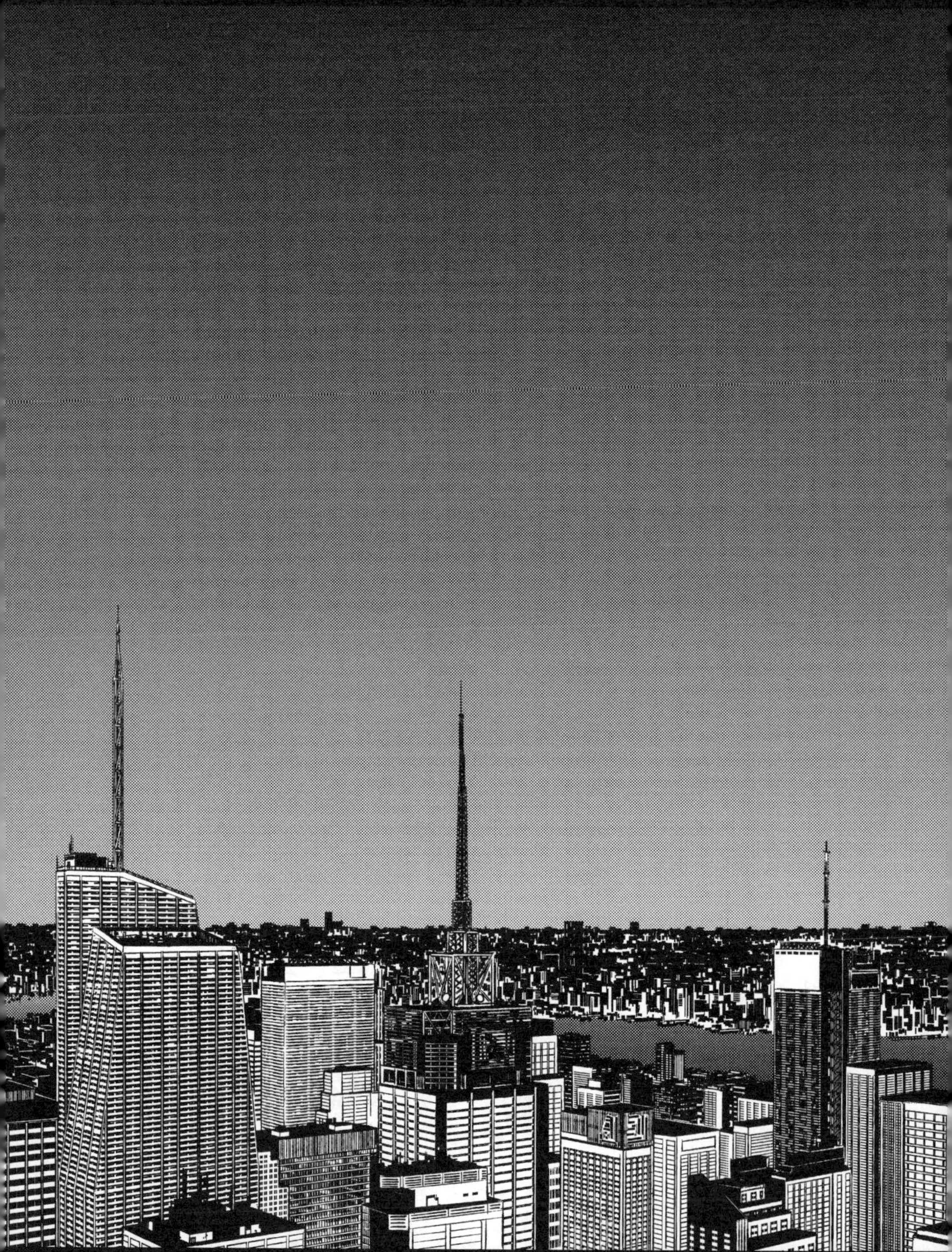

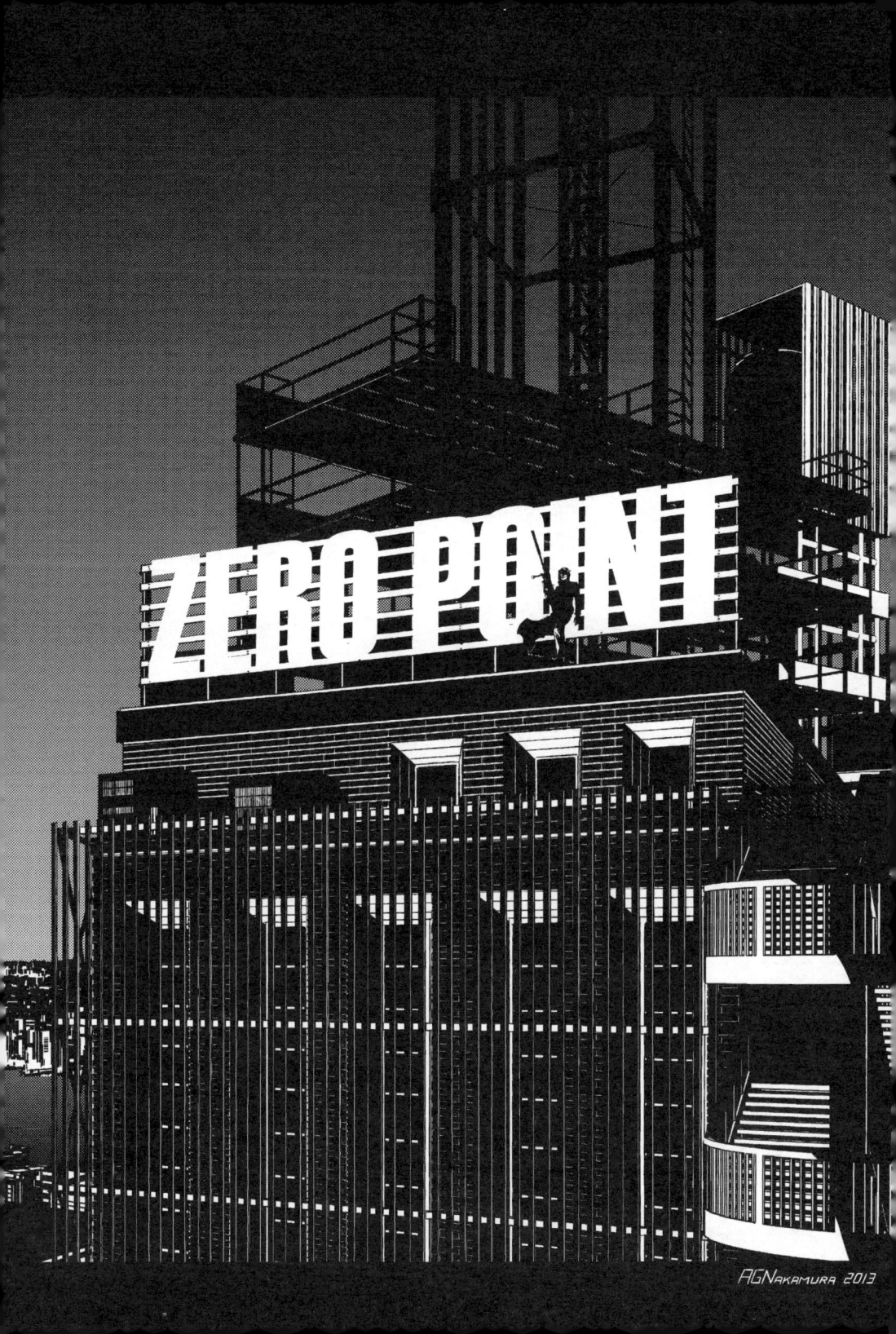
ZERO POINT
AGNakamura 2013

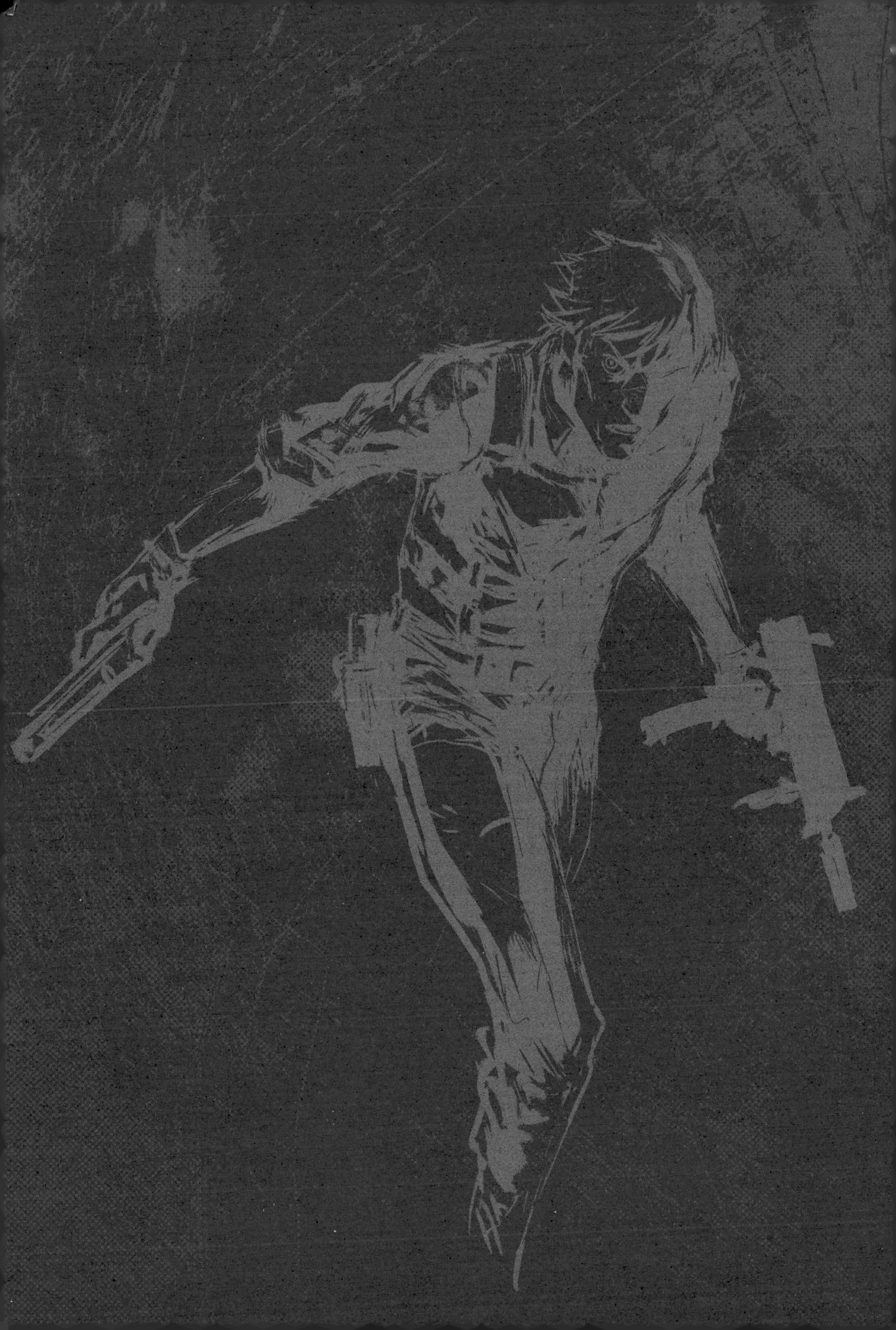

WEAPON FILE: BIRD

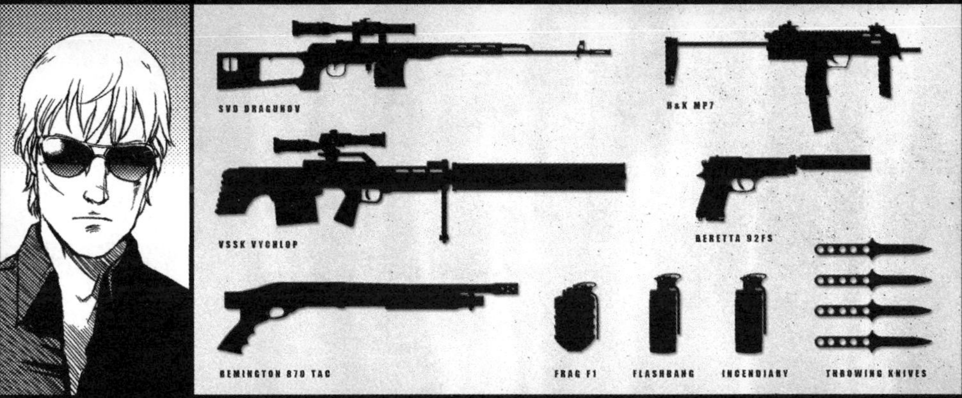
SVD DRAGUNOV
H&K MP7
VSSK VYCHLOP
BERETTA 92FS
REMINGTON 870 TAC
FRAG F1
FLASHBANG
INCENDIARY
THROWING KNIVES

WEAPON FILE: KAT

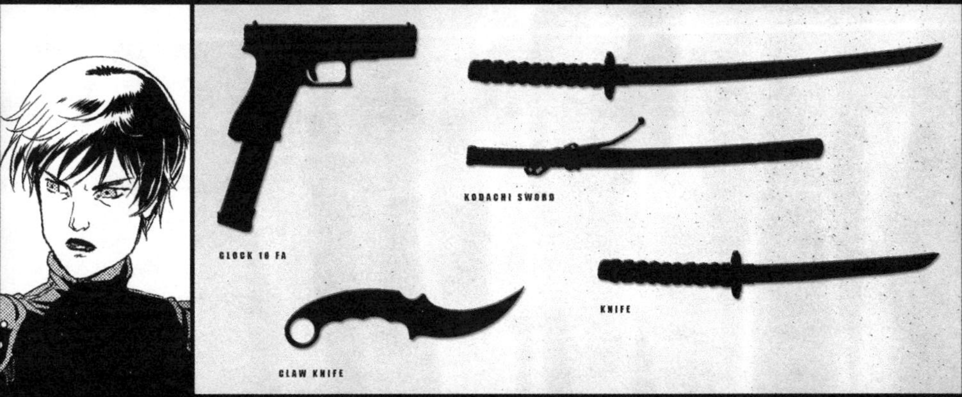
GLOCK 18 FA
KODACHI SWORD
KNIFE
CLAW KNIFE

WEAPON FILE: CROW

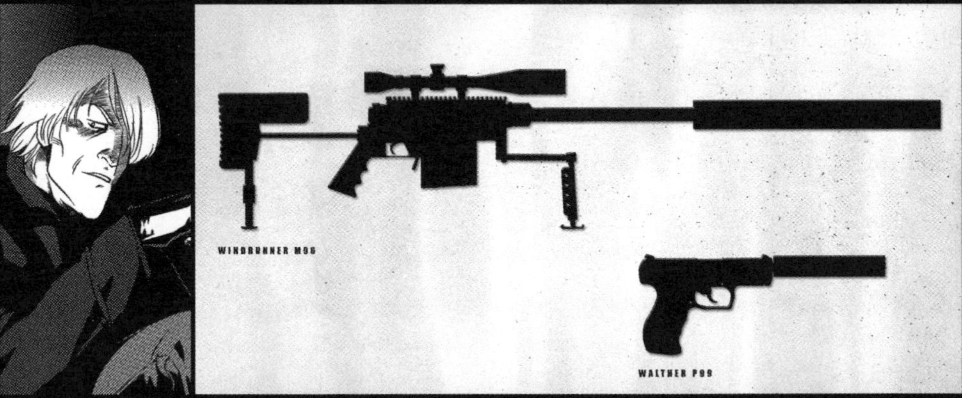
WINDRUNNER M96
WALTHER P99

WEAPON FILE: SWAT

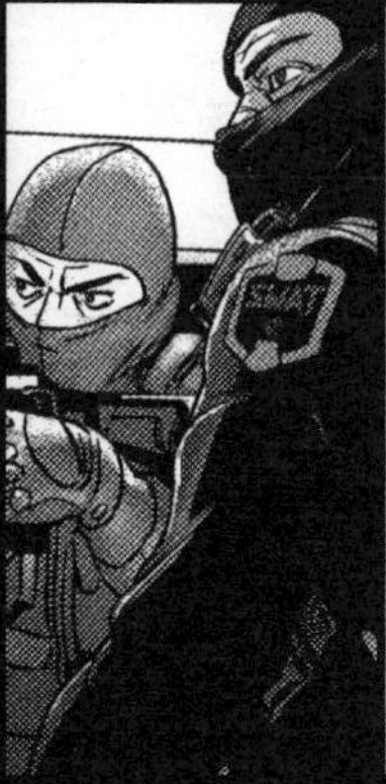

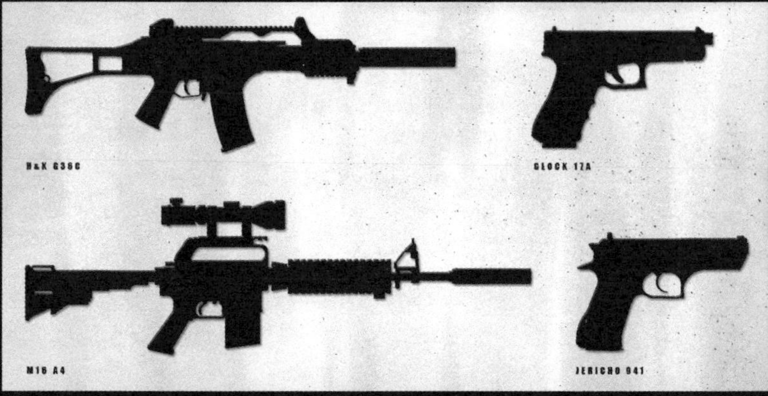
H&K G36C
GLOCK 17A
M16 A4
JERICHO 941

WEAPON FILE: THUGS

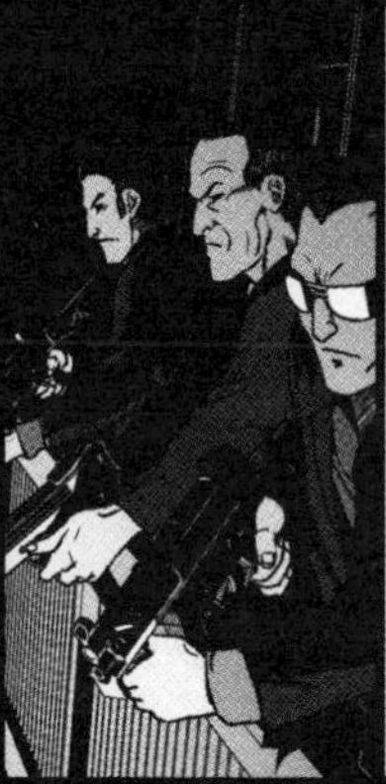

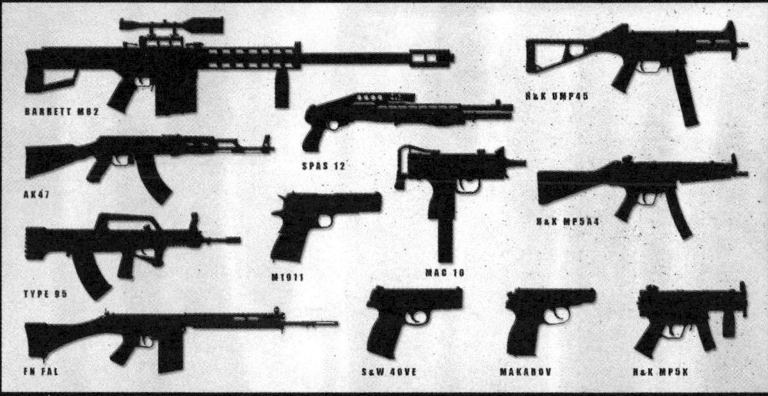
BARRETT M82
H&K UMP45
SPAS 12
AK47
H&K MP5A4
M1911
MAC 10
TYPE 95
FN FAL
S&W 40VE
MAKAROV
H&K MP5K

VEHICLE FILE: McMILLAN

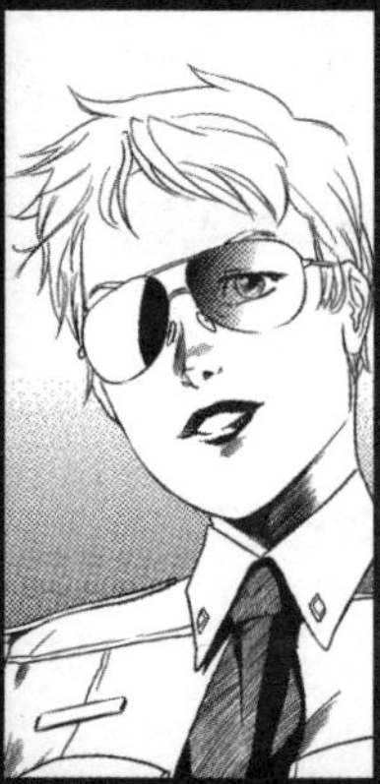

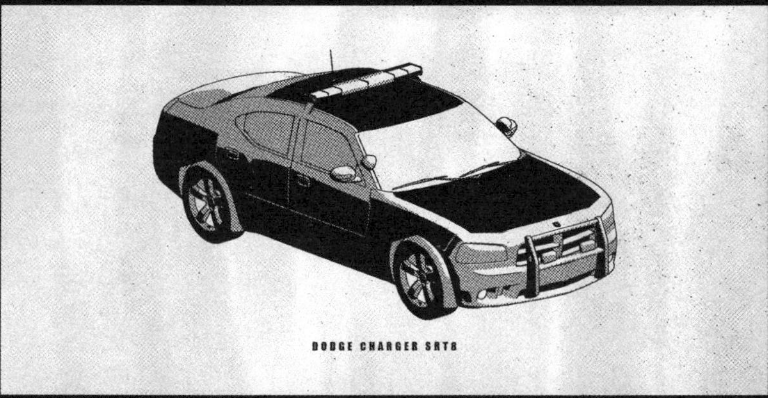
DODGE CHARGER SRT8

VEHICLE FILE: BIRD

CUSTOM CAR. ALIAS: "BOLIDO"

VEHICLE FILE: (UNKNOWN)

KAWASAKI PHANTOM MK1

VEHICLE FILE: CROW

DODGE CHALLENGER 440 MAGNUM R/T

VEHICLE FILE: SWAT

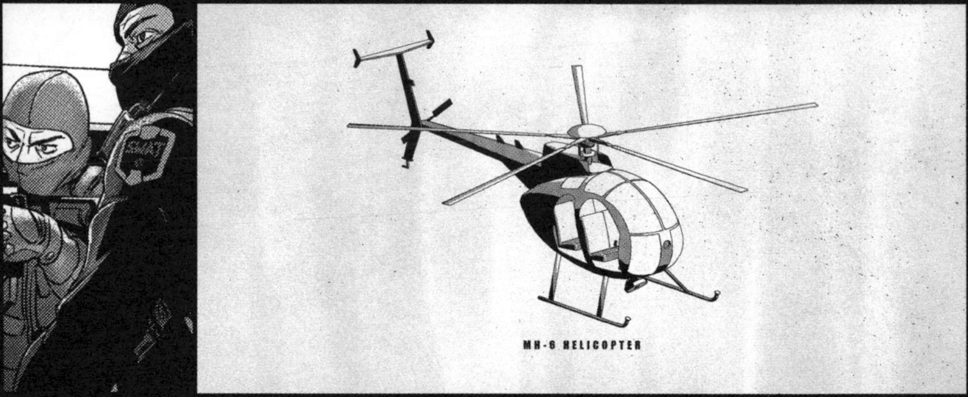
SWAT
MH-6 HELICOPTER

VEHICLE FILE: SECRET SERVICE

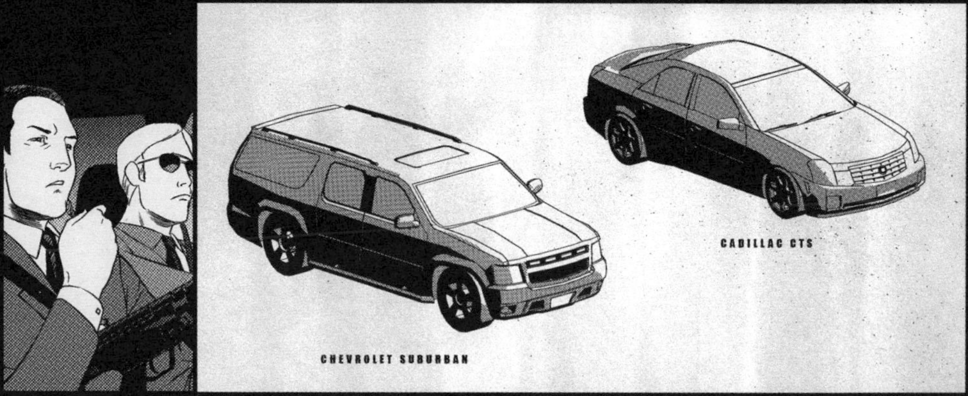
CADILLAC CTS
CHEVROLET SUBURBAN

VEHICLE FILE: THUGS

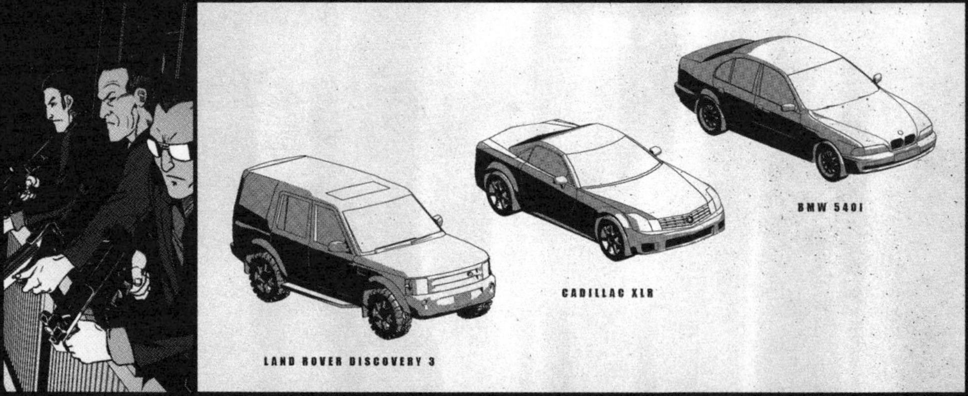
BMW 540I
CADILLAC XLR
LAND ROVER DISCOVERY 3

Agustín Graham Nakamura

An Argentine of Japanese descent, Agustín is a freelance artist who has worked with advertising agencies, film studios, game studios, and production houses. His comics have been published in the United States, Spain, South Korea, Mexico, Brazil, and Argentina. His published work includes *Monogatari* (2021), *INFINITY: Betrayal* (2020), *Terra Australis* (2018), *Wonderland* (2015), *Zero Point* (2014-2018), and *FEAR* (2008). Although it has already been published in Spanish and Portuguese, this is the first time *Zero Point* has appeared in English. Agustín is currently based in São Paulo, Brazil.